BROTHER'S KEEPER

Julie Lee

HOLIDAY HOUSE · NEW YORK

❄ ❄ ❄

Copyright © 2020 by Julie Lee

Map by Chelsea Hunter © 2020 by Holiday House, Inc.

All Rights Reserved

HOLIDAY HOUSE is registered in the U.S. Patent and Trademark Office.

Printed and bound in May 2020 at Maple Press, York, PA, USA.

www.holidayhouse.com

First Edition

1 3 5 7 9 10 8 6 4 2

Library of Congress Cataloging-in-Publication Data

Names: Lee, Julie (Children's fiction writer), author.

Title: Brother's keeper / by Julie Lee.

Description: First edition. | New York : Holiday House, [2020] | Audience:
Ages 8–12. (provided by Holiday House.) | Audience: Grades 4–6. (provided
by Holiday House.) | Summary: Twelve-year-old Sora and her eight-year-old
brother, Youngsoo, must try to escape North Korea's oppressive Communist
regime on their own in 1950. Includes historical notes, photographs of the
author's mother, glossary of Korean words, and timeline.

Identifiers: LCCN 2019052526| ISBN 9780823444946 (hardcover) |
ISBN 9780823448098 (ebook)

Subjects: LCSH: Korea (North)—History—20th century—Juvenile fiction. |
CYAC: Korea (North)—History—20th century—Fiction. | Family
life—Korea—Fiction. | Brothers and sisters—Fiction. | Refugees—Fiction. |
Korean War, 1950–1953—Fiction.

Classification: LCC PZ7.1.L417262 Bro 2020 | DDC [Fic]—dc23

LC record available at https://lccn.loc.gov/2019052526

ISBN: 978-0-8234-4494-6 (hardcover)

✳ ✳ ✳

For my mother and my daughters

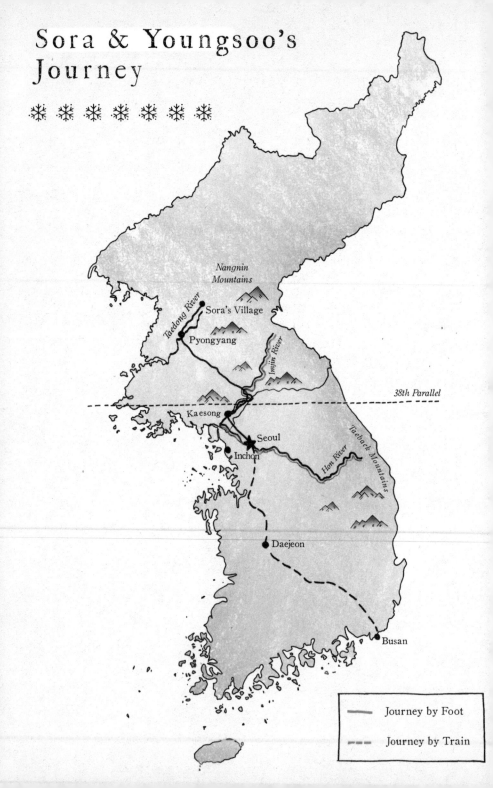

PART I

❄ ❄ ❄ ❄ ❄ ❄ ❄ ❄ ❄

HOME

one · · · · · ·
North Korea
June 25, 1950

I didn't want to step into the river, but I had to. He was floating away.

"Youngsoo!" I stomped in waist-deep, gripping my toes against the sharp-edged clams on the rocky floor. Rushing water swirled around me. I grabbed my little brother's hand and dragged him back to shore.

"Sorry, *Noona*," Youngsoo said, calling me *older sister* in Korean. "I leaned out too far with my net." It wasn't the first time he'd lost his balance and tipped over while fishing, his stomach smacking against the water. He shivered in his wet uniform.

"I told you not to go in too deep. Hold still." I wrung the ends of his shirt and straightened the red scarf around his neck, then took a step back and frowned. What would *Omahni* say? I could already feel our mother's punishment stick snapping against my calves. "How could you have fallen in right before your Sonyondan Club meeting? Your scarf is so wet, it's almost black!"

"Don't worry. It's just a scarf," he said, looking at his feet.

I stared at him. Everyone knew the red scarf was the most important part of the communist youth club uniform. Red had become sacred. It fluttered in the star of our new North Korean flag. Mothers tied and retied it cautiously around their children's necks. And red armbands stood out on the white of the villagers' clothes like a bloodstain.

Youngsoo hung his head low. "I almost caught a fish, Noona. It slipped out of my net."

"I know, I know," I said impatiently. "Every day you almost catch a big one."

But then a pang of regret shot through me, knowing how hard he tried despite always coming home with an empty net.

"I'll make it up to you tomorrow. What kind of fish do you want? Trout? Salmon? Catfish?" He puffed up his skinny chest like a little man and extended his arm toward the river. "Just name it, and I'll catch it for you."

Before I had the chance to give him a stern sideways glance, the kind Omahni always gave me, he smiled earnestly, a piece of black plum skin caught in his teeth. I sighed, wondering if this was how he always kept our mother from staying mad at him too long.

A bell chimed from the schoolhouse on the hill. The teacher, Comrade Cho, stood in front waiting to close the doors, a red band cinched tightly around his upper arm. Stragglers from Youngsoo's third-grade class sprinted past us as we headed up the slope.

"You can't be dumber than the fish if you want to catch them!" a boy shouted at us, his red scarf knotted perfectly.

Youngsoo pushed up his sleeves. "At least I'm not dumber than you! And my sister is smarter than everyone! Right, Noona?"

I groaned. Why did he have to drag me into this?

"Your sister can't be that smart! She doesn't even go to school anymore!" the boy called back, laughing from the hilltop.

My shoulders stiffened. He was right. When I'd turned twelve two months ago, Omahni had pulled me out of school to look after my little brothers.

I glanced at Youngsoo—so drenched and disheveled. Did he even know how lucky he was?

"You'll be late." I couldn't look at him anymore. "Just go."

I pushed him up the hill. Omahni said that skipping even one communist youth club meeting meant Youngsoo's name—no, our *family* name—would go on a government watch list.

And then terrible things would happen.

"What a beautiful day to labor in this socialist paradise!" Comrade Cho announced as the students approached. "Don't forget to continue gathering scrap iron for weapons and bullets, or else your parents will have to pay a fine. Your work is important in making the Fatherland strong!"

Youngsoo joined the wave of red running up the hill, then disappeared inside the A-frame timber schoolhouse. Looking at it, I felt a twinge of loss.

Not for the Girls' Sonyondan Club that I no longer attended, joining my parents at grown-up Party meetings instead.

Not for the new teacher, Comrade Cho, who gave candy to students for reporting anything anti-communist their parents said at home.

Not for the kids in class, who were loyal to the Party first and family second, and could never be trusted as friends.

But for all the learning I was missing. Math. Geography. Science. When I could escape from my chores, I hid behind the willow tree by the school window and eavesdropped on the class.

Today, though, was not a day for escaping chores. I picked up my laundry basket and balanced it on top of my head. The sound of wooden paddles beckoned me back toward the river, and like a funeral marcher, I went.

Downstream, mounds of laundry littered the bank. Women squatted on flat boulders jutting from the sandbars. They scrubbed pants with thick bar soap, their shoulders pumping like pistons, then beat them with flat paddles as if spanking their children. Without any men nearby, the women gossiped about husbands and mothers-in-law as they lifted their shirts to wipe their faces. I looked away.

"*Yah*, Sora! What are you so embarrassed about?" asked Mrs. Lee, her cheeks ruddy from the sun.

I smiled, tight-lipped, and found an open area to set my basket. My long tan skirt was soaked from saving Youngsoo.

"Why's your mom sending a girl to do a woman's job, huh?" a farmer's wife shouted.

"Who else is she supposed to send—her sons? Anyway, Sora's not such a little girl anymore, right?" Mrs. Lee said. "Look, she's even starting to get little breasts now." She poked me in the ribs, and I jerked like a string puppet.

They laughed heartily. My cheeks burned, and I hunched my back to hide my chest. I gazed up at the schoolhouse as if it might somehow reach down to save me, the straw basket pressing against my shins. But it wouldn't, and the laundry wouldn't wash itself.

I took out my brothers' dirty clothes—Jisoo's cloth diapers, Youngsoo's muddy uniform pants—and crouched in the shallows, joining the drumbeat of women. I plunged my raw knuckles into the soapy water, hiding them beneath the cloudy white.

A grandmother came running from around the hill, splashing along the river's edge toward the rest of us, and I watched the waves ripple over my hands. At first I hardly noticed the whispers, the way the women huddled around her. But their murmurs grew, and I looked up at them—their mouths agape, their brows creased—and suddenly everything felt wrong.

The women started hastily packing unfinished laundry into their baskets. I rushed to rinse Youngsoo's uniform pants. Something was not right. I needed to go. The last time a message had spread this urgently, the landlord's son was found floating face-down in the river, his body bloated like a blood sausage. I lifted the basket onto my head and hurried onto the main road through the village center, stumbling past a row of thatched-roof houses, my breath coming fast and hard.

"Noona!"

I spun around and saw Youngsoo running along the bank. He stopped short before crashing into me.

"What are you doing here? Were you sent home? Was it the wet scarf? Are they putting us on a list?" I asked, my voice rising with panic.

"No, something amazing happened!" Youngsoo's eyes shimmered like the river, and he practically sang the words: "We don't have to go to school anymore!"

My stomach clenched. "What do you mean, Youngsoo? That's impossible."

"Comrade Cho told the whole class that 'because of the current situation, there will be no school until further notice,'" he said, carefully repeating his teacher's words. "He even said that 'today will be a day to go down in history.'" Youngsoo jumped high in the air, hollering and hooting at his sudden change in luck. "No more school! No more school!"

My palms turned cold and clammy.

"We need to go home," I managed to say. "Come on."

We walked past streams flowing into rivers, then through plains and pastures until we could see the rice-straw roof of our home. The house was square-shaped to block the bitter winds cascading down the mountains in winter, and it sat squat in the countryside, fifty miles north of Pyongyang, the capital. Although it looked like every other farmhouse in the valley, it was unmistakably home, the rounded edges of the worn, thatched roof hugging the house like a mushroom cap. Around it, fields of corn and millet stirred in the hot wind.

We hurried inside. A broadcaster's voice and the hiss of static rushed to greet us. I set the basket down and stepped into a pair of house slippers.

Abahji sat as motionless as a rock, leaning in to the radio. Deep lines creased his forehead. I had never seen our father look so grave.

Beside him, Baby Jisoo looked up from a pile of clean clothes, yawned once, then went back to his favorite pastime: pulling socks over each of his feet.

Youngsoo and I sat on the floor beside Abahji. I quieted my breathing to hear, but I couldn't understand the announcer's words through the heavy static. I turned to Youngsoo and shrugged, unable to explain Abahji's pensive face.

All at once, the signal cleared, and Youngsoo's eyes brightened as if he had just solved a riddle.

"*That's* what my teacher was talking about. *That's* the reason there will be no more school!" he shouted, pointing at the radio. "War! War! Starting today, we are at war!"

two · · · · · ·

"War is no cause for celebration, son," Abahji said. He shifted on his woven sitting mat, rubbing his knees.

Youngsoo wiped the grin off his face with the back of his hand. He turned bright pink and dropped his gaze to the floor.

"War?" I said, my eyes wide. It was the last thing I expected. "Who are we fighting with?"

Abahji stared at the chipped edge of the low dining table.

"South Korea," he said.

The room was muggy, but I shivered and drew the collar of my short *jeogori* closer. Miss Chun, my old teacher, had once shown a World War II newsreel to our class. It showed soldiers running across hillsides with guns; planes strafing overhead; bombs exploding into giant mushroom clouds. But worst of all, it showed wandering women and children, their clothes in tatters, their hollow faces staring out at me.

"Where is the fighting now, Abahji?" I said. My eye twitched nervously, like butterfly wings, and I pressed my hand over the flutter.

He sighed and shook his head. "Near Seoul."

Seoul. The capital of South Korea.

Youngsoo searched my face, but I wasn't sure what to think. North Korea fighting South Korea. If South Korea lost, would all of Korea become communist, like the North? What if another country swooped in and conquered us both while we were at war with each other?

We'd been conquered before. Japan had ruled Korea before the communists. I couldn't remember much, but I knew the emperor of Japan had banned our *Hangul* language, confiscated almost everyone's land, and ordered us all to take Japanese names. My father became *Yosuke*, not *Sangmin*; my mother became *Chieko*, not *Yuri*. We were treated like an inferior race. Japanese soldiers even kidnapped several girls from the high school. The entire village had mourned, including a Japanese family who lived across the river—proof that not all Japanese were evil, according to Abahji.

After the war, the Russians liberated one half of Korea, the Americans the other half, and the Japanese went home. But our country was left split in two: part communist, part democratic.

The radio blared again:

"On June twenty-fifth, the army of the South Korean puppet government launched an all-out offensive along the thirty-eighth parallel against the northern half of Korea, resulting in the declaration of war."

"But the Korean people need not fear, for the valiant North Korean army has captured the town of Kaesong and will soon enter Seoul to save the South from the U.S. imperialists. Reunification under

communism will soon be possible through the military genius of our Great Leader, Kim Il-sung!"

Abahji looked at our frozen expressions, then straightened his back and cleared his throat. "No worries, my little ones. The fighting will never reach us here. Seoul is almost two hundred miles away." He smoothed the back of my hair and pinched Youngsoo's cheek, but we stayed as stiff as two wooden dolls.

Abahji chuckled and turned down the radio. "Now, let me see if I have another Grandfather in America story."

I sighed in relief when I saw Abahji's smiling crescent-moon eyes return. Surely he was right—the fighting would never reach our small northern village. Youngsoo leaned in closer, all trace of fear gone from his face.

"Oh, I've got one," Abahji said. He paused for a second as if relishing the moment. "When your *harabuji* was in Hawaii working with the sugar planters, he heard that an American president had promised a chicken in every pot and a car in every garage to every citizen. Can you imagine that?"

"What's a garage?" Youngsoo asked.

"It's a house for a car," Abahji said.

"A house for a car!" Youngsoo rolled on his back, squealing and laughing.

A garage. I couldn't fathom such a thing. It was hard to believe that my grandfather had ever lived outside our borders— especially now, when you needed permission just to travel to another *village* for a day. You had to fill out paperwork at the village center asking who, what, when, where, why, and how long the trip would take. And if you didn't report back once you'd returned, the secret police could send you to a labor camp. The state worked you to death there.

"Why didn't Harabuji stay in America?" I demanded.

"You know the answer to that, Sora," Abahji said. "He was the eldest son. It was his duty to return to Korea with his earnings and care for his family."

Just like it was my duty as the oldest daughter to give up school to take care of Jisoo and Youngsoo while Omahni and Abahji worked in the field.

It wasn't like this before Jisoo was born. Back then, I had gone to school, studied, and played with friends. Now it was my responsibility to stay home and watch the baby. At least Harabuji had been *allowed* to go.

I whipped around to Jisoo. "Stop playing with those silly socks. It's almost time for lunch."

"No!" He scooped up the socks and ran away.

I caught him near the wooden chest and carried him toward the table. He squirmed and kicked and knocked me in the chin. I lost my grip, and his bottom hit the floor.

Jisoo wailed just as Omahni walked in from the kitchen carrying a tray of rice and marinated vegetables. She cut her eyes to me. "Yah, Sora. Be more careful with the baby."

"It was an accident," I said, keeping my gaze on Jisoo.

Omahni picked him up, cradling him like an infant. He stuck his tongue out at me. "Omahni, he's not such a baby, right?" I pressed. "He's two years old. Pretty soon he'll start school, and I won't have to stay home and watch him anymore."

Omahni laughed as if that was the stupidest thing she had ever heard. "What are you talking about? Two years old is still a baby!"

Jisoo stopped crying and curled onto Abahji's lap. Omahni tore a piece of *kimchi* and fed it to him. His plump thigh slipped off Abahji's knee, sprawling out as audaciously as some boy-emperor luxuriating across his throne, and I had the urge to pinch that tender flesh hard.

After we'd eaten, Omahni straightened her back and turned to me. "Sora, come help me in the kitchen. Fry the bean pancakes and wash the rice. The Kim family is coming for dinner."

It was the command I dreaded every day, the one calling me into the kitchen. My face must have soured, because Abahji frowned at me.

Ruefully, I followed Omahni from the sitting room and stepped down into the small, stifling space. Buckets of water from the courtyard well sat in a row from largest to smallest on the dirt floor. Omahni was already at the stone counter with her back to the door, her right shoulder rising and falling as she massaged meat in a bowl. Her long hair was coiled in a bun as smooth and shiny as obsidian. I reached out to touch her, but hesitated and dropped my hand instead.

I wanted to ask about the war, but I didn't dare.

"Here, wash the rice," she said, leaning over the wood-burning stove and lifting the gourd off its hook.

I took it from her and poured in two cups of rice, then rinsed the pearly grains, my long hair swaying in front of my face.

Omahni looked at me as if she smelled something foul. "*Tsk, tsk*. Tie your hair back before strands fall into the rice."

"Yes, Omahni." I created a braid.

Her gaze lingered on me. Then, as if there were nothing she could do to change her unlucky fate, she said, "How is it that my daughter got the tan skin while my sons inherited my fair complexion?"

I looked at my olive-brown hands. *Fair as nobility. Dark as a peasant.* That was what I'd always been told.

Omahni handed me the ground mung beans. A pan of hot oil sat on the stove. "Go ahead. Finish the batter and fry the pancakes. You should know how to do this at your age."

I wiped the sweat from my upper lip. I had to mix the mung beans, water, and vegetables, and maybe add soy sauce. And didn't salt and pepper go into bean pancakes too? I stirred the batter and poured small circles onto the pan, then grabbed a palmful of salt from the ceramic jar in the pine cabinet.

"Yah! How much salt did you grab? Only a pinch. Only a pinch!" Omahni scolded.

But it was too late. My empty hand froze over the pan. I stopped breathing. The salt melted into the sizzling batter.

"Aigoo! When will you ever learn to cook? How will I get you married off when you're older?" Omahni sighed and frowned. "Good thing I pulled you out of school. You've had your head in the books too long. You don't know how to do anything else." She pushed me aside and took over.

My head snapped up. "Married?"

"Why do you sound so shocked? Your auntie in Busan got married at sixteen! Don't worry, you won't get married for a few more years. Now cut some fruit for me. Watch how I do it." In one fluid motion, she peeled an apple into a smooth ball, then cored and sliced it evenly.

I grabbed an apple and a paring knife, my head clouded with worry. In four years, I would turn sixteen. A wedding was so much closer than I thought.

First no school. And now this.

The room shrank to half its size. My hands felt tingly and numb, and I could hardly hold the knife. Something sharp stabbed at me.

"Yah! What are you doing?" Omahni said.

I looked down. Blood trickled from my finger. Chunky bits of apple skins lay scattered on the counter, so different from Omahni's peel cut into one continuous spiral, as pretty as the inside of a shell. Her pared apple sat perfectly round on a serving dish, and I set mine beside it—uneven and trimmed to the size of an apricot, its flesh wasted.

three · · · · · ·

The Kim family arrived early that evening.

"Ah, please come in!" Abahji welcomed them with a bow.

"Is that all you do when you greet your closest friend?" Mr. Kim asked. He wrapped his arms around Abahji tightly; Abahji laughed and thumped him hard on the back. Omahni scurried out of the kitchen and embraced Mrs. Kim. They murmured greetings quietly, as if they did not want to be heard.

Myung-gi and Yoomee entered behind their parents. Yoomee bowed and said hello to everyone, but pretended not to notice me. When she walked past, I stared. Something seemed different about her. Ah! It was her bangs; they had been trimmed too short! I swallowed a giggle.

She glared at me, then smirked. "Were you hiding under the willow tree the other day, eavesdropping on my class?"

I choked.

I didn't think anyone could see me under the branches. Had the entire class been watching? I tried to speak, but nothing came out.

"Hmm," Yoomee said, smiling. "I'm sure it was you. I'd recognize your wiry hair anywhere."

My fingernails dug into my palms. I shot her a look that almost burned the silky hair right off her head. God forgive me—I wished her dead, that Yoomee. How could she be so different from her older brother?

Myung-gi strode lithely across the room and set his bag on the floor. He never went anywhere without his books. Omahni said Myung-gi was turning into a handsome boy, and I couldn't argue. But I wasn't sure whether it was his smooth, tan complexion or his bag of books that made me look for him wherever I went.

When we were little, we used to catch dragonflies together, but now that he was fourteen and in high school, he rarely spoke to me. The space between us had widened into an abyss.

"What books were you reading today, Myung-gi *oppah*?" I asked, addressing him respectfully as an older boy.

He dumped his bag upside down, and books tumbled out. My mouth hung open. There were so many—big and small, thick and thin, enough to occupy me for days. I couldn't stop my huge grin from spreading, and I covered my teeth politely, the way I'd always been taught. I picked up a small red book and flipped through its pages, breathing in its comforting scent of ink and musty paper.

Myung-gi snatched the book out of my hands. Had I been rude in picking it up without permission? How strange I must have appeared, inhaling it like a bouquet of flowers. "I'm sorry, I didn't mean to—"

Myung-gi pointed the book at me. "This is a book about

communism. And so are all of these. Don't you remember? The new principal changed the curriculum and confiscated almost everything else." He sighed, then tossed them all into his bag as carelessly as chucking dead clams back into the river. "Sorry," he said, "I'm just tired of reading the same mind-numbing rubbish. Marxist dialectics. Revolutionary principles. Everything for the collective. It's all repetitive garbage."

I'd forgotten. For a second, that red textbook was just another book with that wonderful wood-pulp smell. My face burned in shame. Myung-gi and his family were the only ones we could trust, the only ones in the village who shared our aversion to the regime. I should've known better.

Bowls of rice, bean-sprout soup, kimchi, and pancakes lined the table. Abahji sat on the floor with Mr. and Mrs. Kim on his right and Omahni on his left; the rest of us squeezed in wherever we could. I sat beside Youngsoo and braced myself not to squirm once Yoomee sat on my other side, but Myung-gi dropped down next to me instead. His knee brushed against my leg. I'd never sat this close to him before. I studied his hands—thoughtful and smooth, resting on his lap—and when he glanced at me, I realized that perhaps I'd been staring and felt prickly heat spread across my cheeks.

Omahni jumped up to close the shutters, and then Abahji bowed and said a prayer for the meal. Everyone rolled up their sleeves. No one spoke. Mr. Kim slurped scalding broth from the edge of his bowl, keeping his mouth ajar to let the steam rise.

Abahji bellowed a satisfying *"Aah!"* with each sip. All around the table, I heard a symphony of gulping, sniffling, and burping. I scraped out the last bit of broth and meat in my bowl, leaving it dry.

"Wah, look at how much my son ate. The food must be delicious," Mr. Kim said. He patted Myung-gi on the shoulder as if he'd performed a great feat by simply eating his dinner.

Omahni scrunched her face, unable to accept such a compliment. "Oh, you and Mrs. Kim are blessed to have such a son. He will serve you well in this life and the next."

Mrs. Kim smiled and waved her hands in front of her mouth as she hurried to finish chewing. "You are the one blessed with two sons. You have double the good fortune, and your husband's family line will extend forever."

They laughed, basking in the security of their many blessings. But their tittering pricked at me like tiny icy picks, and I turned my eyes away to dull the sting.

Mr. Kim sucked the stringy tail end of a bean sprout into his mouth and smacked his lips. "Sora-ya, did you help make this meal?"

I nodded.

Mrs. Kim winked at me across the table. "She's an excellent cook just like her mother, much better than our Yoomee. And such a dutiful daughter, too."

"No, our daughter is terrible in the kitchen," Omahni said, her face pink and shiny. "She's a clumsy girl who hates housework. I'm sure we'll never be able to get her married off when she's older."

Clumsy girl—me.

Mrs. Kim scolded Omahni in jest. "That's nonsense. One day, I'm sure Sora will marry a handsome young man of noble blood."

Omahni chuckled lightly into her hand. The sound grated against my ears.

I glanced around the table. Yoomee sat there beaming, and I could hardly stand to look at her. I tried to focus on my favorite daydream instead, the one where I finish at the top of my class.

It's graduation day, and the principal calls me to the podium for my certificate of achievement. Omahni and Abahji wipe away tears of joy. And my classmates, especially Yoomee, watch with envy.

"—No, our daughter is a terrible cook," I heard Abahji say. My head jerked up. "She sprinkled so much salt on this bean pancake that it tastes like the ocean."

Laughter erupted everywhere.

I looked at Abahji. Usually, he complimented my food. I knew that humble parents always criticized their own children in front of others. It was the polite thing to do. But it still felt like a betrayal.

Yoomee livened up at these tales of my shortcomings, her dark pupils sparkling like jewels. With one eye on me, she took a bite of bean pancake, then made a face and guzzled a cup of water, her hand fanning her collarbone. I felt my chin begin to quiver, and when Omahni reached over and smoothed Yoomee's hair saying, "Oh, so pretty," I bit the inside of my cheek until it bled.

Myung-gi glanced at me, and our eyes met. "Shouldn't we tell them now?" he asked his parents, interrupting the laughter.

"Why are you rushing?" Mrs. Kim scolded. "I haven't even finished my soup yet."

"I just thought we should tell them before it gets too late."

I flashed a grateful smile at Myung-gi, but he didn't look back.

"Yes, yes, the boy is right," Mr. Kim said, checking the time on his watch and turning serious. His shirt dampened under his arms. He cleared his throat and turned to Omahni and Abahji. "We plan to escape, and we want all of you to come."

four · · · · · ·

Omahni and Abahji sat still without a word, their faces grave. Abahji turned his gaze away from Mr. Kim. Omahni straightened her chopsticks and bowl, even though they were perfectly aligned.

Escape. The word hissed at me, and I shrank back. Everyone knew that military guards shot anyone trying to cross the border.

But I wrung my hands. If we escaped to the South, we wouldn't have to attend town Party meetings and listen to those never-ending speeches about living in a communist workers' paradise. We wouldn't fear that our neighbors would accuse us of being traitors. We could go to church without being arrested. We could read any books we wanted, instead of just the ones about Mother Russia and the evil Americans. We wouldn't worry about the secret police abducting one of us children on our way home from school, to interrogate us about our parents.

We would lose our fields if we went south. But maybe Abahji could work in a shop or start a business instead of tending crops with Omahni. She could watch my brothers again, and perhaps I would be allowed to go back to school—even against her wishes. I knew school had nothing to do with communism or war or the secret police, but I couldn't stop my thoughts from tangling. What if one kind of freedom led to another?

My heart started thumping. I felt a pull, as if I were standing on a cliff and staring down.

Finally, Abahji broke the silence. "It's too dangerous. There are soldiers standing guard all along the border. If we were caught, they would shoot us—all of us."

Mr. Kim sat straighter, his face animated. "Yes, but with the declaration of war, they'll be too busy fighting to worry about us—or any other defectors. This could be our last chance. Who knows what will happen in the future?"

My stomach churned.

"Where will you settle?" asked Abahji.

Omahni began touching the nape of her neck as if something were there.

"In Busan," Mr. Kim said. "Everyone is heading to the southern coast."

Abahji nodded slowly. "My wife's brother, Kang Hong-Chul, has a house there. I can give you his address. House number 8818—"

"Mr. Kim, of course we cannot go with you. It's too dangerous," Omahni cut in, glaring at Abahji. Beads of sweat glistened on her forehead. "And excuse my words if they seem rude, but you shouldn't have said any of this out loud. It puts us all in a dangerous position. Once you escape, who do you think the police will interrogate? My husband and me. They will accuse us of being traitors, too, simply for being your close friends. If they discover that we knew of your plan and did nothing . . . they will send us away to a prison—or worse!" She jumped up to check outside the window.

Mr. Kim frowned and lowered his head.

A strange tension filled the room. I had known Mr. and Mrs. Kim since I was a baby—they were like family. I had never seen Omahni or Abahji argue with them before.

For some reason, I felt like crying.

Omahni, Mrs. Kim, Yoomee, and I began clearing the table while the men lowered their voices and talked in serious tones over cups of barley tea, Myung-gi sitting on the outskirts of their conversation, stone-faced. I overheard Abahji give Mr. Kim directions to Uncle Hong-Chul's house. *Just a few miles from the Busan station. South of the Gukje Market. He's got a fish stand there, not far from his house.* The radio was flicked on, and an announcer's voice—high strung and staccato—filled the room with rapid-fire war talk.

Anxiously, Youngsoo twirled his wooden spin top across the floor over and over and shouted for me to come see. Yoomee and Jisoo crowded around to watch, but I didn't need to look. I knew it would eventually spin out of control and come to a dead stop.

"Uncle! Uncle! Twirl me again!" I said, reaching up. He spun me like a wooden top, his arms solid as oak when I hung from them.

"He's not your uncle! He's a relative so distant, we're hardly related!" Omahni snapped. "Please, for God's sake," she pleaded to the man standing in the middle of our room, "leave our house. If you have any concern for the safety of my family, please go!"

He deflated at Omahni's words. "I'm so sorry, Yuri. I have no other place to stay. I'll leave tomorrow. I promise. Here, I brought you a gift." He reached inside his bag and pulled out a sack of fresh cucumbers.

"Ai!" Omahni shrieked, snatching the bundle from him. She shook her head and pulled on her hair. "Tomorrow morning, then. You leave at dawn. Aigoo, you must be crazy, helping people escape across the border. If they find out what you've been up to, they'll kill you! You know that, don't you?" Then she stomped out of the house with her laundry basket.

We were alone.

"Sora-ya, you're growing so fast. How old are you now? Six? Seven?"

"Eight!" I said, my face beaming.

Uncle chuckled. "Wah, you're a big girl now. I brought you some peanuts. After you crack them open, you can pretend the shells are earrings. See?" He hung one on his ear lobe.

I giggled and snatched the bag from him.

While I ate, he stared into the small mirror hanging over the water basin and started shaving his face with a metal blade. In the afternoon light, I noticed dark circles under his eyes and neglected stubble on his chin. Even still, he was handsome, his hair combed

back smoothly, thick with pomade. "Is this so interesting to watch?"
he asked, smiling. "Go make peanut earrings."

I sat on the floor and cracked the shells. I was hooking one on my ear
when I heard shuffling outside. Fists pounded on the door. I jumped.

Two police officers barged into the house, pointing rifles at Uncle.

"Do you know why we're here?" one of them shouted,
military-style insignia pointing at me from his padded shoulders.

I looked at Uncle and clutched the bag of peanuts.

"Yes, I know," Uncle said, unflinching. He continued shaving,
gritting his teeth, the white lather disappearing in neat strips.

"Hurry!" The officer flipped the basin into the air. Foamy water
splashed onto the walls.

But Uncle finished pulling the blade across his clenched jaw in
one careful sweep. He wiped his face meticulously with a towel, then
walked out the door, a pointed rifle shoved into his back.

I sat in a pool of urine, the peanut bag crumpled in my hand.

That was the last time I ever saw him—the man who was not
my uncle.

Bowls clattered. I started at the sound.

Omahni was glaring and tossing empty dishes on a tray as
Abahji continued telling Mr. Kim about her brother in Busan. I
knew what Omahni was thinking: the authorities who had taken
the Man Who Was Not My Uncle had executed her aunts, uncles,
and cousins too, just because they were related to an accused
traitor. We were spared by one step in the family tree.

It also helped that Omahni said he had broken into our house, even if that was a lie.

I snuck out the door. The clouds had darkened. I sat against the wooden fence and gazed out toward the millet field. A coolness crept around me.

"Run away with us," a low voice said into the darkness.

I jolted. Beside me was Myung-gi, his wire-framed glasses resting perfectly on his tall nose. Why was he here? Up close, I noticed a small birthmark on the side of his face, a brown spot like a dot of sweet chocolate, and I had the urge to touch it.

"I don't understand," he said. "You always used to tell me how your grandfather lived in America. Wouldn't you like to go there one day, too—or anywhere else in the world? How do you expect to do that from here? We can't even go to the next village without a pass. In South Korea, people are free to come and go as they please."

Come and go as they please.

I mouthed the words silently. Would *I* be allowed to come and go as I pleased?

But then Omahni's frightened face, her skin pulled as taut as the skin of a drum, popped into my head. I imagined creeping through the woods at night, always just steps away from a border guard and a pointed rifle. "It's too dangerous," I blurted. "If you get caught, they'll kill you. Just like they did my uncle."

Myung-gi pushed up his glasses with an index finger, as if to get a better look at me. "Don't you think I know that? But there are some people who've made it across to the South. You can't let fear control you."

"That's easier said than done," I said, without thinking.

He looked down and let out a long breath as if I had disappointed him.

"Your parents are like my parents, and you . . . are like a little sister." He rose to his feet. "I hope you and your family will reconsider."

Then he went inside, leaving the door ajar for me.

five · · · · · ·
June 28, 1950

Days passed, and we acted as if nothing had happened. No one spoke of Mr. Kim's proposal, but it crackled in the air.

Omahni forbade us from seeing the Kims or even mentioning their names, but I knew they hadn't left yet. Myung-gi was leaving his books for me, one by one, under the willow tree by the schoolhouse. Only when I stopped finding old textbooks and novels would I know he was gone.

One summer morning, a lightning storm hovered. Everyone stayed indoors. Omahni sewed a hole in one of Youngsoo's pants, swatting Jisoo away from the sewing box full of sharp needles.

Youngsoo sat across from me at the table, opening a board game. "Noona, do you want to play *yoot*?"

"Maybe later." How could he think of playing games when the Kims would try to escape any day now?

Youngsoo sighed, then said, "You can have one of my schoolbooks. It's your favorite—the history book with all the maps." He nudged it across the low tabletop, nodding in reassurance the way an elder would push a plate of food toward a timid child.

I wondered if he knew that I always looked through this book at night while he was sleeping.

"No, take it back. I don't want it." I pushed it across the table, but glanced at the pretty blue cover as it slid away.

Youngsoo shrugged and put it in his bag. He wasn't trying to embarrass me; his heart was just too big for a small boy—I knew this. But I already had to serve him his food and take him to the school that I was no longer allowed to attend. Wasn't that humiliating enough? How could I accept his charity, too?

"Noona, one day let's go to America together. We can sail across the ocean, and I can be your shipmate." He smiled at me, not giving up.

I gave him a long, hard look. How could those words slip from his lips so easily? America wasn't a dream I dared consider, let alone say aloud—it gleamed so brightly I could hardly look at it. "Youngsoo, maybe you'll go there one day, but not me. You know that." I handed him a slice of apple that I had learned to skin and cut into a perfect crescent moon.

Abahji walked in carrying a bundle of firewood and set it by the kitchen step. I cut more apples into pieces and put them on a plate, and everyone gathered around the table for a break. Abahji pushed an entire slice into his mouth while Jisoo grabbed two, one in each fist.

"Better. You cut it a little better this time," Omahni said through a mouthful of apple.

It wasn't much of a compliment, but like a dog hungry for scraps, I would take it. Finally, I took a bite. Juicy and tart. My lips puckered. I didn't have an appetite.

A man's voice blared from the radio: *"In only three days, our valiant army has captured Seoul, the capital of South Korea! Our South Korean brothers will soon surrender to the bosom of the Fatherland!"*

Abahji clicked the radio off. He stopped chewing.

Silence swelled in my ears. "Abahji, what does it mean? Will North Korea win the war?"

He rubbed the back of his neck. "I don't know."

"Why all the glum faces?" Omahni asked. "Nothing would change for us. We've managed well enough by keeping our heads down and following the rules!"

Abahji whipped around, his face suddenly reddening. "What kind of nonsense are you saying? Everything would change!" I had never seen him so angry. "The entire Korean peninsula would be under communist rule! All hope for free elections, for contact with the outside world, for the right to speak our minds would be gone! Do you like living like this? Constant Party meetings? Fearing our neighbors? Worshipping in secret? Needing permission to visit your parents' graves in Pyongyang?"

Omahni quieted.

I wrung the edge of my blouse tighter and tighter. "What about the Kims?" I asked. Omahni jumped at the mention of their name. "What will happen to them? If the war's almost over, then they won't try to cross the border, will they?" I imagined Myung-gi and Yoomee walking straight into a black cloud of smoke and felt my heart pound.

Abahji took a sip of tea. "I think they will leave any day now. And I think they will make it to Busan." Then he turned to Omahni. "Busan is so far south and so well protected that the North Korean army cannot touch it—the Americans will stop them before they get there. And even if they don't, we'll have a better chance of getting out of Korea from a coastal city. Maybe we should consider leaving with the Kims and settling in Busan, too. We can stay with your brother, Hong-Chul, and his wife."

I stared at Abahji. Was he changing his mind? Something stirred inside me.

Omahni shook her head vigorously. "No, it's too dangerous! How can we possibly travel by foot all the way to the tip of South Korea with three children? We have no money to make the journey. And if North Korea wins the war, then it would have all been for nothing. We would have risked our lives, lost our home, all for *nothing*!" She sniffled, then dabbed her eyes and nose with the bottom of her skirt.

"But what is any of this worth if we have no hope for freedom? Why is your mind closed so tightly? It's as impenetrable as an acorn!" Abahji said.

"And you, my husband, waver like the wind! I thought we had agreed to stay!"

I wondered what we ought to do. My heart raced at the

thought of leaving, but I wasn't sure whether it was from fear or excitement. I tugged on Abahji's sleeve. "Abahji, does *everyone* have freedom in South Korea? Is it true that all the people can come and go as they please?"

Omahni glared at me from across the room.

"Yes, Sora-ya," Abahji said. But his face looked stricken, and I knew there was no easy answer, not even for him. "Your mother is so stubborn," he muttered. Then he brought his fist down hard on the low table—the teacups rattled against its wooden top. He rose and walked out, slamming the door behind him.

In an instant, I felt a gust as Omahni hurtled toward me, her long skirt whipping the air. "Do you think South Korea is some magical place to cure all your ills?" she hissed, her eyes wild with fear. "It's made of the same dirt and rock as here. Nothing will change for you. You'll still be a daughter. You'll still be a noona. You must still follow our traditions. You can't get out of those responsibilities, if that's what you're thinking." Her mouth twisted into a tight knot.

I sat motionless. A steady pressure mounted on my temples. Images from Miss Chun's World War II newsreel flickered in my head—women and children, dirty and ragged, howling by roadsides beside lifeless bodies. And, all at once, the thought of leaving home made me very afraid.

Omahni flicked the radio back on, and the announcer's voice returned like an unwelcome houseguest. She pushed my head toward the sound and said, "Listen to the radio! Do you hear what he's saying? The war is nearly won. There is no point in risking our lives when it'll soon be over. Don't encourage your father! He's a dreamer. Wake to your senses, Sora! A girl must have a keen mind and be as sharp as a fox. How else will you survive in this world?"

six · · · · · ·
June 29, 1950

The next morning, I ran to the willow tree by the schoolhouse. A slick layer of sweat coated my back.

Omahni was right. What was the point in risking our lives to escape? There would *be* no escape if the whole peninsula became communist. I had to stop the Kim family from leaving. They were dreaming, like Abahji.

There were no students running up the hill, no bells chiming from the schoolhouse. The plants out front were already withering. When I closed my eyes, I could still see it, the way life used to be before I had been pulled out of school: girls in the schoolyard making flower necklaces, Youngsoo playing tag with his classmates, kindergarteners running through the grass.

I opened my eyes. The image dissipated like smoke across the empty grounds.

The willow tree stood at the top of the hill, its draping branches hiding the ground and everything on it—leaves, rocks, Han's books. I searched by the trunk but couldn't find anything, not even the red book that he'd angrily chucked into his bag. Had they already escaped? I rummaged through leaves and bushes. Nothing.

The Kim family was gone.

I stopped moving and let the quiet sink in, lonelier than I had been just a second ago. The wind blew in and out of my shirt, billowing it away from my skin as if I were a hollow tree.

I rose and walked. The sky and river blurred into one, and I stumbled home not knowing up from down anymore.

❄ ❄ ❄

"Rumors are circling as fast as a dog chasing its tail," Omahni said to Abahji as I slipped into the house. She tugged on the latch of the storage chest and shoved our folded blankets inside, her face dark as the churning river before a storm. "Some are saying that the Kims were taken to a labor prison. But others think they heard shots."

I gasped. Something cold as liquid metal flowed into my stomach. I started shivering.

"Are you sure about this?" Abahji asked. "I mean, they're gone?" He sat at the low table, his cup of barley tea untouched.

"Yes, I'm sure!" Omahni cried. "And the worst part is that everyone is keeping their distance from our family as if we were a plague!"

From that day forward, Omahni ordered us to stay inside.

We became a target. At the whim of any one of our neighbors, our family could be sent to a hard labor prison in Siberia—all anyone had to do was go to the local Party office and lie. *The Paks are traitors to the Fatherland, just like their close friends the Kims! I heard them say . . ."*

The Party would reward their loyalty—and we would vanish like ghosts.

After the police interrogated Omahni and Abahji, we slept and ate together, never once leaving the house for more than ten minutes. I'd suggest we play school to pass the time, and Young-soo and Jisoo would agree, but by afternoon, they'd be rolling on the floor like sausages. The day would always end with each of us in our separate corners, Jisoo winding down with a thumb and a pile of clean socks.

Soon, our endless games deteriorated into shouting. One person's finger tapping would spark another person's outrage. Even Abahji started barking at us to quiet down. So, after seven days of confinement, when Youngsoo announced that he wanted to go fishing, Omahni didn't object. She just told us to be quick.

I took Youngsoo to the river.

We headed up the dirt road in silence. The swaying trees and whistling birds pacified us. And though I could feel the neighbors watching—eyes past half-closed shutters, curtains rustling without a breeze—I savored the fresh air and refused to hang my head low. I tried to ignore them and imagine Myung-gi running free—*no*—soaring free, high above the trees, away from petty gossip and stifling rules.

"This is a good spot, Noona," Youngsoo said. He crouched in the dirt along the river's edge while I watched him make mud pies and dig for worms. Long, pink bands wriggled on his open palm.

A group of boys came barefoot along the bank, skipping rocks and sticks along the water. Their white shirts were untucked and disheveled, but their red armbands gleamed like fresh blood on snow.

"Look who's here!" a moon-faced boy said. I recognized him as the son of the Suhs. "It's the traitors! If you don't love our country, then you should've been shot with the Kims!" He lunged toward us with a long stick and laughed when we flinched.

I grabbed Youngsoo's hand and walked farther upstream, but the gang of boys followed.

"We should notify the police that these traitors aren't wearing their armbands!" one boy said, holding a piece of candy—the kind that Comrade Cho awarded to students for ratting out their parents.

I recognized him; he was Kunsoo, youngest of the Chung boys. His mother and father had done a day of hard labor for letting Kim Il-sung's portrait hang crookedly on their wall.

The boys surrounded us. So many of them—five, six, seven. My breath grew shaky. I glanced at Youngsoo. His face was white.

"*Trai-tor! Trai-tor!*" Kunsoo and the boys chanted, circling closer.

"Look at this one. Look at the mud on his shirt. This isn't mud from a hard-working proletarian. This is mud from a capitalistic America-loving pig who plays in the dirt all day," Moon-face said, sounding just like the local Party leaders at town meetings. His breath reeked of rotten kimchi. He yanked the worms from Youngsoo's hand and pulled one thin.

"Give it back to him," I said, a hot flare in my chest.

The worm elongated and flattened into a pink line. Stretching, stretching, stretching, until it ripped in half.

"No!" Youngsoo shouted.

Moon-face threw the rest onto the grass. Youngsoo dropped to the ground, picking up the worms that had done nothing to deserve this.

It was then that Moon-face grabbed Youngsoo's arm.

Without thinking, I yanked my brother's sleeve away from him. "Who are you calling a filthy pig, anyway? Have you smelled yourself lately?" I said.

For a second, Moon-face looked at me, as determined as a wolf fixed on prey stuck up a tree. He pretended to walk away—then turned around and jabbed his stick into my stomach instead.

My body coiled. I fell. Tears welled in my eyes, and I closed them.

I felt my stomach. Blood on my blouse. I had to remember to exhale.

There was laughter. Ugly laughter, everywhere. Then howling. Crazy, ferocious howling like a cornered wild animal. I opened my eyes. The boys were running. White river rocks shot through the air like many little arrows. Youngsoo stood over me hurling handfuls of them, a mad howl still blasting from his mouth. Tears streamed down his cheeks.

"I'm fine, Youngsoo!" I said, trying to calm him.

But he wouldn't stop throwing, screaming.

I clasped the sides of his face. "Youngsoo, look at me. It's all over."

He held still. His eyes widened, as if he were surprised to see me. Then he took in a shuddering breath.

I looked toward the woods, hoping to catch a glimpse of Moon-face fleeing. A part of me wanted him back. Here. In front of me. How dare he call us traitors when we had done nothing wrong? I started rehearsing what I'd say to his face—that he was a bully and a brainwashed idiot. I'd tell him that the Kims were smart to run away from stifling, ignorant people like him.

But as soon as I thought it, I knew how dangerous that would be. Instead, I took the last rock from Youngsoo's hand and hurled it as far as I could, then spat on the very ground that I loved.

seven · · · · · ·
August, 1950

Weeks passed. The village began emptying.

Down the road, a hanging basket fell off its hook and stayed in the same spot for days. Miss Chun's house stood vacant, its doors swinging listlessly in the wind. She'd seemed different after her books and teaching materials were confiscated, hardly ever saying hello to anyone, and now she was gone. A family from our old church disappeared in the middle of the night. I could see torn-up floorboards through their window, their found Bible ripped to shreds. Every day their dog sat under the eaves, waiting for them.

One late afternoon, I helped Omahni take down the laundry from the clothing line. Even the air smelled different—earthy and musty—as if the whole village were uninhabited. As if it had been for a long time.

"Where did everyone go?" I asked. "I can count at least four or five families that are just . . . gone."

Omahni scoffed. "Is that all? I can count more than that. What about the Suh family, with the round-faced boy? They left just yesterday," she said, a surliness in her voice. She snatched shirts and pants off the rope and threw them in a basket.

The Suh family. That was Moon-face boy. Even they were gone. "So everyone is leaving, like the Kims?"

"No, they have been taken," she said, keeping up the swift and steady pace of her work. "Like the Kims." She believed what she'd heard—that they had been arrested. I tried to believe that they'd escaped, and that was why they were gone.

"Taken?"

"Yes, taken!" She shook her head in annoyance. "The police have been rounding up anyone they don't like. That's where people go when they disappear—prison! Or worse! They've been arresting pastors, did you know that? Pastor Joh's wife said soldiers came in the middle of the night and took her husband away."

Though she never spared me any details, I started trembling at her matter-of-fact tone. Pastor Joh had been our minister years ago, when church wasn't banned. He wasn't even allowed to preach anymore, so why would they take him? Was he dead? I bit my lip to keep from crying. "Why would they want to hurt pastors?" I managed to say.

"Because they undermine the Reds," Omahni said, as if she was angry with me. "They preach about God and things the communists don't want us to hear. Pastors have the power of ideas. It's not so easy to control people like that."

"But there's no church! There's no preaching!"

"You don't need a church to preach, Sora. The Reds know that."

Red. The color of communism. It burned through the village like a flame. It wrapped around people's arms, squeezing. And when it knocked on your door, there was no hiding. A cold shiver crawled down my back. "Omahni," I said, an urgency coursing through me, "what if they arrest us, too? Shouldn't we run?"

Omahni stopped moving and stared straight ahead, forcing her face into a blank sheet.

"Lucky for us, we're not one of those people with power. In fact, we gained the most from the new laws taking land from the rich and giving it to the poor!" She turned and leveled her gaze at me. "So, no, we shouldn't leave, especially now that North Korea has taken over most of the peninsula. That'd be risking our lives for nothing. Remember, don't go siding with your father on this."

❄ ❄ ❄

As the days cooled, so did the air between my parents. A steely silence grew in the house. Omahni and Abahji hardly looked at each other.

The only thing that got them talking again was the draft.

"They're coming to recruit all able-bodied men into the army," Omahni said one day over a dinner of thin radish soup without rice. She sneaked a glance at Abahji, letting her gaze linger as if she missed looking at his face.

"You think I don't know this?" Abahji cleared his throat and took another sip of soup. "When they come, I'll have to go. But I refuse to fight for them. I will let myself die in combat."

At this, Youngsoo burst into tears, and Jisoo scurried onto Omahni's lap like a startled pup. I could feel Youngsoo's watery eyes on me, begging for some comfort, but I couldn't look at him when there was a tide rising in my own throat.

Omahni slammed her chopsticks on the table. Our heads turned. "We didn't stay just so they could come and take you," she said, her voice shaking. Her eyes were rimmed red. "We'll dig a hole. Hide you away. Keep you safe. Only for a little while. I'm sure this war will end in a few short weeks."

No one spoke.

I turned Omahni's words around and around in my head, inspecting them from all sides. Once, during hide-and-seek, I'd hidden inside a large urn for three hours. Eventually, Youngsoo announced that he'd given up because it was impossible to find me. If the soldiers couldn't find Abahji, they wouldn't be able to draft him into their army. Maybe Omahni had a good plan.

For the first time in weeks, Abahji reached over and touched Omahni's hand. Her shoulders softened with this small gesture.

Then Abahji told me to get the shovels and picks, because he had work to do that night.

❄ ❄ ❄

The next morning, I looked out the window and saw my parents on the edge of the millet field. Mostly hidden by pine trees, they crouched over a gaping hole, a fresh pile of dirt beside it. I ran out to meet them.

"This is where we'll hide your father—just until the war

ends, which will be soon, I'm sure," Omahni said to me, repeating herself from the day before, like a mantra. She straightened and wiped her forehead. Her jeogori was soaked on the back and under the arms. Grimly, she took the shovel from Abahji, and he slid into the dark pit.

I watched in horror as the earth swallowed him whole.

Cautiously, I took a step forward and looked down. Abahji lay on his back as if in a grave. My breath quickened. I thought of those newsreels showing bodies tossed into simple roadside pits. *This is not a grave, just a hole*, I told myself.

Below, Abahji nodded. "I think this is good."

Youngsoo came running from behind. "Can I hide, too, Omahni?" He lit up as if it was his turn at hide-and-seek.

"Don't be silly. This is not a game!" Omahni said.

"Then what is it?"

Omahni kneeled and looked him level in the eye, clutching his shoulders until her knuckles shone white. A frightening calm settled on her face. "This is about keeping our family together. We must protect your father."

After a moment, Youngsoo nodded as solemnly as any soldier called to duty.

Protecting Abahji was the one thing on which Omahni and I could agree. I stood over his hole, my shadow towering like a giant.

"Will he have to stay in there all day and night?" I asked.

"He'll remain in the hole as long as he can," Omahni said.

She shook the brown dirt from her long skirt, and it gleamed white once again.

"But what about food and water?" I noticed my voice rising to a higher pitch, and I cleared my throat.

"He'll have to come in every once in a while. We can also bring him food and water in the night."

I watched Abahji climb out. He was covered in a thin layer of rusty dirt, which had settled into the creases around his mouth and eyes. He looked at me and smiled. I couldn't believe Abahji wouldn't be able to show his face anymore.

eight · · · · · ·
August, 1950

The next evening, Omahni ordered us onto the field. "Today, we practice hiding Abahji in his hole," she announced.

Youngsoo, Jisoo, and I stood before her, scratching behind our ears and fiddling with our clothes.

"Pay attention!" she snapped.

We stopped moving.

"Come, look." Omahni motioned us toward the hole.

I peeked in. Abahji was already inside lying on his back. He tried to sit up, but slipped and hit his shoulder against the wall; a shower of dirt fell onto his head. Youngsoo giggled and Jisoo squealed. But I stared blank-faced, trying to grapple with the indignity of it all. My father. In a hole.

Omahni covered the opening with a wooden board. "Youngsoo-ya, your job is to sweep away all the footprints in the dirt." She tossed him a broom, and he began sweeping up the whirlwind of activity around the hole. "Sora, Abahji slept in the house last night. Your job is to run inside and clear away any lingering signs of him—an extra teacup, his house slippers, anything. Go."

I darted across the field and into the house. Tossed his

slippers under the floorboard where we kept our Bible. Rinsed two teacups sitting on the low table. Swept his undergarments up and into the chest. But what about his clothes, razor, and shoes? How much did I need to hide? Had I overlooked anything? Ai! I ran back out to the field.

Omahni was counting. "Four hundred and twenty seconds," she said to me. "It took you that long to do your job."

I didn't think four hundred and twenty seconds was so bad, considering that the house was at least a hundred yards away.

Omahni turned her attention to all of us. "We must be faster, better."

Later, we sat inside and practiced controlling our faces— loosening our mouths, draining all anxiety from our eyes—so that no one knocking on the door would know our hearts were racing with deception. "This part is just as important as hiding Abahji. We can never let our faces show our thoughts," Omahni said to us. But I worried that mine would betray me, no matter how much we practiced.

"Like this, Omahni?" Youngsoo asked, massaging his cheeks and crossing his eyes. I stifled a giggle.

Omahni put her hand to her lips and frowned. "No, no. Don't look frightened or overly relaxed. Just look normal. No one can know that we're hiding Abahji. Understand?"

Youngsoo nodded.

Jisoo clapped and shouted, "Apah! Apah!" He pounded the low table.

"No, Jisoo-ya," Omahni said, her hands now fluttering in the air. "Don't call your father. He's not here anymore."

Having seen Abahji in his hole just a few minutes earlier, Jisoo squealed and laughed at Omahni's boldfaced lie. "Apah! Apah!" he cried even louder, pointing to the pit.

At that, Omahni wrapped her headache bandana around her forehead and lay on the broad cushion on the floor. "Go outside and play. We'll practice again later," she said.

True to her word, we rehearsed again and again, until one day, we were able to hide Abahji in under two minutes, our faces expertly composed. Omahni stood with her arms raised like the conductor of an orchestra, beaming at us for playing our parts perfectly. "Come, children. I'm so proud of you!"

Youngsoo and Jisoo ran and slammed into her stomach. She hugged them.

"Sora-ya, you come, too," Omahni said.

I went. She reached me with her fingertips.

"You all did very well today. I think we're ready. Our family will stay together. We'll be safe." She nodded fiercely.

I wanted to believe her and would've done anything to make it true. If someone had told me that eating a grasshopper could somehow protect us, I would've eaten a hundred.

❄ ❄ ❄

But I knew there were no guarantees. And it wasn't long before I realized that I *wasn't* ready. That nothing could've prepared me for that late August morning when two military officers came knocking on our door.

"Let us in! It's Byun Tae-joon, Lieutenant of the Korean People's Army," a man shouted.

My stomach plunged.

Abahji was hiding in his hole. Omahni and Youngsoo were out at the market. Only Jisoo sat in the house with me.

I looked around the room. Hadn't Abahji come inside in the middle of the night for a cup of tea and a shave? I flicked my gaze to the table, to the water basin. There were two teacups. And Abahji's razor, still wet on a hook.

Fists pounded. "Open the door!"

I darted toward the hook and wiped the razor dry against my skirt, slicing through the thin cotton, into my skin. A trickle of blood seeped through the white fabric.

"Let us in!"

My hands fumbled. I hung the razor, ran to the door, and turned the knob.

"What took you so long? Are you hiding something?" the lieutenant demanded, his face angular and sharp. Another officer stood behind him. They were grown men wearing black leather shoes and fitted caps.

I glanced at the razor still swinging on its hook. But then a squeal of laughter shot into the room. I had nearly forgotten.

Jisoo.

He clenched a sheet torn from Youngsoo's language book in his fist, the elegant black-ink type now awkward and twisted. "Jisoo, no!" I scolded. Not the precious schoolbooks!

I watched him tear at another page, something inside me ripping, too. I rushed over. "Give it to me," I said, a prickly heat rising on the back of my neck. But Jisoo strengthened his grip on the book, a deep frown drawn across his face.

"Ha, look at the little rascal," one of the officers said, a knife sitting in a sheath around his waist.

"You will not ruin this, too!" I cried, tugging on the book until something wet hit my cheek.

Jisoo was spitting at me.

I loosened my hold in astonishment, and Jisoo yanked another page out of the book. He scurried across the room and crumpled it, squealing in victory.

The officers roared with laughter.

The open book lay on the floor, jagged paper running down the middle of its spine. I felt words bubbling to the surface. "You ruin everything! If it weren't for you, I wouldn't have been pulled out of school!"

Jisoo wailed. "Omah! Omah!"

"Omahni is not here! She's still at the market!" I shouted.

Which made Jisoo cry even harder. "Apah! Apah!" he screamed this time.

I stopped breathing.

"Enough of this nonsense," the angular officer said, no

longer laughing. His eyes narrowed. "Indeed, where is your father, Pak Sangmin? We are here to recruit all able-bodied men into the army."

I couldn't find my voice. My body trembled. I stared at their shiny black shoes. "Our father. He left us. Married another woman," I whispered, then burst into tears.

Jisoo dropped the torn sheet, looked at me, and bawled so loudly that the officers had to cover their ears. His sharp cries surprised me. How much could Jisoo understand? I wanted to pick him up and tell him that it wasn't true.

"Ai! Enough! Enough!" one of the officers said. "Let's go. There's no man in this household." They turned and hurried out the door.

Minutes later, Omahni and Youngsoo returned to a house full of crying.

"What's going on here? Can't you even keep your baby brother quiet?" Omahni said. "And you wanted to leave! How could we ever consider escaping when you make him cry like that? We'd be caught before we left the village!" She headed into the kitchen, muttering, "Can't depend on you for anything."

My head still whirring, I couldn't respond. Instead, I tucked Omahni's words deep inside me, like a tiny gong, reverberating endlessly.

nine · · · · · ·
September, 1950

By September, the mountains blazed with bright oranges and reds. Youngsoo and Jisoo played with the fallen leaves in the front courtyard while I pumped water from the well.

"When can Abahji come out of the hole? He's been in there forever," Youngsoo said, building a tiny village of twigs and leaves.

"Shush. Don't talk about it." Our family had committed such hefty crimes—lying to authorities about hiding Abahji, avoiding his conscription into the army—that I was sure the punishment would be death. For all of us. "Besides, you saw him last night when he came inside to eat and exercise."

"No, I was asleep! That doesn't count."

He was right. Abahji had been in that hole for weeks now, appearing for only a few short minutes in the dark. I'd catch glimpses of him in the late night or early morning shadows, never knowing whether I was seeing my father or his ghost. I missed him.

"What about *Chuseok*?" Youngsoo asked. "Aren't we going to celebrate Thanksgiving this fall?"

I thought of the sweet *songpyeon*, our special meal with the

Kims, visits to ancestral graves, and knew there was nothing to celebrate. "Of course there's no Chuseok this year—use your head and think. It passed anyway."

My buckets were full. I lifted them and shuffled toward the kitchen, water splashing over the sides.

Closer to the house, I could hear Omahni clapping and cheering inside. One of her friends rushed out the door, a scarf covering her smiling face.

I hurried into the main room and found Omahni sitting on the woven mat. She clapped her hands again loudly and grinned, whispering, "Oh, thank you, God. Thank you, God."

"What is it? Why was your old choir friend here?" I nearly dropped the buckets. I couldn't remember the last time Omahni was this excited. Was the war over? Which side had won?

"She received word from the South. Oh, that General MacArthur, he's something else!" Omahni's eyes flickered with determination.

"MacArthur?"

"He's an American general. He launched a surprise attack at Inchon! He defeated the North Korean army there! And now the Americans and their allies have recaptured Seoul. Soon, we may all be free!"

"Does that mean we don't have to leave home?" I asked.

Omahni gripped my shoulders. "I think we'll soon have our freedom *and* be able to stay in our homeland."

My heart leapt. Such promising news! I imagined all the

banned books coming out of hiding, like Abahji from his hole, and I laughed aloud. Then, without warning, Omahni tuned the radio to a lively *pansori* song and danced from side to side. I sat still with rounded eyes, but when the *janggu* drum kicked in, I let go of any reservation and clapped to my mother's beat.

I had heard the janggu drum from a half mile away. We ran down the dirt road toward the sound, Omahni hoisting Youngsoo on her hip and Abahji carrying me on his shoulders. The wide-eyed sun beat down the back of my neck.

Abahji grabbed a passing villager. "Is it true? Did the Japanese surrender?"

"Yes! The Russians have liberated us, and now the Japanese are packing up and leaving! No more Japanese rule! After thirty-five years, we are finally free!"

Omahni burst into tears.

By the time we arrived, the entire village had gathered on the large lot in front of the high school. The Japanese flag was torn in half, and in its place we flew the Korean flag. A group of singers stood up front, cradled by the lush Rangnim Mountains in the background, the river weaving in and out of the hills like a silk ribbon. I stood on the raised roots of a tree to see. They started singing "Arirang."

I looked at Abahji. He closed his eyes and sang. Omahni's mouth quivered with the lyrics. Soon, the entire village was singing in unison, their voices sweet and strong. It was the song of a people constantly besieged, yet hopeful. Always hopeful. Pride swelled in my throat. The melody nearly lifted me off my feet, and I gripped a branch to hold on.

The final note had everyone cheering. Then the janggu drum started thumping again, and a woman's singsong voice rode the rhythm like a wave. Abahji clapped with the music. He grabbed Omahni's hand. "Let's dance," he said. His eyes softened as he stared into her face, and I looked away, feeling suddenly shy. Omahni twirled in the dusty air, her long skirt fanning out like a lily.

"Noona, dance too!" Youngsoo said, toddling toward me.

I laughed and took his chubby hands. We leaned our heads back and spun. Blue sky and green mountain swirled above, colors so brilliant that I had to stop and stare.

ten · · · · · ·
October, 1950

The first bomb came in the middle of the night. When it hit, it rumbled low in the distance.

Youngsoo sat straight up. "What was that?"

Omahni lit a kerosene lamp. I squinted and looked around the room. The large storage chest loomed down at me, its metal front hinges bared like teeth. Youngsoo and Jisoo huddled together on their sleeping mats, their small heads silhouetted against the wall. The nights were turning cold, and I rubbed my arms for warmth.

Omahni glanced out the window in the direction of Abahji's hole. "An explosive," she said. "The Americans are pushing north. They may have reached Pyongyang."

I twisted the edge of my blanket. "Well, we're miles and miles from Pyongyang, so we won't ever be near any fighting. Right, Omahni?" Abahji had said so.

"Distance doesn't matter; they'll be up here soon enough. This is what we must endure if we want the Americans to fight their way north and claim victory. Nothing comes without a price. Now get back to sleep." She blew out the lamp.

But sleep wouldn't come. I lay awake listening to the new

sounds booming in the distance. Could Abahji feel it in the ground? Was he scared outside, alone in the dark?

There were more explosions over the next few weeks, each one growing closer.

❄ ❄ ❄

We never went to the air raid shelter, which was teeming with military police and the most ardent communist supporters. Instead, we huddled indoors as the temperature dropped and morning frost glistened in the fields. Omahni heated rocks in the stove, then wrapped them in towels and put them inside Abahji's hole. I couldn't stop shivering—whether from cold or fear, I could no longer tell the difference.

We were eating dinner one day when it happened. A long whistle sliced through the air. Omahni, Youngsoo, Jisoo, and I looked at one another around the table, listening to that high-pitched sound, knowing that we were doomed.

Before anyone could speak, the Earth collided with the Sun. The floor shook. Dishes crashed in the kitchen. Straw blew off the roof. And terror pummeled my heart into a bruise.

The house stilled.

I peeked through my fingers and saw Youngsoo's trembling body covering Jisoo, and Omahni's thin arms shielding them both. Then came the sound of debris raining down on the roof like crackling corn, followed by an unbearable silence—until the next bomb, which could drop at any moment.

"Are you okay? Is everybody okay?" Omahni asked, her eyes wide.

I nodded, but couldn't stop shaking. How close had it come? I scrambled toward the window and saw thick black smoke rising from a neighbor's field. So close. What about next time?

I wanted to run and hide, but there was nowhere to go. Jisoo kept blinking and looking around as if he couldn't figure out what had just happened.

"What about Abahji?" Youngsoo cried. "Apah!"

At that Omahni jumped up and darted out the door, the long hair fraying from her bun. Youngsoo ran to the window beside me, both of us peering out into the dark. Through the thick pines, we could see her clawing at the wooden board covering the hole, then Abahji's dim figure climbing out, stumbling, and righting itself. They clutched each other like they were both made of water, their arms grasping for something solid to hold on to.

❄ ❄ ❄

Every night I waited for it to come, the one that would land right on top of us. I wore that worry like a noose around my neck.

But it never came. Instead, after a few more strikes in the fields, the blasts eventually dwindled to a distant rumbling, like thunder.

"Children! Children!" Omahni said one day, waving us close to the radio. "God has rewarded us for all our suffering and patience. The Americans have finally taken Pyongyang and are marching north toward the Yalu River. The communists will soon lose this war!"

She held a leaflet—the kind that South Korean planes had started dropping overhead. It showed a picture of a white man with the name "General MacArthur" promising humane treatment to any surrendering North Korean troops.

I couldn't believe it. This was really the end. Abahji could come out of his hole. The North would become free like the South. We'd all be allowed to come and go as we pleased. I imagined going back to school, having my own books, going to America.

Over the next two weeks, I noticed the hard knot between Omahni's shoulders loosen. And I even thought I heard a sigh escape from the house itself.

❄ ❄ ❄

On the day the Americans came to our village, everyone stood outside in their coats, cheering and waving homemade South Korean flags like spectators at a parade.

"Children, come out! They're here! They're here!" Omahni called from the front courtyard, holding Jisoo on her hip.

Youngsoo and I ran out the door, past the gate, and down the path, stopping at the edge of the road where we wedged ourselves between a group of small children and an old couple dressed in their finest clothes. Through the trees' bare branches, I could see a line of trucks, jeeps, and soldiers heading toward us from the top of the dirt road. I wouldn't have believed they were really here if it wasn't for Abahji's familiar field behind them.

I'd never seen Americans before. The men towered over

us. They wore heavy green coats. Dark metal helmets rounded the top of their heads. Tall noses and deep-set eyes complicated their faces. Their skin came in different shades—white, brown, black—and I wondered how anyone could know they were American only by their features.

I joined the clapping. Omahni stood beside me and wept. The soldiers strode past us, smiling and waving, a few even bowing. One soldier swaggered, laughing with a cigarette hanging from his lips. Another one caught my eye and winked, flashing a smile that made me turn a deep shade of red. I marveled at the ease in their step, at the way their faces were open, not closed.

"Gooks," a freckled soldier muttered, glaring at us.

"'Gooks'?!" a silver-haired officer demanded angrily. He spat out his cigarette, mashed it with his heel, and started to yell at the soldier.

I couldn't understand what they were saying. But I knew something was wrong. Something about Gooks. I turned to Omahni. "What does 'Gook' mean?"

Omahni squinted hard, perhaps trying to remember—or trying to forget.

When she wouldn't tell me, I knew that "Gook" couldn't mean anything good. And I was sure Omahni understood this, too. But we continued waving and cheering anyway. They were here to save us, and for that we would endure almost anything.

"Tootsie Rolls! Tootsie Rolls!" a dark-skinned man shouted from a truck.

Handfuls of candy rained down on us: long, skinny rolls in brown wrappers. All the kids shrieked, scrambling to collect the sweet gifts. Youngsoo jumped in the fray, disappearing for a moment, but reemerging triumphant with the edge of his coat drawn and cinched like a bag. Unsure whether I was too old to join, I picked up only the stray pieces that had landed near my feet.

Youngsoo held his coat full of candy as if it were a pot of gold. "Here, Noona, have some." He grinned, showing a mouthful of dark brown goo.

I took one, peeled off the wrapper, and slipped it into my mouth. I bit down, and it stuck to my teeth, the creamy sweetness rolling over my tongue.

All the remaining villagers were here, finally showing their true faces, laughing and talking freely: *We had always dreamed of America, didn't you know? How could we have told you the way we really felt when the Party was always listening? It was either your family or ours that would be called traitors; no hard feelings, eh?*

I listened—my mind spinning amid the loud cheering, candies falling, children scuffling—and didn't know what to think. Was the war over?

That was when I spotted Abahji standing outside instead of hiding, for the first time in weeks. His jacket hung at sharp angles around his shoulders. His complexion had paled to pure white. In the light, his holed-up body, now exposed like a snail out of its shell, glowed translucent along the edges. When he saw me, he laughed and cheered with the sun on his face. My arm flew up and wiped my eyes. I rushed over and pressed his hand into mine.

Abahji looked as if he was expecting me to say something, and when I didn't, he only smiled and asked, "Is the candy delicious?"

I nodded and savored the last bit, letting the sweetness linger for as long as it could.

The Americans stayed for only an hour before continuing their push toward the North Korean–Chinese border. Jeeps rumbled down our narrow dirt road. One camouflaged in green beeped its horn in a few short bursts. Everyone wished them luck, thrusting both arms up and shouting "*Mee-gook!* America!"

I squinted through the clouds of dust. The soldiers' long torsos and unlined faces made them look more like boys than men, not much older than Myung-gi. I felt an affection for them that took me by surprise, as did the gratitude that caught in my throat. They sat in trucks heading to their next battle, lined in rows like easy targets.

I wondered if they might die as I watched them rattle down the road until they disappeared completely.

eleven · · · · · ·
November, 1950

Weeks later, we listened to the news broadcast that would change everything. The announcer's voice faltered in and out through the static:

"This war, which was started by South Korea, the puppet regime of the evil U.S. Imperialists, will soon... to an end..."

I glanced at Abahji. He sighed and shook his head. It was the lie they'd been telling us since the beginning of the war: that South Korea and the U.S. had attacked first. We knew it wasn't true, because Omahni's friend, the old choir member, had a black-market radio that could receive foreign broadcasts from the rest of the world—all of which reported that North Korea had invaded first. And the regime had lied to us before, about the whereabouts of the disappeared and even about the existence of God.

"Our Chinese friends have joined heroic North Korean units and decimated the filthy American dogs and their allies in a crushing military defeat... Hook-nosed American monsters, who wish to wipe Korean... from the face of this... now tremble in fear and flee in retreat below the thirty-eighth parallel."

Abahji turned off the radio.

The winning and losing sides had flip-flopped once again.

Our joy had been almost as short-lived as Liberation Day, as those precious few hours when the Russian soldiers had become our saviors—until they started taking whatever they wanted, especially the men's watches, which they wore five in a row up their arms. In the end, the Soviets were the same as the Japanese.

"Those American soldiers. Dead. All dead," Abahji said. He pounded his fist against the low table.

I sat by the window and tried to remember their faces. Cigarettes hanging from the sides of their mouths. Dark sunglasses sitting high on tall noses. Dimple-capped smiles. Just a few weeks ago, they were here, but now they were gone. Even the freckled soldier who had said something about Gooks. His sergeant who scolded him. The man who had tossed Tootsie Rolls from the truck. I couldn't believe it. I was sorry, so sorry.

"We must go. Tonight, when it's dark. No one will see us," Abahji said. He sat on the floor rubbing his knees until I thought he might wear a hole in his pants.

"What?" Omahni cried, sitting beside him. "Tonight? Are you crazy? It's too late now—it's almost winter. We'll all freeze to death!" Her face hardened.

"The Americans are leaving. Once they're gone, we will be trapped here forever." There was a sharpness in Abahji's tone that I rarely heard. "This is our last chance to escape. We need to stay ahead of their retreat."

"You don't know that! The Americans were winning! This is

just one small setback. We don't need to leave. They'll free us all!" Omahni jumped up and started wiping the floor with a rag.

Abahji stood and put his steady hands over hers so she'd look at him. "We can't be sure that the Americans will win. This war is too unpredictable. How long do you want to continue living in fear? We saw what they did to your relatives. The Reds have no morals, no God, no loyalties, except to the Party. We cannot continue being amongst these brainwashed people who walk around like the living dead," Abahji said, his voice quivering.

"*Then you go alone!*" Omahni cried, flinging the wet rag across the room. "The trek is too dangerous! Soldiers will shoot us at the border! I know how to keep my head down and follow the rules. The children and I will stay here!"

The floor dropped out from under me. She couldn't have meant it. She was just angry. She would take it back.

Please, Omahni, take it back.

I looked at Abahji—at the way his shoulders hunched as if he'd just been struck with an arrow—and waited for him to say something. But he sank down mute at the table, leaning his entire weight on one arm as the rest of him went slack.

Something inside me ticked louder and louder. Every day, our lives seemed only to worsen: smaller rations, greater fear, more vanishing people. If we stayed now, Abahji would have to go back to hiding in a hole. But in Busan, people could come and go as they pleased—maybe even *I* could come and go as I pleased. My breath grew shallow, and my head felt faint.

Tonight could be our last chance.

"Abahji," I said, hardly able to keep my voice from shaking. They both turned to look at me. My face burned under Omahni's intense glare. "I . . . I think we should go."

Omahni pressed her lips together in a severe line. Her eyes reflected every wrong thing I'd ever done to her.

Abahji smiled and bent to smooth my hair. Then he straightened his back. "Sora-ya, you're even braver than your father, who has been hiding in a hole."

I started to speak—I wanted to tell him that he was wrong—but shook my head instead.

Abahji took a deep breath. "Everyone, pack quickly. We're leaving now."

Now? I looked around the room, staring hard at every object, trying to soak up the memories. Youngsoo's fishing net on the floor. The small cast-iron stove that warmed our backs. The low dining table, lacquered in black and inlaid with fake mother-of-pearl. The sturdy teak wardrobe that Abahji had made. I couldn't believe we were leaving so suddenly, leaving the house that I'd lived in all my life. Everything—the mud walls, the stone floor, the thatched roof—began to blur, as if already escaping me.

"Snap out of it, Sora!" Omahni said angrily, pulling her jacket from a drawer. "You asked for this, so hurry up and gather your things!"

I knew she never really wanted to split the family apart. In the end, my voice mattered—it was two against one. She had no choice.

But it was a shaky triumph at best. Omahni would be giving me the evil eye for the rest of my life. I avoided looking directly at her.

"Abahji, what should we pack?" A faint blast rattled the windows.

"Sora-ya, pack only essential items. Nothing too heavy. Warm clothes, coats. Quickly!" Abahji marched across the room carrying a sack of rice.

But I grabbed Youngsoo's history book off the floor and frantically turned to my favorite page—the world map—and cringed as I ripped it out. A mangled edge of paper ran down the middle like a fresh wound. I thought of Jisoo tearing sheets from this book and couldn't believe that I had just done the same. But an entire book was too heavy to pack, while a single page was weightless. I folded it carefully and tucked it deep inside my coat pocket.

Omahni yanked undershirts and sweaters over Youngsoo's and Jisoo's heads. She crammed their fingers into gray wooly mittens and their arms into padded-cotton coat sleeves. When she was finished, my brothers stood in the middle of the room like tree stumps. I changed into my warmest pants and put on my thick, quilted coat. Abahji swung the *jigeh* onto his shoulders— an A-frame backpack loaded with rice, blankets, and a small pot—and helped Omahni tie Jisoo onto her back with a long strip of cloth. Jisoo was lost in a swaddling of blankets, only his face peering out like a baby owl from its tree hole.

"Okay," Abahji said. "Let's go. Quietly."

I glanced around for a final goodbye, a dull ache rising in my chest. Would I ever see our home again? The waving millet fields? The majestic mountains? The sparkling river under the afternoon sun? Then that dull ache sharpened to a stab, and I clutched the edge of my coat.

PART II

❄❄❄❄❄❄❄

ESCAPE

twelve · · · · · ·
November 26, 1950

Abahji opened the door. It was dark. The clouds had swallowed the moon whole.

"It's too black out. We need a lamp," Youngsoo said, tugging on Abahji's sleeve. I knew he was afraid of the dark.

"No, son, a lamp will only put a spotlight on us. Now be quiet."

We followed Abahji out the door.

"Make sure you hold Youngsoo's hand," Omahni whispered to me as she adjusted Jisoo on her back. "He's your responsibility."

I nodded and held on to him.

An icy wind swept around us. In the distance, deep rumbles made the air vibrate, as commonplace now as any hooting owl or chirping cricket. I took guilty comfort in the dull, muffled sound of those faraway blasts—they proved the battle raged farther north instead of here.

Dried cornstalks waved in the wind. With a thick scarf and hat covering most of my head, my ears seemed stuffed with cotton. And, like a dream, my eyes grappled with dim and nameless shapes as I plodded through the darkness. Was this all really happening?

I shivered. No one spoke, not even Jisoo. I walked behind Abahji, Youngsoo by my side, while Omahni stayed close with Jisoo on her back. Every few seconds, Abahji would turn his head to check on us.

For hours, we marched in silence down the dirt road alongside corn and millet fields, the swish of corn leaves whispering around us. My canoe-shaped rubber shoes felt hard and stiff, and the sides of my feet chafed. I winced.

"Youngsoo, stop leaning on my arm. You're too heavy." I nudged him off, and he whimpered in reply.

Abahji halted.

I stopped breathing.

We listened for footsteps—and heard some.

Seconds later, Abahji gestured toward the cornfield. I hurried between the rows, the blisters on my feet vanishing.

The field teemed with stalks as tall as my father and as numerous as an army. Dried leaves brushed my face like paper blades. I crushed Youngsoo's hand into my fist as we wove in and out of the densely packed corn. Deeper and deeper. Not caring whether we'd ever be able to find our way back to the road. I tried hard not to rustle the stems.

At last, Abahji stopped. We huddled to the ground and didn't move. The pungent smell of fertilizer stung my nostrils and tickled my throat, but I pushed down a cough and squeezed my eyes shut. The pointy tip of a dried corn leaf stabbed at my cheek.

Jisoo stirred and shifted on Omahni's back. A low whining

started from his throat, like a tiny snowball rolling downhill, bigger and bigger. I seized up.

He was going to do it again. Ruin everything.

I had heard Jisoo whining from halfway down the road.

I was walking home from school holding my final exam—the only one in the entire grade marked with a perfect score. A gust blew, and I turned the sheets sideways into the wind so they wouldn't crinkle. These papers wanted to fly.

Omahni ran out to the side of the road, waving for me to come. "Hurry, Sora-ya. I need your help. Watch Jisoo so Abahji and I can sow the millet before the sun goes down." She ushered me into the house.

Jisoo sat on the floor crying over a mitten that wouldn't fit on his foot.

"From now on, you must look after your brothers so I can work in the field," Omahni said matter-of-factly. "I'm taking you out of school. Today was your last day."

"Last day of school?" Blood drained from my face. I felt my lip tremble.

"Sora-ya, you're overreacting! You'll learn how to keep house. It'll be good for you. You need this for your future."

Whose future? This was not the future I wanted. "But I'm going to be a writer one day."

"What? A storyteller?" A bubble of laughter popped from Omahni's mouth. "Sora, put your feet back on the ground."

Omahni walked into the kitchen. Pots and pans clanged. I could hardly gather my rushing thoughts. "But Yoomee goes to school," I blurted.

Omahni poked her head into the main room and frowned at me. "Does Yoomee have little brothers to look after? Does her mother work all year long, harvesting potatoes in the spring and rice and millet in the fall?" She exhaled loudly. "As close as our families are, the Kims are different from us, Sora. Yoomee's father is principal of the high school. He thinks fancy books are more important than anything, but we're more practical than that."

I stared at her. In just a few words, as plain and gray as rocks, she had explained away my future.

"Give Jisoo rice. I'll be back by sundown." Omahni hurried out the door.

Jisoo crawled to the low dining table and tipped a pot of hot barley tea onto the floor. He yelped, then wailed—his hand turned bright red, and a blister started forming right before my eyes. I wanted to pick him up, but I couldn't move, couldn't breathe.

Just like that. On my twelfth birthday. My life was over.

Jisoo's hand smacked me on the shoulder as he wriggled on Omahni's back, ready for his nighttime milk. He opened one hungry eye and looked at me, then at the cornstalks towering above us.

"*Hush!*" I whispered angrily. "Be quiet!"

He crinkled his forehead and frowned. It was an expression

I knew well—the look right before he would rear his head back and let out an ear-splitting howl. In the grainy darkness, I could see Abahji press a single finger against his lips.

"I'm sorry, Jisoo!" I said.

But the apology could hardly get past my clenched teeth and sounded like an angry hiss instead. He squirmed and whined crossly, letting out quick and heavy breaths like he always did right before crying.

Omahni bobbed him up and down, quietly shushing him with a soothing sound that swept up and mingled with the wind. My parents looked at each other.

"Come out from where you hide!" a man shouted through the darkness.

I jumped and nearly screamed. A piercing voice. Sharp and clear. All this time, I had been walking in an eerie dream, but the reality of our treacherous escape came rushing toward me, as real as the cold air sweeping across my cheeks through the corn.

I looked at Abahji, his brows twisting in alarm, as Omahni flashed me a razor-sharp look. My face burned. How could I have angered Jisoo like that? I imagined Omahni's scolding: *A daughter with a temper is worse than having no daughter at all.*

"Come out, or I'll shoot into the cornfield!" the man threatened.

We sat frozen amidst the stalks. Even Jisoo quieted.

"Don't shoot! We're coming out!" a woman cried.

Corn leaves rustled a few feet away. An old woman and her

husband walked out of the field onto the dirt road. "Bombs have been dropping near our village," she pleaded. "What do you expect us to do? Stay and die?"

"Shut your mouth! How can you and your husband abandon your country? Our Great Leader has called upon all of us to fight against the evil Americans!" The man's tone was vulgar and sharp. "And you *dare* speak that way to me? Traitors! You're under arrest."

The exchange drifted into muffled words, stifled sobs, shuffling feet, then silence.

But still we waited.

Finally, Abahji signaled us up. I struggled to stand; my knees buckled. My jaw ached from clenching my teeth.

Abahji led the way back toward the dirt road, and we tunneled through the maze of corn until the air opened up around us. Far away, on the other side of the field, a small ray of light—a lantern—moved away from us. My throat was dry. I swallowed.

"Thank God it was not our family that was found," Omahni whispered, her voice wavering.

"But what will happen to the old couple?" I asked.

No one answered.

thirteen · · · · · ·
November, 1950

"There's a house," Omahni said, hunched, Jisoo slumped on her back. She pointed down the dirt road, her face long and drawn. "We need to rest. Let's stop there for a little while."

Abahji nodded.

We had walked for hours. A timid dawn was spreading across the sky. My legs ached. The blisters on my feet stung. Youngsoo dawdled behind me, unusually quiet.

"It's not far, children. We can sleep there," Abahji said encouragingly. He hoisted the jigeh higher on his back and quickened his step.

Up ahead, I could see it. A stone house with a straw roof, fallen leaves covering the courtyard. In some ways, it looked like home, but without the crawl space for firewood under our porch or the warm wooden beam that hung over our door. This stone house was cold and coarse like a chiseled piece of mountain. I hoped the people who lived there would be kind.

Abahji was as brazen as a drunkard, strutting up to the front of the house and marching right inside as if he had lived there all his life. I stopped and stared, wondering if it was possible to become drunk with exhaustion, but when Youngsoo and

Omahni shuffled past and went inside, too, I followed them through the door.

"The owners clearly fled months ago," Omahni said, wiping the dust off a table with her fingers. A portrait of Kim Il-sung hung crookedly on the wall, a stray nail on the floor just below it. Omahni untied Jisoo from her back and set him down. He swatted the thick spiderwebs rounding the corners of the room, then stomped on the dried leaves nestled behind table legs.

Abahji dropped the jigeh from his shoulders with a dull thud and rubbed the back of his neck. He raised his arms and stretched his body from side to side, half smiling and half grimacing. And then, without wasting a single minute more, he announced that he would search for firewood and went back outside.

Immediately, Omahni whipped around to me. "What was that about back there in the cornfield? How could you make Jisoo cry like that? Do you want to get us all killed?"

I stared at my feet. If I could go back in time, I would undo all of it—shushing Jisoo in the cornfield, leaving home. Omahni was right: What was I thinking?

I snuck a sideways glance at Jisoo, who was pulling the map from inside my coat pocket.

"No, Jisoo! That's mine!" I snatched it from him. He howled, and tears sprang from his squinty eyes.

Slap.

Omahni's handprint burned into my cheek.

Her eyes flashed like a wild animal defending its cubs. Only,

I was the danger she had defended against. My stomach tightened. Wasn't I one of Omahni's children, too?

"Get some sleep. All of you. We need our rest before we walk again," Omahni said. She pounded her lower back with a fist and headed slowly into the kitchen as if every joint in her body ached.

I sat on the floor and yanked off my shoes. Youngsoo and Jisoo stared at me.

"Are you okay, Noona?" Youngsoo asked quietly.

"I'm fine. Why wouldn't I be?" I said. I felt something wet and wiped the side of my face. Was I crying?

"Because your cheek . . ." Youngsoo said, pointing.

I found a silver spoon on the low table and checked my reflection. My cheek was bright red, but I could no longer feel the sting.

A hard knot formed inside my chest. Little brothers would always cause trouble. And I would always be their keeper. The realization sank like a rock to the pit of my stomach.

I peeled my damp socks from my blistered toes; the sores oozed, but I blew on them till they dried. Until we reached Busan, I just needed to do my part by not messing up. I folded the map and tucked it back inside my coat pocket. It was still whole, though I'd worried away the edges overnight.

Abahji returned with the smell of the outdoors. He carried firewood for the stove. "Why are you children still awake? Get some sleep."

Loud blasts echoed over the mountains, closer than before. The windows rattled slightly.

Youngsoo and Jisoo spread blankets on the floor, then fell asleep in seconds. Jisoo sucked his thumb hard, as if trying to draw milk from a stone.

I curled up beside them. How odd it felt to help ourselves to a stranger's house, even if it *was* dim and musty. But our own home was now just a memory. It had been only one night since we left, yet it already felt like a lifetime ago.

I closed my teary eyes, my head heavy. Soon, I slipped into sleep the way that fish glide through waters, to a place so deep even dreams couldn't go.

※ ※ ※

Hours later, the starchy smell of rice filled the house, waking everyone. Omahni was rolling the sticky grains into perfect little balls.

My stomach rumbled, but I waited for Abahji to take one first, then my brothers. Finally, I ate. *Mmm. Soft, warm, and slightly salty.* Nothing ever tasted so good. I barely chewed, swallowing so fast that I had to pound my chest with a fist to coax the food down. Who knew that a simple rice ball could be so delicious?

Youngsoo couldn't stop grinning. He popped the rice balls into his mouth as if we were sitting at a picnic. "When we get to Busan, I'm going to buy us a big house," he announced.

Abahji laughed. "Is that so? And how will you pay for that house?"

"Busan is by the ocean, so I'll be a fisherman. And I'll catch fish for dinner every night for you, Omahni."

This time, Omahni laughed.

"Noona, what kind of fish do you want?" he asked.

I didn't answer.

"No, really." He stretched out his arm as if offering me the world. "What kind of fish do you want? You can have your pick of any fish in the sea."

fourteen · · · · ·
November, 1950

During the night, it snowed heavily. After a breakfast of leftover rice balls, Youngsoo stood and stared out the window. "Look. There are hundreds of them."

"What, snowflakes?" I said underneath a blanket.

"No, people!"

I went over to see and pressed my face against the glass. A long procession of people marched through the snow-covered valley. Dressed mostly in white, they looked like ghosts.

Abahji leaned over my head. He ran his fingers through his hair, locking his gaze on the steady stream of marchers. "We can't afford to stop and rest while everyone else heads south. Let's go. Quickly."

In a flurry of activity, Abahji and Omahni gathered our belongings. I found my socks drying by the kitchen stove and pulled them over my blistered feet, the warmth soothing my soreness. A good rest and hot food seemed to have worked a miracle on my aching body. Omahni strapped Jisoo onto her back while Abahji hoisted the jigeh onto his shoulders.

Youngsoo tugged at his sliding-down socks and drooping

pants, gathering himself together like a boy made of sand, everything slipping through his fingers. He had slack shoulders and puffy half-moons under his eyes, and I wondered suddenly if the journey would be too hard for him.

Abahji put his hand on the doorknob. "Is everyone ready?" He looked at me.

I reached into my coat pocket. The folded map was still there, its corner dull against my finger. I nodded.

We stepped outside. Snow-capped mountains jutted up into the sky like many daggers. The air nipped my nose, and snow crunched beneath my feet. I braced against the bitter winds that funneled through the valley.

Before us were the refugees. Their expressionless faces floated by in a white fog of snow, as if passing from this life to the next. I shuddered, but I fell in step with their silent march. What choice did we have? It was safer to travel in a group than alone, and we joined the long line of others heading south.

"Elder Sohn!" Abahji called suddenly.

A gray-bearded man with a furry hat turned to look. He pushed a bullock cart filled with his belongings. "Pak Sangmin? Is that you?"

Abahji grinned. "Yes, it's me! It's been so long!"

Elder Sohn bowed and clasped Abahji's arm. "It's unfortunate that we meet under these circumstances." He pointed to the jigeh. "Take that load off your shoulders, old friend, and put it in my cart. I can push it easily for both of us."

"No, no, no." Abahji shook his head. "I can carry it."

"Don't be a stubborn mule."

"Then let me push the cart. I'm younger and stronger."

"There you go again. Just like the time you objected to my nomination of Mr. Chung as church elder! Stubborn as always."

"Stubborn, but right," Abahji said.

They chuckled, then grew quiet, as if they could hardly believe there was a time when deciding who should be church elder mattered at all.

Youngsoo lagged two feet behind me, his nose running and his head drooping. "Noona, wait for me."

"Hurry, Youngsoo. We have to move quickly," I said.

He shuffled closer. "Are we almost there?"

"Where?"

"Busan."

I stopped and looked at him the way Omahni looked at me when I said something stupid. "Of course not. Busan is on the southern coast of South Korea."

He squirmed and rubbed the back of his neck. "Well then, how long will it take?"

I sighed and kept walking. "Weeks, months. Not sure."

"When will we be able to go back home?"

"Maybe after the war."

"When will that be?"

"I don't know!" I shouted. "Save your breath and stop asking so many questions."

He wiped his wet nose and then reached for my hand, but for once I pulled my arm away.

I looked out at the crowd and noticed other children. Some were younger and crying; others were older and solemn. Many clung to their mothers' coats, but a few marched on their own, an irritable stomp in their step. Several of them—girls—were around my age.

I found myself hoping to make a friend. But I never got the chance.

fifteen · · · · · ·

A speck from the edge of the sky headed toward us.

As its buzzing grew louder and louder, everyone in the crowd stopped to look, squinting toward the sun. A fighter jet was soaring across the thinning clouds, swooping down low.

"A white star! A white star!" a woman said, pointing at the belly of the plane. "It's the Americans!"

"No!" a man cried from behind us. "It's a red star! Communists!"

I held up a shielding hand, but only caught a glimpse of the star. It was red. No, it was white. No, red. The sun glinted and danced against the sharp metal wings, playing tricks on my eyes.

All at once, everyone ran.

Feet rushed. Voices rose. Faces streamed past in a blur. The crowd broke apart, running amok in thoughtless chaos. They scattered in all directions—across the white lowlands, through dried cornfields—but mostly toward a hill. I stood rooted like a tree.

"Omahni! Abahji! Youngsoo!" I shouted, hardly able to hear myself.

Faces flashed past like the flicker of a newsreel. A mother

with a baby strapped to her back. Boys with gray mittens. A man with a jigeh on his shoulders. I spun in confusion.

"Move! Move!" a woman screeched, shoving me to the ground.

I fell on my hands and knees. So many feet trampling. Around me. On top of me. Someone gripped my head as if it were the knob of a wooden post. "Get off!" I screamed, struggling up.

On top of the hill, the crowd regrouped, raising arms above their heads. "Look at us!" they cried in a chorus. "We're civilians!" They waved their tattered sleeves, held babies up toward the sky, unraveled their long scarves to flutter in the wind like an SOS.

I clutched my chest—I was nothing but a pounding pulse. My legs wouldn't move. I looked toward the hill. Should I run there? Or stay here?

Then, through the thinning crowds, I saw him.

"Youngsoo!"

He stood alone, his mouth distorted in a terrible cry. Tears streamed down his face. I felt strange, as if I were looking at my own heart ripped from its body.

I raced toward him, grabbed his hand, and then ran left and right, stopping and going. What was I doing? Where should I run? Omahni, Abahji, and Jisoo had to be near, but there was no one left on the icy road. How could they have disappeared so quickly?

Overhead, the jet roared.

My brother and I looked at each other.

"Let's run to the hill!" I said. Nearly everyone had rushed to the top. Maybe Omahni and Abahji were waiting there, hoping we had the sense to follow the crowd.

We ran across the snowy lowlands. Toward the hill. Where we'd be safe.

Our feet punched through the snow. Our breaths shuddered in and out. Our legs couldn't pick up fast enough. But we were nearer. I could see faces. Elder Sohn with the furry hat! Girls with long braids!

"Faster, Youngsoo! Faster!" I screamed.

It was loud and close when it came—the deep rumble that rippled through the air.

I stopped, yanking hard on Youngsoo's hand. We stood motionless as the jet swooped toward us with the focus of a hawk falling on its prey. I squinted at its star, still unsure. To the Reds we were traitors. To the Americans we were communists. There was nowhere to hide.

I looked up, mesmerized, its shadow covering us.

Time slowed as I watched the plane bank and then dive toward the crowd on top of that hill. These were the people who had walked alongside us, whose breath had warmed the air all around us.

I threw my arms up toward the sky, somehow hoping to hold that flying monster back. But it continued. And I saw something drop from its underbelly.

In an instant, a deafening blast struck me to the ground.

A white flash went off before my eyes.

Silence whooshed through my ears. I lay on my back, stunned. Youngsoo was moving his mouth, but I could hear no sound. Where was I? Why was I so tired? Had I just died?

How good it felt to rest in peace and quiet, the blue sky looking so pretty, birds gliding on the wind. I was in a bubble, floating.

I floated on my back in my cotton swimsuit, the sun warming my face. The water was shallow enough to feel the pointy leaves of water thyme along the river bottom.

I stretched my arms and closed my eyes, letting my ears dip below the surface. Now the world was muffled, the way I liked it. No little brothers nagging. No Omahni barking. No wooden paddles banging. The currents rocked and swayed me gently, as if I were in a cradle.

Splash.

Water in my face. I gulped and coughed, getting on my feet.

Jisoo had stomped into the river. He was naked.

"Go, Jisoo!" I said.

But he wouldn't leave. He clapped and splashed. His chubby belly jiggled up and down.

"He's just trying to play with you," Abahji said, gathering wood for a firepit.

"That's right. If you children can't play nicely together, then no picnic. We all go home," Omahni warned.

I got on my stomach in the shallow water, my eyes and nose just above the surface, like a crocodile in waiting. I watched him teeter toward me, his arms reaching closer and closer. What was he doing?

He waddled forward. Small hands gripped the sides of my face. Then, a slobbering kiss on my cheek.

Feeling strangely calm, I watched silent clouds of black smoke begin to creep across my view . . . until curdling screams flooded my ears. They were deep-throated wails and moans—sounds so full of mortal grief that I knew I couldn't be dead.

I scrambled to my feet, scattering snow. Black smoke and a blazing fire raged on top of the hill, and I stumbled backward, surprised by the intense heat against my face. I could no longer see waving arms or hopeful faces, only charred lumps, thick smoke, and roaring flames. And all those people . . .

What if? What if?

No, I couldn't believe it. Omahni, Abahji, and Jisoo couldn't have been on that hill.

My stomach twisted.

Something stirred by my side. A mitten-covered hand slipped into mine. Youngsoo stood beside me, staring at the fire. I looked at his face, then looked again. Somehow, he seemed different. The tears were gone, his cheeks washed bare, his eyes sapped of all emotion.

And all at once, I felt it too.

Emptiness.

sixteen · · · · · ·

The roaring plane disappeared as suddenly as it had appeared.

A blustery wind spiraled down from the mountains. My teeth chattered, and I clamped a hand over my mouth.

Only the cries of women and children punctured the whistling winds. Creeping out of the woods, mothers and grandmothers stood frozen on the roadside, clutching their chests as if trying to catch all the broken pieces of their hearts. Small children were rooted to the ground, calling out for Mama.

We stood by the hill, staring for what felt like hours. Then a blast struck the earth just beyond the mountain. I jolted. People began emerging from the trees—more than I had expected—trickling, then streaming out from their hiding places. They were all heading south on the dirt road once again.

I ran toward them, grabbing their arms and searching their faces. A few yanked themselves away. Others clucked in pity. And some didn't respond to my tugging, their expressions hollowed out like a gourd.

If Omahni, Abahji, and Jisoo weren't here, then maybe they were on that hill. A sickening feeling came surging, and I vomited on the side of the road.

A grandmother with lines raked across her forehead picked up her bundle of things and stepped toward us. "Children, you must continue walking south. You cannot stay here. The Reds are not far behind. They'll be here soon." She shooed us along with her arm.

I nearly slapped her hand away. I knew this *halmoni* was trying to only help, but I wasn't leaving until we found our family.

"No," Youngsoo told her, working himself up into a coughing fit. "We need to find our parents and baby brother! I know they're here!" He clambered up a large, icy rock, gazing out at the stream of passing faces.

"Children, you have to go. No one is staying in the North. Your parents are probably traveling south too, moving along with the crowd," the halmoni said in a softened tone. "I'm sure you'll meet up with them again if you continue—"

She hadn't even finished her sentence when a collective scream rolled in from behind. In the second that I glanced away and back, the old woman was already gone. I grabbed Youngsoo's hand.

Shots fired in the air. A megaphone echoed: *Comrades, return to your Fatherland! Don't abandon your country! The South is a puppet for the imperialist Americans!*

Bullets whizzed past. Bodies fell. Everyone scattered.

We had no choice. We had to go.

Youngsoo and I ran away from the place where our parents could be. Past the woods. Through a valley filled with frozen cornfields. Farther and faster. My mind wrestled every step, but my feet kept moving. The landscape changed like a slideshow—from farmland and terraced hills to mountains and evergreens. We ran until everyone was gone.

Finally, I stopped and looked around.

Youngsoo and I stood gasping for air, our backs bent. The pine trees were taller and skinnier than the ones at home. Where were we? How had we gotten here? Where had everyone else gone? The sun was setting, and I shivered uncontrollably. There was no way we'd find our parents now.

"What do we do?" Youngsoo asked, his chin jittering.

I wanted to confess that I had no idea, that I was terrified. But Youngsoo had the wide-eyed look of a cow about to be slaughtered, so I bit my lip and fought the overwhelming urge to burst into tears. I told him we should keep going south.

❆ ❆ ❆

With no one to tell us when to stop, we walked for miles into the night.

This was no different from when I was in charge of walking Youngsoo to and from the river, I told myself. But, of course, this *was* different. What happened to Omahni, Abahji, and Jisoo? Were we heading in the right direction to find them? What about food and shelter?

I took a deep breath and felt the hairs inside my nose crackle and freeze. Snow soaked the bottom of my pants. If we didn't find a place to stay for the night, we would freeze to death.

The temperature dipped dangerously low, until I could no longer feel my toes. But we continued trudging side by side as miserably as two yoked mules.

I noticed Youngsoo's wet nose and glassy eyes. He was getting sick. He needed a warm bed, a change of dry clothes, and a meal.

Wouldn't Omahni expect us to meet at home if we were lost?

I thought of everything I had hoped to do once we reached Busan—go to school, have my own books—but an explosion echoing off the mountains shattered my thoughts into a million pieces. It was getting dark, and I wasn't sure where the bombing was—it was *there*, then *there*, then nowhere. Going back would be easier than forging ahead into unknown territory.

"Let's go home," I said.

Youngsoo wheezed, and his cheeks flushed. "But that halmoni said we should continue heading south. She said no one is up north anymore."

"But maybe Omahni and Abahji headed back thinking that we would meet them there. There's no other way for them to find us, is there? Come on, we're not too far from home. We should go back."

A wind blew and trickled into our coats. Youngsoo rubbed his arms for warmth, then nodded.

❄ ❄ ❄

We turned around and headed north.

As the hours wore on, we passed small groups of people

traveling in the opposite direction. "You're going the wrong way! No one is left up north!" they called.

I ignored their warnings. Youngsoo needed to go home. If Omahni and Abahji were alive, *surely* they would expect to meet us there.

We continued walking, encountering fewer and fewer travelers on the road. The forest fell away, and snowy fields stretched out on either side of us. A distant blast illuminated a barn perhaps a half mile away. I shuddered, then pulled Youngsoo's hand and trekked toward the shelter, my muscles stiff and frozen. I was struck by the stillness: there wasn't even the rustling of leaves in the copses of trees, or the caw of a bird in the distance.

"Noona, do you know the first thing that I'll do when we get to Busan?" Youngsoo asked through chattering teeth.

I frowned at him, wondering how he could talk nonsense at a time like this. I kept my mouth shut, not wanting to relinquish the hot breath in my body, but Youngsoo waited. Finally, I answered, "I don't know."

"I'll give everybody a hot steam bun as big as my head."

I laughed, and felt my precious warm breath hit my face. "If they made steam buns that big, I'd dig my frozen fingers and toes into it."

"I'd sleep with it like a warm, squishy pillow."

I played along with his little game. "Then, when you woke up in the morning, you could just eat your pillow for breakfast."

This time, Youngsoo burst out laughing, and I smiled. I imagined cradling that gigantic steam bun and thought I felt warmth rise from the center of my body.

But when he went further, saying, "Jisoo would probably get sticky dough all over his hair," we both fell silent.

Youngsoo believed that Omahni and Abahji were alive, that Jisoo was somewhere sucking his thumb. A few hours ago, I had too—it was why I had turned around. But now, in the dark, I was beginning to believe only what I knew: I had not seen their faces in the crowd; there was a good chance they had run to the top of that hill; and we should have found each other by now, passing on the road. I remembered that Youngsoo could sometimes be a silly little boy, and a crushing burden of responsibility pressed down on me.

I looked around. Fire burned on the horizon; on the far edge of a cornfield, dried cornstalks were ablaze. Skinny trees, creaking in the wind, dotted the snowy farmland. Abahji had thought I was brave when we had decided to escape. But my voice had shaken when I said I wanted to leave; was that still considered brave?

Strange sounds began cropping up—clicking noises, drifting snow, whistling winds. Perhaps it was just animals. But there were footsteps too; I was sure of it.

"Do you hear that?" I asked suddenly—dried leaves grinding underfoot, slow and measured.

Youngsoo stopped walking. "Hear what?"

I listened. There was only the distant rumbling like thunder.

"Hear what?" Youngsoo repeated.

"Nothing," I said, letting out a long breath. "Let's go."

But then I saw it: the flutter of a coat behind a tree.

seventeen · · · · · ·

"*Omah*, it's just two little children," a teenage girl called out, her voice flat.

She and a woman emerged from the shadows. The girl had dirt on her face, but so did her mother. Stained quilts hung over their shoulders like shawls, and they had hardly any possessions, just one small bag—although it was wartime, they seemed worse off than most. I exhaled in relief at seeing this simple family instead of armed soldiers.

"Are you two traveling alone?" the mother asked. Her hair was pulled back, exposing a grimy face as round as a pumpkin.

"Yes," I said. "But we're looking for our parents and baby brother. We're heading back home to find them."

"You're going north? No one is up north anymore."

The wide-open plains swirled around me. Every side looked the same. I was losing my sense of direction. "Then can you tell us which way is south?"

The mother cocked her head. "Your parents just left you?" she asked, ignoring my question.

"No, we lost them in a crowd. I'm sure they're looking for us, too. Can you please tell us the way to Busan?"

"Do you have bags? Anything you're carrying?"

"No," I said. "Please. Can you tell us which way is south?"

The daughter stared, her gaze cold and unflinching. The mother sucked her teeth with her tongue.

In the quiet of this deserted place, it was all I could hear. And suddenly I knew my decision to head north had been a terrible one. There wasn't a single person left in this valley, except for the woman, the girl, and us. I glanced at Youngsoo; he frowned.

Uneasiness crept over me, like burning paper turning black.

"You two better stick with us. It's not safe for children to be out here alone," the mother said, finally. She grasped my arm tightly.

The teenage girl grabbed Youngsoo's arm. "There's a storage barn up ahead. Let's stop there for the night."

"No!" I blurted, my heart kicking. "My brother and I will go on our way. We don't want to trouble you." I didn't know where we would sleep if not the barn, but we needed to get away.

"It's no trouble at all," the mother said. She forced a smile underneath her stony eyes.

They pulled us toward the barn. When we stepped inside, it was dank and cold—somehow even colder than outside. Bales of hay towered against the far wall under a ceiling of exposed beams. There were no animals, but the smell of horse and dung gripped me.

The mother lit a kerosene lamp, casting huge shadows on the walls. Then she set her bag down, and a small chicken popped its head out.

"I can't believe you don't have anything on you." She examined me up and down. "Not even a little bag of rice? Your parents didn't have you carry anything? A girl practically grown like you? They must have spoiled you."

I huffed in indignation.

The daughter laughed.

"Here, take some of this hay." The mother tossed a bale at me. "Use it for bedding."

It hit me in the stomach, and I stumbled backward. Clumsily, I began to tear out fistfuls of straw and lay them on the floor. It scratched my hands, but I hardly noticed—I was too busy pretending not to listen as the mother and daughter spoke in low tones.

"We could always sell her to soldiers," the mother murmured. "I'm sure they could find a use for her. She looks old enough." For a second, she stared at me. "Such a pretty girl, too."

"She's not that pretty," the daughter said. "What about her brother?"

"Too little. He's not worth much. We'll decide everything in the morning. For now, let's get some rest. There's nowhere for them to go." They spread thick hay across the floor.

Youngsoo started to speak, but I pinched his arm, and he shut his mouth. A sob swelled in the back of my throat; I swallowed it down. Somehow, I mustered the courage to say, "I wish we'd had some of this hay to sleep on last night!" and pushed out a carefree laugh, which I worried came out as a petrified bark. A forced smile quivered on my cheeks.

The mother seemed too busy smoothing the hay to notice. But the teenage girl looked at me and grinned. In the eerie light, her impish face looked like a carved wooden mask.

Before the kerosene lamp turned off, I studied the location of the barn door—about twenty paces from where I sat. I noted the door's latch and how it worked—slide across and lift up. I memorized the exact spots where the mother and girl lay—one on my left and one on my right.

Then everything turned black.

eighteen · · · · · ·
November, 1950

Youngsoo lay trembling beside me. I listened, motionless, the darkness amplifying every sound. The mother smacked her lips; the girl turned from side to side. Eventually, the barn quieted, until I was left with only a loud thumping in my ears.

Was it a trick? Were the mother and girl really sleeping?

I thought of Omahni, Abahji, and Jisoo, and how I might never see them again. "Abahji," I whispered. Tears welled in my eyes, and there in the dark with no one to see, I let them flow freely.

I watched Abahji stir in the early morning shadows. Everyone else was still asleep. He sat up to put on his shoes.

"Abahji, you're working more every day," I whispered, lying on my mat.

"I have to work hard to take care of all of you," he said.

"But we hardly see you anymore."

Abahji looked out the window. "Hmm, it snowed. First snow of the season." He paused. "Get your coat, Sora-ya."

I scrambled to my feet, careful not to wake the others. "What are we doing?"

"Go to the kitchen and get one of Omahni's trays. A big one. Then meet me out front." He walked out the door.

I scurried to the kitchen, grabbed a lacquered tray, then slipped out the side door. Soft drifts of snow covered the dirt road and the earth. It was barely light out. Nighttime foxes still padded through the woods, while early morning cranes began their delicate walk across the stubble fields.

"Sora-ya, up here!" Abahji called from the top of the sloping road between our house and the millet field.

I ran toward him.

"Set the tray down and sit. I'll give you a little push," he said.

I plunked it on top of the hill, then stopped. "Shouldn't we wake Youngsoo?" I asked.

Abahji rubbed his chin. "Not this time. You're ten now, and soon you won't want me to push you on a sled anymore. I'm sure he'll understand this once." He winked at me.

I grinned. It was what I had hoped—only better. He pushed and spun me at the same time, and I slid down the road in circles. I laughed and ran to the top again.

"One more time, please?" I held my breath.

"No, Sora-ya. I have another surprise for you. Look." He pointed at the horizon.

Streaks of pink and orange covered the sky. A piercing diamond light peeked over the edge of the mountain. I gasped. It grew bigger and bigger, until it rose high enough to shed light on all things ordinary—thatched roofs, picks and shovels, wooden carts.

"I have to go to work now. Get back inside before everyone wonders where you've been." He tousled my hair.

My shoulders deflated. I watched Abahji swing an axe over his shoulder, then head toward the pine trees. The day had begun.

A ray of sun hit me in the eye. Through the barn window, I could see a brightening sky beyond the mountains. It was dawn; stray beams of light were shafting in.

Youngsoo snored beside me in the dim. I tapped him on the shoulder, and he groaned.

"Shush!" I pinched him hard.

He jerked awake, and I clamped my hand over his mouth. Our eyes met, and after a moment I could see he understood: *Be quiet.* I rose slowly with him, blood pulsing in my ears.

Holding his arm, I took a step toward the door. Hay crunched under our feet as loud as broken glass.

I froze and held my breath. Surely, they could hear.

No. They slept on. Nineteen more steps to go, an eternity away.

We crept like cats already arched, on the verge of tearing across the room. But I held back and went slowly, quietly, until we reached the door. It was huge and heavy, wide enough to fit a bullock cart and horse. The latch was cold and my fingers stiff. I slid the metal bolt.

It squeaked.

Someone shifted on the hay. The hen stirred. I whipped

around and saw the mother turn on her back, yawning. But how could I see her in the dark? *Ai!* I flicked my gaze to the window. Golden light flooded the barn.

The sun had risen.

My thoughts raced. What did the mother even mean—sell me to soldiers? Why would they ever pay to have me? I couldn't understand it, but it scared me more than guns or bombs. My hands shook.

Youngsoo hopped from foot to foot. "Noona, hurry!"

"Shush!" I hissed.

I wiggled the latch. The chicken started clucking. Someone stirred and moaned.

A blast of cold air shot inside as I pushed the door open. I shoved Youngsoo through and darted out behind him.

Then I grabbed his arm and ran.

We trampled over thorny brush and knotty hills, through drifts of snow and ice. Biting winds slashed our faces. We didn't stop until the sun was high—two small figures on the frozen plains.

nineteen · · · · · ·

After running all day, we found shelter in an abandoned cottage. House slippers lined the wall by the door, and red armbands lay neatly folded on the dresser, as if the owners could return at any moment. But I knew they wouldn't. Dust covered the furniture, and all the bedrolls were gone.

"Help me move this table," I said, grabbing the wooden legs on one end.

"Where do you want to put it?" Youngsoo asked. He stood in the middle of the shadowy room, shivering.

"Against the door."

"Why?"

"Because the lock is broken, and we don't want anyone coming in." I glanced toward the window at the trees' moving shadows— they sometimes looked like bodies with arms and legs.

Youngsoo lifted the other end, and together we carried the table across the room. "What if someone tries to separate us again?" he asked.

"It won't happen. I promise." But I couldn't look at him when I said it.

We pushed the low table flush against the door. It wasn't

much of a barrier, but it would have to do. I lit a match to a kerosene lamp sitting on a wooden chest, my hands trembling slightly. Youngsoo, still standing, didn't say a word.

We needed food and water. I was so hungry, I felt nauseated.

"I'm going to check the kitchen for something to eat," I said. "I'll need to take the lantern. I'll be right back."

"I'm coming, too!" Youngsoo said, rushing to my side.

The kitchen was only feet away—even if I brought the lamp in there, it would still glow into the main room—but I let him follow.

I stepped down into the tiny, dirt-floor kitchen, banging my head against a hanging pot and ladle. They swung on their hooks, clanging into each other like noisy footsteps. My hand shot up and stopped them mid-swing.

I paused to let my heart settle.

A large earthen jar sat on the floor, big enough to fit two small children. Straining, I managed to shift its heavy lid with both hands—it scraped against the top of the jar, stone against stone, like a rock rolling away from a tomb.

We peered inside and gasped.

"Kimchi!" Youngsoo said.

My hands couldn't move fast enough. I reached for two tin cups on the open shelf, fumbling and knocking over plates and spoons. I filled each cup with the kimchi and its juices, handed one to Youngsoo, then tipped back my head and coiled a long, speckled cabbage leaf into my mouth. It was fresh from *kimjang* season, when everyone made batches of kimchi for the winter. Crisp and tangy. Perfect.

"Why would they leave it behind?" Youngsoo asked, between bites.

"Because it's too much. How could anyone pack and carry all this kimchi?"

I crunched on the thick base of the cabbage leaf, my favorite part, then drank the juices. And for a second, I forgot myself, and this dark place, and the winds whistling outside like a woman screaming.

"Noona, can you believe we were almost kidnapped?" Youngsoo asked. He coughed into his arm, then took another bite of kimchi.

I stopped to think. It was unbelievable. "Kidnapped," I said, as if to convince myself that it had really happened. "We were almost kidnapped by those people."

"And their chicken," Youngsoo added.

We looked at each other, then broke out laughing. "If that chicken was here, we'd be having it with soy sauce right now!" I declared.

Youngsoo's head popped up from his bowl. "Ooh, Omahni makes the best chicken with soy sauce."

We stopped laughing.

"Noona, do you think Omahni, Abahji, and Jisoo are looking for us?"

"Of course. We just have to keep heading south, and we'll run into them," I said, turning my face away to hide my worry.

"But how do you know which way is south?"

"Well . . . there are guides like the North Star. And we can follow the trails people are leaving."

He paused to consider this. "How do you find the North Star?"

"Well, it's the brightest one in the sky, isn't it?"

"They all look pretty bright to me," he said, blowing his nose against the bottom of his shirt.

I wanted him to stop talking. "Let's go to sleep. We'll need our rest," I said, stepping back into the main room.

We huddled on the stone floor, and Youngsoo fell asleep. But the kimchi churned inside me, its acids burning a hole through my stomach. In my mind, I retraced our steps from the barn to here. Had I gone the right way? I hadn't looked at the North Star; I was never good at finding it. The map crinkled softly inside my pocket, and I reached in and pulled it out. The Korean peninsula was so tiny compared to the rest of the world; when I put my thumb on it, it disappeared. Which animals lived in Africa? What foods did people eat in France? Were there really hairy cowboys in America?

The room grew colder. A strong wind blustered, rattling the windows. Something light and tinny, like a watering can, blew against the side of the house. I squeezed my eyes shut and waited for morning.

twenty · · · · ·
Maybe December, 1950

For the next few days, we found deserted homes full of kimjang kimchi and ate nothing but pickled cabbage to sustain ourselves. Sometimes we curled into balls, our stomachs cramping and gurgling, but we ate it anyway.

We never stopped walking. Hillsides, once full of rice paddy terraces, were stripped bare. An ox lay on its side, vultures feasting on its abdomen. Thatched-roof houses were charred to the ground. Fallen trees, destroyed by bombs, were everywhere. Walking south according to the sun was easy, but at night, I lost the North Star in the sky.

Finally, we came across a line of windburnt refugees heading south through a snow-covered valley. There were at least fifty people. Was it a mirage? Were there really others like us here? Youngsoo and I looked at each other, our hopes rising. I dropped his hand and sprinted toward the group, ducking between strangers and searching their faces.

But Omahni, Abahji, and Jisoo were not among them.

I found Youngsoo at the back of the line. "Let's stick with these people. It's safer to travel together," I said. I didn't need to tell him that I hadn't seen our parents.

He nodded.

But I knew the group couldn't stay together for long. How would we all fit in one house? At nightfall, everyone would splinter off in different directions. I studied the crowd, searching for a person we could follow, someone we could trust to look out for us. We couldn't be alone anymore. Youngsoo had caught a cold; he needed a mother to take care of him. And I needed someone to lead the way.

A lady and her little daughter walked on the edge of the crowd. The scarf wrapped around the woman's head came together in a tight knot under her chin, the two ends hanging perfectly even. I watched the way she walked with her arm around her daughter's shoulder, the way she took bits of food from her bag and fed the girl at just the right times to keep her going. In the evening, when the crowd split into different houses, I followed the group that the mother had chosen into a small stone cottage.

Inside, there were chests and a table covered in dust. An old man stepped into a pair of tattered house slippers left behind by the owners. I pulled Youngsoo across the crowded floor to where the mother and child sat, and we settled ourselves beside them.

The woman was busy spreading blankets when she glanced at us and smiled. "Joonie-ya, say hello," she said to her daughter. The girl smiled shyly, a beauty mark dotting the edge of her upper lip.

Youngsoo peeked around me, his eyes brightening. Then he

dropped my hand and rushed to Joonie's side. My mouth hung open in disbelief. Now I knew: one pretty girl, and Youngsoo would desert me in a second. I smirked and pretended to glare at him.

The mother laughed, then handed us a bowl of cold rice from her bag. I bowed deeply. Youngsoo took half but had to stop after three bites, his cough unrelenting.

"Is he sick?" the woman asked, eyeing him carefully.

"It's just a little cold." I tried to flash the same smile that always got Youngsoo out of trouble with Omahni, but I knew I had failed when she frowned at me. "It looks like Youngsoo and Joonie have become instant friends," I tried, hoping to win her back. "My brother is eight. How old is she?"

"Seven," the mother said, studying the dried snot on Youngsoo's sleeve. I tucked his arm behind me. She looked at me and smiled slightly. "You have a lot of common sense."

I wasn't sure how she would know, or whether it was even true, but I beamed anyway. I couldn't help it. Omahni would never have said so.

The woman turned her attention away from me. "Joonie-ya, come sleep on this side." She patted the space on the floor farthest from Youngsoo and me. Joonie went and curled up in the curve of her mother's body.

In the middle of the night, Youngsoo broke into a wheezing, coughing spasm. I patted him on the back, not wanting him to wake the entire house; a man across the room was already sighing and grumbling.

"It'll be okay," I whispered, my eyes half-closed, soothing him long after he had quieted and fallen back asleep.

❄ ❄ ❄

The next morning, I awoke to an old man looming over us.

"Did you get any sleep with all that hacking, boy?" he asked, his voice hard.

"Yes, sir. I did," Youngsoo said, bolting upright. The old man walked away to gather his bags, muttering a string of profanities.

I looked around the room. Everyone was packing to resume the daily trek. But where were the mother and daughter?

I saw the back of Joonie's shiny long hair flutter out the door. They were quick. I nearly missed them.

"Hurry, Youngsoo, let's go!" I said, shaking his shoulder. "We don't want to get left behind!"

Without any possessions, we needed only to button our coats, scramble to our feet, and run out the door. There were fewer people walking south today. I grabbed Youngsoo's hand and searched the loose chain of marchers for Joonie and her mother until I found them walking briskly in the middle of the line.

"There they are!" I said. I pulled Youngsoo so we could walk alongside them.

Joonie squirmed out of her mother's grasp to hold Youngsoo's hand. He grinned. I knew he would start offering her gifts, even though he had almost nothing to give. Maybe he would promise her any fish in the sea.

Instead, he pulled a river rock from his pocket. I watched him wipe it clean against his coat, smudging the tan fabric with dirt before handing it to Joonie.

"Joonie-ya," her mother said. "Don't touch that. It's dirty. Come, hold my hand."

Something about the way she said "dirty" made my cheeks hot with shame. The girl frowned, but returned to her mother's side.

The woman wrapped a protective arm around her daughter, her long coat flapping like a curtain between us. A nameless fear swelled inside me as I watched her clutch Joonie close.

Youngsoo shrugged and wiped his nose against his sleeve. He continued walking, undaunted, like his fishing days by the river. It wasn't the first time he'd ever walked away empty-handed, and I supposed he was used to it by now.

We marched in silence, following a churned-up road. At dusk, when the group separated into different shelters, different abandoned homes, we followed Joonie and her mother. Days passed this way; I couldn't keep count. Our group kept changing as newcomers joined and others fell away, but Joonie and her mother were always there—I made sure of it.

It was dark one night when our group entered another deserted home. The house looked hollow and sad, like a family member left behind. The rice-straw roof had partially blown away. The eaves drooped on one side. Spiders had moved in.

An old halmoni dropped to the floor and began rubbing her feet. "We're getting close to Pyongyang. I can feel it!" she announced.

"How do you know?" I asked.

"Because I grew up there," she said. "Besides, all roads end at the capital, and we're almost at the end of this one!"

I shivered thinking what the end of this road would bring. What would a city look like? How could two country bumpkins like us find our way through its streets?

There were ten others in the house tonight, including Joonie and her mother. As always, I waited for them to sit, so we could settle beside them.

The mother looked at us and sighed. She offered us another bowl of rice but didn't smile or say a word. I accepted it with both palms facing up, my head bent low. Was I begging? Or was she offering?

Youngsoo grabbed a clump from the bowl, and I noticed the grime under his nails, the dirt creased in the dried skin of his fingers. For a second, I wished we had washed our hands in the snow. I glanced at the mother, and her eyes darted away. I wondered if she disapproved. But how else would we eat in the middle of a war, if not with our dirty hands? I chewed neatly, covering my teeth and minding my manners.

I spread our coats on the floor and told Youngsoo to get some rest. He curled into a ball and closed his eyes, and we huddled close for warmth as winds screeched outside the door.

We were asleep when the woman nudged me. "Wake up. Your brother is having another coughing fit." There were deep grumbles across the room as Youngsoo rasped uncontrollably. Hardly able to keep my eyes open, I patted him on the back and hushed him, hoping he hadn't annoyed anyone. We wouldn't want to get kicked out of the house. That was all I could think as I fell back asleep.

❄ ❄ ❄

Hours later, still exhausted, I nearly missed Joonie and her mother leaving before dawn.

The mother packed her bag quickly, making every effort not to make a sound. Why the rush? Why so early? I looked around the dark room. No one else had yet woken.

Then, all at once, I knew.

She had fed us but never agreed to take care of us.

I sat up and touched her arm in the dark. "I know how you feel about my brother. But he can be really sensitive sometimes, so I'll make sure he doesn't find out why you left us," I said, my voice breaking.

"Left you? You were never with me. You don't even know my name, child," the mother said, her face tight and guarded. "Listen, I have my daughter to protect, and I fear what your brother has is contagious. He is your responsibility, not mine. You're all that he has left."

My face burned in embarrassment. All this time, I had been chasing. And she had been running—from us.

Of course he was my responsibility, not hers. Had I tried to unload the burden of caring for him? A yarn of guilt balled up in my throat.

The woman's face softened. "Let me give you some advice. You won't have much of a future as an orphan girl. Your only saving grace is your brother; at least he is a son who can carry your family name and support you once he has grown. Take care of him; put his needs before your own. That's how you survive in this world."

It was just like Omahni talking. Telling me my worth. Hot tears stung my eyes. I couldn't look at her. I knew that everything she said was true.

twenty-one · · · · · ·
Maybe December, 1950

It took another day to reach Pyongyang on our own.

The city was on fire.

Two months ago, it had been bombed and captured during the Americans' push north, but now the communists were pushing back—and the battlefront was close. We could hear shells bursting somewhere beyond the outskirts.

Flakes of ash fell from the sky like black snow. Morning light filtered through burnt, wiry treetops. I stopped to catch my breath, but choked on the bitter taste of smoke; a haze had settled over everything.

I'd never been in a city before. The roads were paved, but they were lined with rubble. The buildings left standing were two and three stories tall—some of them pagodas, others pitched-roofed—their windows all blown out and charred. Only the framework of the railway station was still standing, like a skeleton.

Down the road, huge portraits of Kim Il-sung and Stalin hung on the brick façade of a school, their faces riddled with bullets. And past that, on the next block, wooden-fronted stores—a fruit and vegetable shop, a cold-noodle shop—were empty, their doors hanging at crooked angles.

When I half closed my eyes to blur the ruined buildings, Pyongyang *could've* looked like an ordinary city—if it weren't for the tanks and the overturned trucks on the sidewalk; a cow ambling in the middle of the road, its rope dragging behind; and the occasional body on the ground, bent at unnatural angles. I covered Youngsoo's eyes and looked away.

People were crisscrossing the city like sleepwalkers. Women carried bundles on their backs and heads, and most men wore baggy white pants and shirts with vests, as Abahji had—they were farmers, like us, finding their way south. But there were city folk too, some of them even wearing simple, Western-style button-downs tucked into zippered pants—nothing too fancy, because not even the rich of Pyongyang wanted to show their wealth. The government might arrest them as *bourgeois* and *anti-communist*.

Youngsoo and I followed the crowd until we reached the Tae-dong River. It cut through the middle of the city like a sword. South Korean guards stood along the bank, checking for North Korean soldiers trying to infiltrate the South, opening bags, shoving back men. Along the muddy shore were hills of sandbags, and behind them stood abandoned houses, crumbling from neglect like so many broken shells washed up on shore.

I looked up and saw a destroyed steel bridge, its girders mangled and jagged like the ribs of a carcass. It swarmed with black dots.

I rubbed my eyes and realized that the dots were people

scaling broken girders a hundred feet high. They had strapped their belongings onto their backs and now crawled across the ruins of the bridge in a careful procession, desperate to reach the south bank.

On the ground, thousands of people waited in line to do the same. An eerie silence hung over the crowd; everyone seemed to hold their breath, afraid that the slightest sound would break a climber's concentration.

A young mother stood in line with a baby on her back. She closed her eyes, murmuring to herself. "'Though I walk through the valley of the shadow of death, I will fear no evil, for Thou art with me . . .'"

"What happened to the bridge?" I asked, tugging on her arm.

She opened her eyes and looked at me. "Blown up. It was bombed to keep the Reds from crossing over. But now we're trapped on this side of the river with them."

Trapped.

The word batted with frenzied wings inside my chest. We'd fallen slightly behind the Allied retreat; they'd already bombed the bridges and left us all for dead. And now the communist soldiers were coming to reclaim this shattered city.

We weren't just running. We were being chased.

I stared at that tangle of broken metal. A black dot plunged into the icy water.

"Noona, should we cross the bridge?" Youngsoo broke into a coughing fit, his shoulders jerking uncontrollably.

I looked at him, at the way he couldn't keep his cough under control or his body still. Then I gazed upstream. The river seemed to go on for miles with no end in sight. There *had* to be another bridge. A safer bridge.

"No," I said. "There must be another way across. Come, let's go."

I grabbed his hand and hurried upstream. Up close, the Tae-dong gleamed deeper and darker than the river back home. A large chunk of ice floated by, rotating slowly as if it were alive.

"Noona, we can build a raft. I saw some firewood back there!" Youngsoo pointed to a cluster of houses.

"Don't be stupid! We can't build a raft." I wove through the crowds, quickening my pace. I knew I must have hurt him. Sometimes my tongue really was as sharp as Omahni's. "Don't worry. We'll be fine," I added.

"But how will we get across?" he asked, frowning.

I didn't know, and I didn't trust myself. Yet every decision was up to me—our lives depended on it.

The farther upstream we ran, the more the crowds deterio-rated into desperation and chaos. The grave silence by the bridge soon gave way to crying, shouting, and fighting. A mother ran with her baby slipping from the sling on her back. An ox strad-dled with luggage lumbered beside me, its hooves sinking deep into the muddy ground, its labored breath hot against my face. A man waded into the freezing water, kicking twenty feet off shore before turning blue and sinking.

I needed someone wiser and older. But I continued running upstream, pretending that I knew what to do, even though I couldn't stop shaking, couldn't stop my heart from pounding.

Eventually, we reached a stretch of river where even the mud had frozen. I'd started retreating inside my head, too tired to talk, too tired to run; Youngsoo shuffled alongside me, just as quiet and withdrawn. I didn't want to look at that dark water anymore, even when the crowd stopped moving and started clustering along the shore.

But then, a collective gasp. I turned and pushed my way in to see, dragging Youngsoo.

Halfway across the river, a canoe nosed through small chunks of ice. But it was weighed down with too many people—mothers, grandmothers, infants. Water spilled in over the sides. The crowd screamed, and my mouth hung open. I watched the women and babies sink, the murky water devouring them whole.

A man wearing a straw rice-paddy hat pulled two other canoes ashore onto the north bank. "Only women and children on the boats!" he hollered. "*And not too many!*"

A din of protest rose from the mob. But I was glad, because I was desperate enough to take this way across.

"Youngsoo, that's us! We're children! Let's go!"

I pushed and shoved, and grown men pushed back—men old enough to be my father, but without any concern for me at all. Here, I was no one's daughter, and my eyes stung with hurt. Then someone knocked Youngsoo off his feet, and he burst into tears.

"Stop crying! Stop crying!" I said, my face turning tight and red.

But we had missed the boats. I pulled Youngsoo to his feet, and we continued running upstream.

A heavy blast echoed just beyond the city, and I imagined the Reds appearing right at our heels. Afraid, I yanked Youngsoo's arm harder, and when he tripped, I scolded, "Watch where you're going! They're *coming*!"

Were there more boats? I couldn't find any. Instead, I kept thinking of that mangled bridge: Was it our only way across? The thought nagged at me. What if we were wasting time running away from it?

We ran until our frantic sprint dwindled again into a weary shuffle. A bit of bloody sock stuck out of a hole in my shoe.

I gazed upriver. Even though it was bitterly cold, the midday sun hung brightly overhead and I had to shield my eyes. Maybe there was no way across—such truth had been lurking for a while. I had been running like a skittish squirrel and didn't know which way to go anymore. In fact, I never had.

I squinted in the sun, thinking I had *such* poor judgment, when a glint of light shimmering against ice caught my eye.

And then I understood what stretched before me.

"There!" I said, pointing half a mile up the river. "The water froze, and people are walking across!"

I laughed, then grabbed Youngsoo's hand and ran, the rocky ground hurting my feet through the thin soles of my rubber shoes. But I didn't care, for now I could see it clearly: plates of ice stretching across the river. Hundreds of people on the bank. Tenuous figures walking on water.

"Yah!" an old woman said near the icy edge, when we arrived at the frozen bank. "You can't have too many people on the ice at once. It's not that thick. It'll break. Get back!"

I pushed through the mob, ignoring her—we *had* to cross. But someone shoved back, and I fell to the ground.

"We were here first!" a woman said, clearing a path for her twin boys. They looked around Youngsoo's age; their heads were shaven and their faces round as if they hadn't suffered a hungry day in their lives. She was the one who had pushed me down. She had no right—there was no line!

Without thinking, I got back on my feet and tried to reach the ice. Her firm hand shoved me aside again.

"Uh-muh! The nerve of this girl. I said we were here first. Let my sons through!" The woman glared at me.

Fighting back tears, I stood aside and let them pass. One of the boys lowered his stubbly head in apology.

Finally, another small break opened in the crowd by the water's edge. I squeezed through it with Youngsoo. The sun shone off the frozen water, the ice gleaming like a heavenly road that had miraculously appeared for our crossing. But up close I could see it had broken into separate pieces, like stepping-stones across the frigid water.

I took a step, and the ice rocked under my feet. Youngsoo

let go of my hand, extending his arms to steady himself as he followed me onto the floes. We slipped and slid across the river like new fawns trying to find our legs.

We were more than halfway across when there was a splash and scream directly ahead—and then an ear-piercing cry. The mother of the two boys crouched over the edge of an ice block.

"No, no, no!" she cried, peering into the murky water. A shaven head bobbed near the surface. And another. Short, fat fingers gripped the edge of the icy slab.

I felt lightheaded.

"Help!" the woman pleaded. Every time she leaned to lift her sons out of the water, her chunk of ice tilted.

We were the closest. I hurried forward and offered my hand to help steady her, and she yanked hard as she reached for her children with her other arm. My feet slipped, and I fell, the firm ice smacking against my chin. The block tilted forward, and I started sliding headfirst toward the dark, icy waters.

"Noona!"

Someone stomped hard on the back end of our block. The ice righted itself. I gripped the edge.

"Help! My boys!" the woman screamed, her hands grasping at me.

"I can't. I can't! I'm sorry!" I shouted back.

"Noona! Get up! Keep walking!" Youngsoo shouted.

Yes, keep walking. I rose slowly. The ice swayed. I was a mouse, light and quick on my feet. Youngsoo followed close behind.

We passed the woman. She moaned and pressed her cheek to the little blue hands now frozen stuck to the ice's edge.

I turned my gaze forward, hardening my heart, biting down on my lip until it bled. The other side was only a few feet away. *Almost there*, I told myself.

Step after step, we crept on, until the solid earth rose to meet us. We had made it to the southern side of the Taedong.

I fell on my back on the frozen ground and stared at the sky. Those shaven heads. That screaming mother. Tiny blue fingers. I couldn't stop shaking.

The afternoon sun beat down on my face, and I wondered what would happen if the ice bridge melted, and everyone on the other side was trapped forever.

"The Reds are here," Abahji had muttered to himself. It was our turn to host a Party meeting.

Omahni glared at him. "Don't cause any trouble. Let's just get the red stamps on our ID cards; we could use the extra rations."

Abahji got up to open the door, his jaw clenching.

Feet stomped into the house. Wouldn't they take off their shoes? Jisoo crawled under the table to hide. Men in button-down work shirts pushed heaping spoonfuls of rice and broth into their mouths. One woman sat squat on the floor like a mudslide that had landed in our home. Omahni chattered away behind a taut smile, her cheeks flushed and her back straight. She scurried in and out of the kitchen, serving bean sprout soup for dinner. The portrait of the Great Leader we had hung for the meeting stared down at us, all-seeing. It wasn't long before Omahni and Abahji were too busy to mind us children.

I washed dishes in the kitchen. Youngsoo stood beside me.

"What is the Workers' Party, anyway?" he asked. "And why do we have to be here?"

"Shh, don't talk too loudly," I said. "The Workers' Party is kind of like your Sonyondan Club, but for adults. And our whole family has to be here, especially me, since I don't go to Sonyondan Club anymore."

"Oh." Youngsoo scratched his head.

I ladled soup into two bowls "Here, eat what you can before our guests eat everything."

"What about Jisoo?"

We poked our heads into the main room. It pulsed with pumping fists and loud talk: Long live the Red Army! Persecute the bourgeoisie! Hail to the working class! Omahni went back and forth, serving food and gathering dirty bowls. Abahji sat listening, the tight lines around his mouth about to snap and splinter. And under the low table, trapped on every side by seated strangers, lay Jisoo.

Someone pounded on the tabletop and shouted with a red face. Jisoo's little body quivered, a dark wet spot forming on his pants. He followed Omahni with his eyes, waiting for her to notice him. A sharp pang hit me in the center of my chest.

twenty-two · · · · · ·
December, 1950

We left Pyongyang and never spoke of the river that ran through it, the one with a voracious appetite for women, infants, and boys with shaven heads.

Youngsoo and I spent the next week trekking across frozen hills and lowlands, avoiding others as much as we could. The people we'd encountered so far had either abandoned or taken advantage of us—I no longer trusted strangers.

There were deserted villages everywhere, so we never had trouble finding shelter for the night. In each house, I knew to get the stove burning, so heat ran through the piping and soothed our frozen feet on the *ondol* floor. I knew to check the clay jars buried outside, often full of fermenting kimchi. And I knew there was always a chance of finding rice, and became good at discovering its hiding places—under the floorboard, stuffed into socks, inside an old chest. Like scavengers, we relied on the food left behind by others.

But the house we had chosen this night had no kimchi or rice.

"Ai! I can't believe this rotten house doesn't have a single thing to eat!" I kicked a wooden table—*hard*—and my toe throbbed.

"Don't worry, Noona. I'm not even hungry." Youngsoo lay on his side, coughing.

How could he not be hungry? I studied him. He looked different—darker, leaner—like a boy in the wild. There were shadows under his eyes. His hair had grown, curling like snail shells. I knew I had changed too. My calves had hardened. The calluses on my feet were as tough as horses' hooves. And I had become good at running—especially running away.

I found a blanket and spread it on the floor. Youngsoo and I curled up on it, back-to-back, like bookends. There was nothing to do now but sleep.

We listened to jets zooming overhead, one after the other. The fighting was heading our way fast.

How far could we walk the next day without having eaten? How could we outrun tanks and planes and men?

It was our bad luck that had brought us to this house with no food. If we had taken a different path, found a different house, we could have ended up with bellies full of rice and kimchi. I blew out the kerosene lamp and dreamed I was being chased by wolves.

❄ ❄ ❄

When it came to chance, though, it turned out that luck could turn just as easily from bad to good.

The next day, we walked for hours, our steps heavy and slow. An icy wind blasted our faces, and we sputtered to catch our breath as if we were drowning. But up ahead, in a forest of pine trees, a pearl of light shone through the branches and smoke curled above the treetops. I could even see a bit of a thatched roof.

"Youngsoo, let's head toward that house. We need to find a place to stay for the night."

"But it doesn't look abandoned," he said between shallow breaths.

We stared at the light. After traveling alone for more than a week, we had grown accustomed to solitude. In some ways, it was easier like this—just the two of us—although I still worried whether I was taking us in the right direction.

"It's getting dark. We need to stop," I said, finally. "We're going in." At least there would be a fire.

In the growing dim, the trees were beginning to look like witches with spindly arms, and their bumpy roots tripped us the entire way. The cold bled in through our every buttonhole and seam. I felt a tremor of anxiety. What if we were walking right into the hands of another person who wanted to sell me to soldiers? I prayed that the people inside would be kind.

By the time we reached the cottage, I felt faint with hunger. It was surrounded by a low cinder-block wall, and a tree grew inside its courtyard, the heavy branches hanging down outside the fence, creaking and groaning.

Youngsoo stood with his mouth agape. "Noona, it's a persimmon tree."

We looked at each other, hardly believing our eyes. I'd nearly forgotten that these fruits ripened in winter. I'd nearly forgotten persimmons existed at all.

Most of them had been picked, but I could still grab one, two, three! A few squashed ones lay in the snow right by my feet. It was a miracle!

We crouched to gather as many fallen ones as we could. Soon, a small mound of bright orange formed between us, and we quickly pulled off our mittens. I snatched one and squeezed its solid mass, full of juice and ripe pulp. Its waxy skin yielded soft and tender in my hand. I took a bite.

The fruit burst in my mouth and squirted across my face. Youngsoo squished one open and gorged on the glistening flesh, juice running down his chin. I laughed and took another, splitting it so its sticky insides broke apart in my palms. I lowered my face and lapped the pulp and juices, my cheeks smeared with orange flecks. When was the last time I had eaten something so sweet and good?

Youngsoo looked at me.

I looked back.

And we cackled in delight. We sat there like scoundrels, hovering over our mound of treasure and gorging ourselves until our lips looked bruised.

I licked my fingers and admired the mess we had made, thinking how I could've never done this back home. In this strange place, I didn't have to cut the fruit into pretty pieces. I didn't have to serve it on a plate to my brothers. I didn't have to hide my teeth when I ate and laughed. Here, lost in the middle of a war, crouched under a stranger's persimmon tree, it didn't matter who I was, and for a second, I thought I had glimpsed into heaven.

twenty-three ······

I wiped my mouth on my sleeve. The last of the light was fading. A cold wind swept around me, and I remembered that we still needed to get inside the house.

I went to the wooden front door. Youngsoo clutched the edge of my coat and looked up at me. I forced a smile, then knocked hard.

"Hello? Hello?" I called out. The cold stung my eyes, causing them to well. "We are two children without our parents. We want to spend a night inside away from the cold. Please let us in!" A blast of icy air blew across my face, and I dug deeper into my coat, touching the edge of the folded map in my pocket for comfort.

The door opened, and brightness flooded the entryway. In the glow stood a man whose hands were calloused and weathered, his nails dark with dirt.

I took a deep breath. That smell of grain and damp earth. That familiar silhouette, medium build. I only needed to see his crescent-moon eyes to know. My heart thumped, and I blinked to clear the bleary haze from my eyes. From behind, a high-pitched cry.

"Abahji!" Youngsoo shouted. *"Abahji!"*

I burst into tears.

"I'm sorry, children, but you must be mistaken. I'm not your father," the man said, his chin quivering. In the light, I could see that his face drooped like a hound's.

I closed my eyes, wishing that this strange man would turn into my father, wishing that he would lift me up and swing me around and hug me tightly. I opened my eyes.

The man kept sighing apologetically, looking as though he might cry too. All at once, I felt sorry for him. I wiped my eyes and reached for Youngsoo's hand.

"May we please come in from the cold?" I asked, a flatness in my tone. I couldn't hide my disappointment.

"Of course, there's always room for more." He stepped away, and I gasped at the number of people crowded inside. There was hardly a place to step or sit. Everyone lay on the floor, practically on top of one another.

I made my way to an empty space in the corner where water stains had darkened the oiled-paper floor. The smell of so many bodies, soiled and unwashed, was sour and potent. Youngsoo settled beside me. He coughed and wheezed. His nose dripped. I put a hand to his forehead; he had a fever.

"Aigoo, orphans. So sad and pitiful," a grandmother said. "Hurry, children, eat." She handed me a blanket and a bowl of rice with sweet black beans.

Orphans. I winced at the word. "Halmoni, we're not orphans.

We became separated from our parents, but our father always knows what to do. He'll find us again," I explained.

"*Tsk, tsk.* I feel so sorry for you poor children!" the old woman wailed, beating her chest with a fist. "If you haven't found your parents by now, dears, then you are orphans for sure!" She moaned, shaking her head. "Oh, this terrible war! Terrible war!"

"Will somebody please tell that crazy woman to shut up?" a man hollered from the middle of the room.

Was it true? Were we orphans?

The truth had always been there. But hearing it aloud seared a hole in my chest. I slumped to the floor and hugged my knees.

Youngsoo whimpered beside me.

I tried to recall the sweet smell of sticky rice and sesame oil in our house, the sound of Omahni shaking out our quilts, our father's stories of America and its outlandish promises. The memories were already cloudy, as if it had all been a dream. "Abahji," I whispered. "Who will look after us now?"

I bowed to the halmoni for the rice and black beans, then gave everything to Youngsoo. I told him to eat all of it, and when he did, I exhaled in relief.

"And what about you? Don't you have to eat?" a teenage girl asked, sitting across from us. Her hair hung loosely in a ponytail. Omahni would've *tsk*ed at her tan skin and small eyes—a plain face, a peasant's face. But the girl leaned over and closed my hands around a small mound of anchovies wrapped in a cloth.

"I'm not hungry, but I'll take it for my brother," I said. "Thank you."

The girl tilted her head back and laughed. "If you're going to take it, you must eat some for yourself! This is no place for martyrs."

I flushed.

"I know your type," she continued. "You're a good girl. You always do as you're told. There's nothing wrong with that . . . just know your worth, too."

No one had ever said that to me before. Looking at her again, she didn't seem so much like a lowly peasant—just an ordinary girl, like me.

Her ponytail swished to one side. She studied Youngsoo's feverish face and said, "You're no good to him if you don't take care of yourself, too." She opened my hand, unwrapping the anchovies. "You're a courageous girl. Eat some. You deserve it."

I accepted the food, but my face crumpled with emotion upon hearing those words. The girl's kindness broke me, and when I tried to say thank you, my voice turned ragged.

I opened the cloth and slipped a tiny, salted anchovy between my lips. My throat swelled with gratitude, and I could hardly swallow. I looked over at Youngsoo, who lay on the floor, his face hot with fever, and tried to pass an anchovy to him too, but he shook his head. After a few more bites, I wrapped the rest for later.

That evening, I sat and listened to the adults discussing their travel routes south.

Which way will you go? Through Kaesong? Across the Yellow Sea? No one seemed worried anymore about border guards—only about staying ahead of the battle line. If we got stuck behind the front, we'd be trapped under communist control again, maybe forever. And if we got stuck in the fighting . . .

"Noona, we're almost there, right?" Youngsoo nestled deeper into his blanket.

"Yes, we're almost at the border. As soon as we cross over, we'll be in South Korea." The words felt strange against my tongue.

"Then we'll be safe?"

"Yes, I think so," I said, my voice wavering. But what if—after all this—the Reds swept across the border and took over the South anyway? There would be no safety. Not even in Seoul. And our parents would have died for nothing.

Youngsoo exhaled, then hardened his voice. "They're still alive, Noona."

Abahji. Omahni. Jisoo.

"I know, I know. Get some sleep."

I curled into a ball, my limbs heavy. Could I really lead us the rest of the way? Worry darkened my mind. I lay there wondering about the land across the border. What kind of life awaited us?

twenty-four · · · · · ·
December, 1950

Dawn had not even broken when my eyes flew open. The house felt emptier, stiller, colder.

"Wake up. We need to go," I whispered into Youngsoo's ear.

Many people had already left, abandoning possessions too cumbersome for the rest of the journey: pots, blankets, utensils. There was little time to waste, but I scavenged through the mess, gathering a spoon, two small pots, and rice, wrapping everything in a blanket.

I stood over Youngsoo, who looked at me with glassy eyes. "Noona, everything hurts. I can't walk out there in the cold."

Panic fluttered in my chest. "You have to. We have no choice. I'm not strong enough to carry you."

"But I can't."

"Yes, you can. If you don't . . . I'll leave you behind, I swear. Now get up!"

Youngsoo's eyes widened. "Don't leave me!"

I sat down and covered my face. "Of course I won't leave you, idiot." I sighed shakily.

A second later, I felt a small hand on my back.

"Noona, you can go," he said, blinking and swallowing hard.

For a second, I saw it in my mind—walking out the door without him, light and quick on my feet. I took a deep breath, then wiped my face against my sleeve. "No. Don't be ridiculous. I'll *never* leave you."

Nearly everyone had gone by now. Only the elderly lingered by the stove.

"Take my bullock cart," one of the grandfathers said suddenly. His face looked as soft and lined as kneaded dough. "I'm not able to push it any longer. This journey is too much for my aching bones. I plan to stay here in this old house. I've lived my life, but you, children, must go. Push your brother in the cart."

I looked out the window and saw a sturdy wooden cart—not too big, not too small, just the right size for me to push. My heart leapt. I knew I should politely refuse his offer, at least once, but I was too afraid to let it go.

"Thank you. *Thank you*," I said, hardly able to speak. I bowed deeply.

"Hurry, now. Take the cart," the old man said, shooing us with his arm. "The Reds are coming."

Omahni tossed an armful of pine bark into her wooden cart, then stuck a knife into a tree and peeled off another layer. Rice was short this winter, and we gathered bark to fill our bellies. After Omahni stripped and steamed it, it was slightly sweet, but it would never be my favorite food.

I sneezed, and felt my head swell and my nose clog.

"You've caught a cold," Omahni said, hacking through layers of bark.

The air nipped. A wintry wind chilled me to my bones. I shivered.

"Go back home," she insisted. "I can handle the rest."

I didn't move. When was the last time Omahni had ordered me not to help?

"Go!"

I jumped. "Yes, Omahni." I folded my arms to keep warm. My sleeves were too short, the elbows thin and bald. I had worn this same jacket since I was seven.

Omahni slipped off her coat and tossed it to me. "Here, take it."

"But you'll freeze, Omahni. I have a jacket."

"Eh, but it's too thin. Just take mine and put it over yours. It's a long walk home."

I draped it over my shoulders; it was still warm, and I sank into it. "I'll send Youngsoo back with your jacket once I get home."

She glared at me. "Don't even think of doing that. He's too little to make it here alone. I'll be fine. Just go."

I left, the cold wind on my back. I looked over my shoulder and saw Omahni's slight figure crouched by the towering pine trees. The wind blew and bent her like a thin plank. Was she really that small— my mother, the one who kept planets in orbit and the universe in order?

When I opened the door, a gust of wind rushed to greet us as if it had been waiting on the doorstep all night for our return. I cringed and tucked my chin inside my coat.

The cart was by the side of the house. I spread a blanket inside and told Youngsoo to climb in. He curled up, and I covered him with a quilt, tucking the bundle of pots and utensils in the corner.

I grabbed the handles and looked at him. "Are you ready?"

"I guess so," he said, sniffling.

twenty-five · · · · ·
December, 1950

Over the next week and a half, a forest of skinny pines closed in. They surrounded us at every turn, each tree the same as the next. We had long lost the trail left behind by others, and I began to wonder if we were traveling diagonally instead of straight. Or if we were lost.

But I continued pushing the cart, trudging through valleys and stopping at abandoned houses along the way. We had no other choice. Youngsoo's cough had filled his chest, but I could hardly hear his constant wheezing through my own sniffling, my own clogged ears.

What Youngsoo and I talked about during those strangely quiet days of travel still lingers in my mind. He told me that sometimes he wished he weren't the first-born son.

"Too much pressure," he said. "Everything depends on me. But I'm not smart enough to live up to something like that."

I never knew that he felt that way, but I understood.

He kept talking, coughing, talking about his wish to grow up like Grandfather, to be as adventurous as him, as responsible, to make a lot of money in America so that he could buy a big house for our family.

"I think you are like him," I said.

Thunderous blasts drew nearer and nearer, but we ignored them, tamping down the spring-loaded screams ready to catapult from our throats.

As I pushed the cart, he told me about the time older boys teased him on his way back from gathering pine tree bark—poor man's food. And how he'd lied and told them it wasn't for our family but for the lame-footed boy who lived across the village.

"I'm sure you're forgiven," I said.

"But it was worse than that," he confessed. "When they called the lame-footed boy a beggar, I laughed and called him one, too."

I was quiet for a second. "We all do things we regret sometimes."

He sniffled once, then nodded, his small head poking out from under the blanket.

One day, he told me that he thought it might be his birthday. "I wish I had noodle soup to celebrate," he said. It was what we always ate on birthdays—the noodles represented long life.

I paused to think. His birthday was December 20. Today could very well be that day. "Happy birthday, Youngsoo. That means you're nine now." I reached down and hugged him, sorry that I had no noodle soup to offer.

He only nodded, too exhausted to say another word, like a wind-up doll that had suddenly run down.

A bright flash lit up the dim morning sky as if it were midday, exposing the jagged mountaintops around us. Gone were the plains and lowlands of the west. The land had become truly mountainous, and I worried we had gone too far east.

I pulled out the map and examined the line of the Taebaek Mountains to the east of Pyongyang. We hadn't gone that far, had we? Was it possible we were in the foothills? My hands were raw and blistered from gripping the barrow's handles, and the paper quivered in my grip; I refolded it and put it back in my pocket. The explosions were even closer now—I could feel them underfoot. As the ground trembled, I imagined a stomping giant hurtling toward us.

I moved to push the cart, then froze. Something was creeping across my waist and back. It tickled intensely, and I scratched long and hard. Maybe it was a strand of hair. I lifted the edge of my shirt to check—and screamed.

Youngsoo sat straight up. "Noona, what's wrong?"

"Sesame seeds!" I cried in disgust.

"What?"

"There are sesame seeds in the seams of my clothes!" I tried brushing them away, but they were stuck. Puzzled, I checked my pants—and that's when I saw the seeds moving, scurrying across my waistband.

"*Lice!*" I screamed.

All at once, my entire body turned into an impossible itch. I writhed and scratched like someone possessed. I imagined the tiny bugs creeping down my back, up my neck, into my hair. I yanked off my coat and beat it on the ground.

"Noona! Stop!"

I looked at Youngsoo. His lips trembled. He stared at me as if I'd gone mad.

"What about you? Do you have any lice?" I flung open his blanket, tore off his coat, and lifted his shirt—then drew in a sharp breath. "My God!"

Nits were buried in the creases of his clothes, and red sores dotted his skin. But more than that, it was a bag of bones I saw curled up inside that cart. Underneath all the layers, Youngsoo was wasting away. I could even see his thin chest pulsing, nothing but skin and rib cage separating his heart from the air.

Worry paced inside my head. I had to do something.

I pulled the cloth satchel from my pocket and unwrapped it. The fishy scent of anchovies filled my nostrils; there was only a palmful left. My stomach rumbled, but I slipped a few into Youngsoo's mouth. He chewed slowly. I fed him another and another until only a few slivers remained.

I couldn't look at him when I slid the last ones between my lips and licked the salt off my fingers. Then I remembered what that ponytailed girl had said, and I ate because I needed it too.

It was dusk. Sleet blew horizontally into my face. My hands were red and throbbing, and my body stung with lice bites. I couldn't push the bullock cart anymore.

"Youngsoo, get on my back."

I left the cart against the side of a hill, thanking it under my breath for granting my brother some rest. Then, slowly, he climbed on, as light as air. I strapped him to my waist with a blanket and hugged the bundle of foraged items. His frailness weighed heavily on my heart.

We didn't have any food left, and now itchiness rivaled hunger and coldness, all hard to ignore. What if the next abandoned house didn't have rice? How long could we go without?

I was too busy thinking and scratching to notice them heading toward us—two dark figures through the white valley.

twenty-six · · · · · ·

Closer and closer they came. South Korean soldiers in dark green fatigues.

I wasn't sure where they'd come from. Maybe we were close to the thirty-eighth parallel and they were part of a regiment fortifying the border. All I knew was that there was nowhere to hide.

"Stop!" one of them shouted, rushing toward me, his rifle cocked. He wasn't really any older than Myung-gi, his frame tall and lanky. Under the strain of the loud command, his voice had cracked. "Are you traveling alone?"

"Yes, my brother and I are . . . orphans." My mouth turned dry.

"What are you?" he barked. "North or South Korean?"

"South."

Loud snickering. "Really? You're South Korean? Is that why your North Korean accent is so thick?"

My heart started kicking.

"Just because we're from the North doesn't mean we're communists," I said, daring to look him straight in the eye.

The lanky soldier rammed his rifle under my chin. His finger rested on the trigger.

I gasped. "Please. My brother is sick. We need to find my uncle and aunt in Busan."

The roar of approaching jets rumbled in the distance.

"Let them go, birdbrain," the other young soldier said, his face pocked and pimply. "They're just kids."

"She's not such a kid. Look, she's even kind of pretty. How old are you?" the lanky soldier asked.

"None of your business!" I cried, covered in cold sweat.

Jets thundered overhead.

The soldiers looked up.

But I gazed past them, the long, dark valley calling me. Every muscle tensed. The slope of my back shifted. One foot inched forward, even with the rifle still under my chin. *I could run for it. Knock the barrel off my neck before he could shoot. Cut between the mountains.*

"Don't do it, Noona," Youngsoo whispered over my shoulder.

"Don't do what?" the lanky soldier asked, the jets disappearing.

And just like that, the moment passed. "Nothing," I said, a thick and tarry gloom settling over me.

"Let them go." The pocked soldier stepped closer, adjusting his too-wide helmet. "You can get into serious trouble for mistreating civilians. You'd be breaking the international laws of war. It's *wrong*."

"So? Who would know?" the lanky one said, grinning.

The pimply soldier raised his own rifle, aiming at his friend. "Me."

My neck ached, the hard-metal muzzle still pushing into the soft flesh under my chin. I held my breath, thanking God for the laws of war—and for this pimply soldier who followed the rules, even when no one was looking.

The lanky boy stared right at me, rocking slightly in his boots. "Fine. Just go," he said, lowering his rifle.

Everything came loose inside me, and I rubbed my throat, wanting to burst into tears.

But I only nodded and started walking away, trying to remember to breathe. It wasn't until I turned a corner around a hillside and could see a small forest that I broke into a sprint, threading through the trees, branches clawing at my face. Faster and faster. I ran until my lungs burned, until my legs lost their feeling, until all noises fell behind.

I never thanked Youngsoo for saving me that day. I hope he understood.

"You'll thank me one day for my vigilance. Now hide this," Omahni said, handing me the Bible.

It was small and brown, its woven cover fraying at the edges. I lifted the floorboard by the doorframe and dropped it down below. "Why do we have to hide it? No one comes to our house except the Kims."

"If you're reckless in private, then you'll be reckless in public," Omahni said, folding Abahji's shirt and putting it in a drawer. "What if Youngsoo were to slip it into his schoolbag along with his

other books by mistake? What if he brought it to school?" She stopped
*folding laundry as if she hadn't thought of that until just then. Her
face paled.*

*My hands turned cold. I tamped down on the floorboard with my
foot, making sure I had closed it completely. "Omahni, does everyone have to hide things in holes? Even in South Korea? Even in
America?"*

*"How should I know?" Omahni snapped, picking up Abahji's
pants and smoothing out the creases.*

Eventually, we saw others heading in our same direction, rag-
gedy and loaded down with bundles. I sighed in relief at the
sight, knowing they were like us—refugees, not soldiers.

We followed them until we came to a deep valley ringed in
mountains, hundreds of people funneling through it like sheep.
It wasn't long before the crowd slowed, as if the people in front
were waiting their turn for something.

I climbed the side of a hill to see. Water shimmered in the
distance. My heart dropped.

"Another river," I whispered.

Youngsoo's head turned to me. "How will we get across?"

I had no answer. All I could think about were those boys
with the shaven heads—a boat filling up with water—the
black Taedong River devouring women and children whole.
The sun hit the edge of a mammoth peak and cut a shadow
over us.

We headed toward the water. There was no other way forward.

The Imjin River—that was what the others were calling it. It wound back and forth on itself like a snake, and I knew we might have to cross it more than once. The sun shone, round and steady, thawing the winter's day as if it were spring. Youngsoo relaxed over my shoulder, but the sudden warmth made me uneasy. How could an ice bridge form if the temperature wasn't freezing?

Finally, we reached the river's edge. There were so many of us: men and women carrying bundles on their backs and heads; old couples and their farm animals plunking through the water; and toddlers, their lips so pink, following in a line behind their mothers.

But no one looked like our family.

Everyone walked along the bank or in the shallows, not crossing yet. I took off my socks and shoes and followed them, hoisting Youngsoo higher so his feet wouldn't get wet. We needed to get to the border and make sure that we crossed at night in the dark.

"Excuse me," I said to a woman walking alongside me. "How can I get to the border?"

She grinned until her gums showed. "You'll be crossing soon. Part of the thirty-eighth parallel cuts right through this river!"

"Will anyone try to stop us?" With Youngsoo on my back, I sank deep into the muddy ground.

The woman patted my arm. "The Reds won't. They're not here yet."

I pointed my face toward the sun, finally taking in the spring-like day. Across the river, fluffy clouds floated over South Korea, and I wanted to reach up and touch them. Abahji would've swung us in the air at this news.

"Did you hear that, Youngsoo? We're crossing the border right now, and there's no one to stop us." He coughed, then squeezed my shoulder.

Families walked hand in hand, pants rolled high as if traipsing through a stream looking for clams. One woman reunited with her sister, splashing across the water to hug her. They cried and held each other's faces, their hair pulled back in buns. Youngsoo poked me in the shoulder, pointing and smiling, and the hope in me grew stronger. I dared to believe our parents were alive again.

We walked for hours. I searched every passing stranger, and though it was never them, I told myself that if they weren't here, they were in Busan. Others on the journey said as much, talking about their own plans to meet up with lost relatives who had fled there too. A load lifted from me, and I let my mind wander to luxuries like books and Tootsie Rolls and school.

"Sora-ya, is that you?"

I whipped around. A familiar face! It was Mrs. Lee, the ruddy-cheeked laundry woman from back home who'd poked me in the ribs. Except, her hair had grayed. She carried her three-year-old daughter on her back. I never thought I'd be so happy to see her. "Yes, it's me! I'm Sora!"

"I thought it was you!" She pounded me hard on the shoulder, using her scrubbing arm. "Where are your parents?"

"We lost them, but we're going to meet up with them in Busan," I said. "I'm sure of it."

Mrs. Lee nodded, her wide smile half closing. "And what about your brother here? Is he *trying* to look like a wet noodle?" She stuck her finger in Youngsoo's side, and he started cackling and coughing. It felt good to hear him laugh again.

"He's caught a bad cold. But I think he'll be fine once we get to Busan. Are you heading there, too?"

"Oh, no. I'm going to Daejeon. My sister, her husband, and their children are there. But we can travel part of the way together."

Part of the way was better than nothing. I wanted to wrap my arms around her hefty middle.

It was time to cross the water. She waded in first, her belongings floating behind like a tugboat. The little girl on her back clapped and shook her head, her two braids swinging back and forth like a rattle drum.

I followed, the water reaching past my waist. The air had warmed, but the river was still freezing. Youngsoo's legs and stomach dipped below the surface. "Cold!" he cried.

"Just pretend you're fishing back home and fell in. You've done this before." It was the only thing I could think to say to keep his mind off the water creeping up our sides.

"I'll t-try," he said, his chin jittering against my shoulder.

My fingers and toes tingled and could hardly move. I focused on my armpits, the one spot that was still warm. Oh, and I couldn't forget the back of my neck. I put my hand there.

The river floor began sloping upward, and the water dropped to my knees. People at the front of the line had already walked out onto snowy grass. Up ahead, I could see nothing but dry land and mountains.

Had we crossed over into the South? Not even one border guard to stop us? No impassable spots on the river?

I shivered through my wet clothes and told Youngsoo we'd stop and make a fire to dry ourselves soon. He coughed and nodded. I imagined a crackling fire hot against the back of my knees, the soaked fabric drying to a crepey texture, warm air enveloping me in fluffy clouds like the ones I'd seen floating over the South.

This was what I was thinking right before I heard the first shots.

Behind us. On the far bank. Foreign men in uniforms shooting at us. People screaming, splashing through water, falling facedown. A stampede swept us up like a wave of water buffaloes. I ran, Youngsoo clinging to my back.

Shots. And more shots. Mrs. Lee falling facedown. Two little braids sinking into water.

The Imjin River turning red.

Cries echoing up and down the valley.

I kept running. Didn't look back. Prayed Youngsoo hadn't been hit over my shoulder.

twenty-seven · · · · · ·
December, 1950

No matter how hard I scrubbed with snow, I couldn't get the blood off my pants.

Blood stained pink—the color of a woman's gums, a toddler's lips, a laundry woman's ruddy cheeks. Scenes kept running through my head: Something brushing against my leg. Bodies floating past like driftwood. A bare back—its shirt lifting up in the water—rotating like a tortoise. But neither of us had been hurt.

We were in Kaesong—a small city not far from Seoul, according to my map. It had taken us four days to get here after crossing the Imjin River; the land was hilly, with mountains connecting in the distance. Electrical poles lined the town's narrow dirt roads, shorter than the ones in Pyongyang, glowing in the dusk. Tile-roofed houses stood so close to one another that their eaves overlapped, lights shining in all their windows. None were abandoned.

Youngsoo had picked one, and I had knocked on the door, my hand shaky and tinged red. A middle-aged woman had answered, and when her eyes moistened at the sight of us, I knew we had chosen the right house to spend the night.

"Just call me *Ahjuma*," she had said.

Now she sat on her floor at a low table, cutting egg pancakes into diamond shapes. I was still rubbing the hem of my pants. "Don't fret over the stain, child. Would you like a pair of my pants?"

"No, thank you." Omahni had cut and sewn these herself. "I'll wear mine." I sat beside Youngsoo, clutching our bundle of belongings.

"Well, at least let me take your things and set them over here."

"We have nothing of value!" I blurted.

Ahjuma's eyes grew wide, and she stared at us. Youngsoo crumpled under her gaze the way he had when his teacher scolded him for forgetting his homework.

"I only want to help. And in case you've forgotten, you were the one who knocked on our door, so mind your manners," Ahjuma said, pushing bowls of rice and dumpling soup toward us. "Now, go ahead and eat."

I looked around her house. The ondol floor was warm and clean. Clothes lay neatly folded in the corner. An electric iron sat plugged into the wall. My face burned in embarrassment. Why would this lady want anything from two dirty country bumpkins like us?

I set down our bundle, then grabbed a spoon and took a bite of rice, making sure to lower my face so she couldn't see the red spreading across my cheeks. Neat cutouts of egg floated in the broth as a garnish, perfectly trimmed. I glanced at Youngsoo.

He slurped from the edge of his bowl, then wiped his mouth with the back of his hand and burped. It was the most appetite I'd seen him have since we left home.

Ahjuma clapped and squealed. "*Yeobo!*" she called. "Come see how well these children are eating!"

A paper door slid open, and a man limped into the room, a scowl clinging to his face. "Where did these children come from? Why are they here? Whose are they?" he demanded.

"Yeobo, they said they just came from the Imjin River. Poor things. Look at them." Ahjuma shook her head. "They're all alone."

"Imjin River?" the man said. He looked directly at me, his bushy brows rearing up like two black bears. Had we done something wrong? Why was he staring? I started squirming.

"Did they shoot at you? The foreign soldiers?" he asked.

I nodded.

"They're on the South's side. Did you know that?"

My head snapped up. The South! "Then why were they shooting at us?"

"Because," he said, his scowl deepening, "the Reds have been infiltrating the South. Dressing in plain clothes, traveling among the refugees . . . Pah! Evil times, everywhere!"

I couldn't believe it. The whole war was stupid.

Youngsoo sidled closer to me, but I nudged him away. He started coughing.

"Oh, you must have caught a bad cold," Ahjuma said, pouring a cup of herbal tea for Youngsoo.

He sipped it and stopped hacking; Ahjuma patted him on the back. His cheeks seemed a little rosier.

The man took a seat on the floor by the low table. "Give me my dinner. Now. I'm hungry."

Ahjuma served him a big bowl of dumpling soup and rice, and small side dishes of kimchi and marinated vegetables. Her husband drank a whole bottle of *soju* before picking up thin metal chopsticks with thick fingers and snapping at the food like a crocodile.

Ahjuma went into the kitchen and returned with a towel and a water basin. She told us to wash our faces, but then she cleaned Youngsoo herself, tenderly wiping spots of blood and grime from his cheeks. "Children, you should stay with us for more than one night. It's very dangerous out there," she said gently.

I bowed respectfully. "Thank you, but we need to hurry to Busan. Our parents are waiting for us there."

Ahjuma looked down. She fiddled with a piece of tissue, folding and unfolding it like origami. "Children, your parents may not be there," she said, avoiding our eyes. "I know this is hard, but you must be realistic. If you've been separated, who can say what's become of them? You're already in the South. You don't need to go all the way to Busan."

I wanted to throw down my bowl and cover my ears. Why was she talking like that? She didn't know anything about our family—about Omahni's plan to keep us all together, about Abahji's way of always knowing what to do.

Not *anything*.

"You can't fool me! I know what you want, woman!" the man bellowed. He slammed his fist on the table, spilling the soup. "We're not keeping them. I won't have it!"

"Yeobo," the woman pleaded, "how can we send them back into the cold with all that fighting?"

"Ahjuma," I said, my heart beating faster, "we'll be fine. We've made it this far."

"You heard the girl! Let them go and find their parents." The man opened another bottle of soju, then wiped his nose with a knotty finger.

"Yeobo, please. I think the boy is sick. Look at him. He's so thin."

Youngsoo grabbed my arm, his eyes round and watery. "Noona," he whispered, "what's going on?"

"She wants us to live here," I hissed, while Ahjuma and her husband argued. "But we're not going to. We have to get to Busan as soon as we can, remember? That's where Abahji and Omahni would be. It's where we want to go."

"Where do you want to go after you've completed your schooling? What do you want to be?" Miss Chun asked.

We were in the classroom, and all of the students had just left for home. Light streamed in from the window.

"I'm not sure. A writer, maybe? A teacher, like you?" I blushed.

"In all my years, I've never seen a student as exceptional as you," Miss Chun said, sitting back in her chair. She pointed her chin down, then looked at me as if asking whether I understood. Which I didn't. *"You know, your mother was here today."*

My eyes opened wide. *"She was?"* Omahni never visited the school.

"Sora." Miss Chun leaned forward. *"No matter what you want to be when you grow up, you should get a university education. Don't stop with your schooling. Go as far as you can. Make that your goal. Don't let anyone stop you. Do you understand?"*

"Yes, thank you." I bowed, then packed my book bag and headed home.

University! That's where Myung-gi wanted to go. I didn't know anyone smarter than him.

A soft thud made my head turn.

Ahjuma had thrown herself to the floor, weeping, as if the prospect of our leaving had drained her of all her strength. Her skirt crinkled like a withered flower. She covered her face with both hands.

Her husband touched her back. "Fine! Just one." His speech was slurred. "We can only afford to keep one."

I stared at him.

"Yeobo, we can't just take one! We have to take both!"

"No," the man said. "This is where I draw the line. The girl can stay for a few days, if she likes. But it's the boy we'll keep. A son is worth more than a daughter."

I watched the man's greasy lips move up and down. *A son is worth more than a daughter.* I'd heard it a million times before. And I refused to hear it again.

"I'm so sorry, dear," Ahjuma said, her head lowered toward me. "I promise to raise him well."

"It's settled, then." The man took another swig from his bottle. "The boy can be my farmhand. I was going to hire someone, but this will be cheaper, won't it? And he can look after us once we're old."

Youngsoo latched on to my arm; his hands squeezed with fear. Everything within me screeched to a halt.

"You can't have him," I burst out.

The man turned to look, as if he'd only now realized I was fully human. "Don't be spiteful, little girl. In a few years, you'd be of marrying age, and then we'd have to pay a dowry and send you off to live at your in-laws' house. That's why we can't adopt you. We don't have the money for a worthless mouth."

My insides blazed, his words a lit match tossed down my gullet. "I never asked you to adopt me."

He narrowed his eyes. "You outspoken, ungrateful little—"

"And you're taking my brother over my dead body!" I added, all in one breath.

The man turned red, took another drink, and bellowed, "You dare deny my wife what she wants?"

He staggered to his feet, and when he raised the back of his hand to me, I grabbed Youngsoo's arm and our bundle and rushed out the door.

We ran.

The frigid night air burned my face, but I sucked it in. A cool calm filled me when I realized we weren't being chased. Looking over my shoulder, I could see Yeobo's and Ahjuma's figures in their lit doorway—the man in profile, shouting obscenities at the woman—and knew more than ever that Youngsoo and I needed to get to Busan.

twenty-eight · · · · · ·
December, 1950

We walked for days along wide roads, beside noisy travelers and silent deer. We saw few houses, but we found enough scraps of food in them to keep going. Tiny towns in ruins were scattered throughout the mountains.

Hundreds of people like us—weary and cold—shared our route, passing by us in a stream. Sometimes we walked with a group, other times we went our own way, not wanting to take even one more chance with strangers.

A few kind travelers tried to warn us that we would come across more rivers as we headed south, that all the bridges had been destroyed, that the Reds were coming fast. They weren't wrong. But the temperatures dropped and turned the waterways into ice bridges.

I trudged through the snow for miles and miles, often carrying my brother. One day the sky dimmed perfectly, turning deep orange and pink, more beautiful than I would've thought possible during war.

Sometimes, we were granted these small gifts, perhaps as reminders that the sun would still rise and set on this world— even if it had gone crazy.

❄ ❄ ❄

I was walking along the foothills, Youngsoo hoisted on my back, when I saw it—a patch of gray flashing between boulders on the hillside. I stopped.

"Did you see that?" I asked over my shoulder.

Youngsoo barely lifted his head. "No." His voice was weak. "What did you see?"

I saw it again, only fifty feet away. It stole my breath.

"A wolf," I said.

Youngsoo's legs clamped tighter around my waist.

The animal had the high ground, which couldn't be good. It pulled its lip back in a snarl, its yellow eyes glowing.

I froze, but my heart pounded to be let out. I couldn't remember any lessons that I'd been taught about this. Should I scream? Run? Grab a rock?

The wolf stared intently, keeping a cool gaze on us. I couldn't look away, my body paralyzed under its power. Its gray fur bristled against the stark white snow, like brushstrokes on a canvas. Was it a dream? I'd had nightmares like this, but I always woke up.

"Noona, where is it?" Youngsoo asked.

"There," I hissed, pointing up the steep slope. How could he miss it? It was right in front of us.

"Where?"

"*Shush.*"

"Noona, I don't see it."

"Quiet," I said. "Now, listen carefully. I see a house through those trees. Let's make a run for it. Hold tight."

He nodded.

"One," I whispered. "Two. *Three*."

At the count of three, I ran, roaring like a savage beast, riding on all my fears. I hurtled toward the house, raced inside, and slammed the door.

We pressed our backs against the wall. I slid down and listened for howling.

What if there was an open window? A hole? A broken latch? Youngsoo sat beside me quivering.

Something breathed deeply through the gap under the door, inhaling our scent, scratching to get close. I gripped Youngsoo's hand, pulled him closer to me. We huddled together and listened to a low growl in the dark.

❄ ❄ ❄

We must have fallen asleep that way, exhausted, because in the morning I found us slumped together in the same spot.

It was quiet outside. I knew the wolf had gone.

Stiffly, I got up and searched the freezing house for food. We had to eat.

In the kitchen, empty jars lay on their sides. Burnt pots sat on the stove. Tables and shelves were overturned. Others had already been here, and there was nothing left. The realization struck me like an arrow in the heart.

A few kimchi leaves clung to the insides of the jars. I tasted one; it had gone bad, but I collected every piece. I checked the pots and scraped out the crunchy bits of scalded rice stuck inside.

"Noona, where are you?" Youngsoo called from the main room.

"In the kitchen. Coming!" I rushed back with a small bowl of rotten kimchi and blackened rice. Maybe it was the way I bounded in, but he startled upon seeing me.

"Eat!" I barked.

He picked at the food, wheezing. "Noona," he said, not looking at me. "Are you all right? You seem . . . different."

"Different? What do you mean?" The hard globs of rice were like pebbles, but I crunched on them anyway.

"I don't know. Like you could kill a wild animal with your bare hands."

That stopped me mid-chew. I looked at him, a piece of rotten cabbage leaf hanging from my mouth. He looked back, and we burst out laughing.

"Look, I'm a wolf," I said, tearing another slice of kimchi with my teeth. "Of course I can kill wild animals! *Arooo!*" At that, Youngsoo doubled over and could hardly catch his breath.

But maybe he was right: I *was* different now. All I cared about these days was food and shelter—no better than an animal, no better than a wolf. School and home were things I had hung in the back of my mind for safekeeping. They felt far away.

Had I *really* seen a wolf last night? Or was it just my imagination—shadows playing tricks on my mind? I shook my head, no longer laughing. "I might be going crazy. The stress is finally getting to me."

Wind whistled sharply under the door and kicked up a cloud of ash and dust. I couldn't think of what else to say. Out of nowhere, tears dripped onto my shirt.

Youngsoo's face turned serious. He held a ball of burnt rice between his hands like a small woodland animal. "Noona, you're the least crazy person I know."

I chuckled and wiped my eyes, then sat there like a tree stump and let him hug me.

Sunlight streamed into the barren room. We heard the distant growl of bombing blasts, getting louder. It was time to move on.

I sniffled and wiped my eyes. *Had* I hallucinated that wolf? Did it even matter? Like any nightmare, real or imagined, I knew it would be back at dark. We needed to get to Seoul before then.

I packed our belongings in the quilt, strapped Youngsoo to my back, and headed out the door.

twenty-nine · · · · · ·
December, 1950

The Red army was closer than I thought. They were almost at the gates of Seoul itself.

When we reached the outskirts of the city, Youngsoo limp on my back, I realized we were just barely ahead of them. The city police blocked hundreds of us from going any farther on the main road, the dull thunder of artillery in the distance; they blew whistles until they were red in the face, trying to divert all refugees to crowded ferryboats on the Han River.

"Why?" a woman demanded in a thick Northern accent, one of her front teeth missing. "Let us past!"

"No, take the ferry! The boats'll take us to the south side! The north side of the city is too dangerous!" a man in the crowd called out. When we all turned to look and saw him wearing a wool coat and suit, everyone listened. "The Reds'll shell the north side first!"

Throngs of people pushed and shouted: *Please, we've come a hundred miles from the North! Let us through, we're Seoul residents! I have a silver watch and two gold brooches!* I pushed my way toward the front, and one of the officers grabbed Youngsoo and me and set us on a boat. We sat on the ice-cold seats, grateful that we didn't have to get into the water to cross.

"You know," said the young woman sitting next to me, her eyes glazed, "the last time the city fell, I survived by hiding in the bathhouse under a bench. The Reds rounded up all the 'anti-communists' for execution—all kinds of people. Whoever they wanted. Their shiny black boots marched right past my nose . . . . Right past." She paused, staring at the city. "I don't think I'll be as lucky this time."

Youngsoo and I shivered and said nothing.

"Seoul is like a dream," Yoomee's father had said to Abahji over a late-night bottle of soju. *"A thriving city full of churches and businesses, all doing well."* I had lain in bed listening to their wistful sighs, their low conversation, the soft clinking of glasses in the front courtyard, and imagined a city with streets paved in gold.

But when we stepped off the ferry, Seoul was burnt and in shambles.

The roads were covered in ash. The wires between the streetlights were cut. It was afternoon, but the city was eerily quiet—the only sound, besides the shuffling of refugees, was a loudspeaker crackling instructions to go to the main train station. There were bombed-out buildings—four and five stories tall—with nothing but their facades and back walls still standing. Abandoned cars sat on the sides of the road, their windows shattered and bloodied.

"Noona, I don't like it here," Youngsoo whimpered softly on my back.

I blew out a white cloud of breath. "That doesn't matter. We're going to the train station as soon as we find food."

"I'm not hungry."

"You have to eat."

"I can't. Everything hurts."

My temper flared. "Don't you know that if you don't eat, you will die? You *will* eat and that's final." The sound of my voice—still as short as our mother's—took me by surprise. I had wanted to be gentler.

I felt Youngsoo's shuddering breath, then wet tears, on the back of my neck.

A gang of boys around Youngsoo's age ran down the middle of the street, black army caps on their heads, their faces smudged in filth. They disappeared like rodents behind a crumbling wall.

I continued walking, not knowing which way to go. I saw only strange sights. A chimney stack still standing while its building lay in a heap on the ground; a single arch untouched amidst a sea of rubble; a mess of dirt, burlap, and sheetwood inside a blown-out shop. We were in Seoul, but we were lucky and unlucky at the same time, and I couldn't help feeling as if every step of our journey was nothing but a game of chance.

And then I noticed it.

A thin cross on top of a steeple.

It was just over a hill, past piles of ruins. I blinked a few times to make sure it was there. I hadn't seen a church in so long.

"Look, Youngsoo!" I cried, climbing a sandbag hill. "Do

you remember how Pastor Joh used to hand out food to the poor and crippled? I bet that church over there would help us, too!" We needed to eat before getting on any train. Who knew how long the ride would last? I rushed us forward.

Dozens of people littered the churchyard, living in the shadow of the spire. An old halmoni walked out of a house made of cardboard as if it were nothing at all to be living in a cardboard house. And maybe it wasn't: countless other box shelters covered the grounds, leaning toward one another as if for support. I rubbed my arms for warmth. Could those thin boxes do anything to block the bitter cold?

A woman hunched over a boiling pot slurped stew with a metal spoon, delicious steam spiraling up into the air. My mouth watered. A gnawing feeling had permanently settled in the pit of my stomach, and I found relief only when I slept at night and saw myself eating sweet, sticky *dduk* or salty short ribs. On those nights, my belly was full of dreams.

The woman peered at me through the steam. "You're wondering how I made this stew? Go back down the street, about a fifteen-minute walk," she said, pointing. "There are a few women selling things like dduk and bread. If you're lucky like I was, there might be a lady selling American C rations."

I stared at her, blank-faced. C rations? I'd never heard of such things.

"Don't you know, C rations? Canned rations?" the woman said a decibel louder, as if I were deaf. "They're cans of food for the

American soldiers. They stay fresh until you open the lid. Inside are meats and vegetables. Oh, it's the best." She looked off dreamily, then pushed another spoonful of stew into her mouth.

"But I don't have any money."

The woman laughed, and a piece of chewed-up meat fell from her mouth. She snatched it from the ground and stuffed it back into her hungry face. "Well then, little miss, you're going to have to steal. I hope you're quick on your feet."

"What about the church? Aren't they handing out any food?"

"Who's 'they,' exactly?" the woman said, squinting at me. "There's nobody working in the church—they were all shot by Reds or run off. It's partially collapsed. We're just using it for shelter."

That flicker of hope inside me blew out so fast, I was speechless.

I bowed and thanked her, but wished she had offered me stew instead of advice. How could I steal food? I'd never stolen anything before. And what about Youngsoo? How could I be quick on my feet with him on my back?

Loud booms resounded in the darkening sky.

I turned to him over my shoulder. At first, the words wouldn't come out, but I knew I had to say them. "Maybe . . . maybe you should stay in the churchyard with all these people while I go get food. You'll be safe here."

"What? You're leaving me?" His mouth was agape.

"No—well, only for a little while," I said, blinking fast. "Don't worry."

But the words rang hollow in my head. What if I got lost on these unfamiliar streets and couldn't find my way back? What if a bomb landed on him or on me or somewhere in between? I untied the blanket around my waist, and when he cleaved away from me, I felt split in half.

But I settled him with blankets under the overhang of the church building. He sat there, frowning. I wanted to tell him that my heart was pounding through my ears, that I didn't think I could steal food, that going alone scared me more than anything, but he was little, and I knew it would do no good. A cold wind seeped through my coat, and I felt thin and vulnerable without him on my back.

I knelt beside him. "There are lots of people here. Look at all the campfires just a few feet away from you. You'll be warm and safe." But when I said it, my voice sounded too loud, too cheery.

He didn't answer.

"Okay, well, I have to leave before it gets dark." I waited for a response, and when there was none, I stood up on leaden feet. Out of habit, I reached for his arms around my neck.

I didn't say goodbye, and I didn't look back at my little brother—sitting alone, painfully thin, biting down on a sob. Even still, I could feel his eyes watching me go.

thirty · · · · · ·

I crossed the churchyard and headed toward the street. Past the smoking city, mountains towered in the distance. My hands wouldn't stop shaking.

The smell of the woman's stew still lingered, even if only in my mind, and for a moment I closed my eyes. When was the last time I had *galbi?* My mouth watered with the memory.

Plates of galbi, scallion pancakes, and rice cakes had lined the table. The families were very generous for this year's church picnic—the last one we would have for years to come, although I didn't know it then. I lowered my face over the galbi and breathed in the rich smell of barbecued beef.

Youngsoo poked his finger between the strips of meat, then licked off the sweet, savory sauce. Omahni and Abahji didn't notice. They were talking with other parents across the grassy churchyard.

"Stop it, Youngsoo," I said, wishing I were five like him—too little to know any better.

"That's right, don't touch the galbi, Youngsoo," Yoomee said. "My family brought that meat, so it's ours, not yours." Galbi was

expensive, but since Mr. Kim was principal of the high school, he had more money than most families in the village.

"Your parents brought the galbi to share with the entire church. So it's not just yours," I said, wishing that we could've afforded to buy all that meat.

"Well, it's not just Youngsoo's either, so he shouldn't stick his finger in it."

I couldn't argue; she was right.

"Uh-muh. She's such a showoff. Just because her dad has money," a teenage girl said, glaring from the far end of the table.

"That's what you call a spoiled brat," another girl said.

I glanced at Yoomee. Her arms were crossed. She looked off to the side until I saw a tear roll down her cheek. Then she wiped it and walked away.

The girls laughed, each taking a piece of galbi, and I wondered how they could swallow past the shame.

"Bread for you, miss?"

I came back to reality. It was dark now, but I could still make out this woman's face, as brown and lined as a dried-up riverbed, a makeshift marketplace around her. Beggars stood beside peddlers, their hands cupped toward passersby, their eyes deep in their sockets. I cringed at their oily smell.

"Oh, thank you," I said, reaching for a loaf the length of my hand.

The woman swung it out of my reach. "No! You must pay."

"I'm so sorry, but I have no money. Please, my brother is sick. If he doesn't eat, I'm sure he will die." I knew, suddenly, that this was the truth. My lip trembled.

"You think you're special? That's everyone's story these days. Just look around. We're all going to die if we don't eat, including my children and me. So pay up if you want bread."

"Please! Just half a loaf would be enough!" I said, dropping to my knees. I held on to the bottom of her tattered skirt, which reeked of urine.

"Get off, beggar!" The woman yanked at her skirt. When I wouldn't let go, she kicked me in the chest, then walked away.

Beggar.

I didn't know why it shocked me. I looked and smelled no better than them. What was I doing if not begging?

But for some reason, I felt no shame. The smell of bread still lingered in the woman's wake. My stomach hardened. I thought of that wolf on the hillside, sniffing deeply under the door, and I breathed it in.

I got up and dusted the back of my pants. There were others with food.

One woman peddled worn cloth and shoes, which I imagined had come off the dead. Another was selling dduk and potatoes. There was even a young girl bartering kimchi and rice. But no, those were not what I wanted.

I searched the road until I found her. An old halmoni held one canned ration in the air; the others she kept in her bulging coat pockets. I remembered what the woman by the church had said—there were meats and vegetables inside those C rations. I stepped closer.

"What kind of currency do you carry? South or North Korean?" the halmoni asked me.

I froze, thinking. Should I tell her I had no money? If I begged, wouldn't she kick me away, like the bread lady? Then I'd never get a chance at one of those C rations. I thought of Youngsoo waiting in the churchyard.

My heart starting thumping.

"Yah, are you deaf and dumb?" the halmoni asked, squinting at me.

But maybe she would be kind, like the halmoni who had shared her sweet black beans. Maybe she would be dignified, like the man who had given us the wooden cart. I gazed at her, silently, imploringly.

The woman turned and covered one nostril, then shot out a line of mucous from the other. "Yah, either pay or move away from me," she said.

It was then that I knew what I had to do. I stopped to brush the hair from my eyes. And then my body moved on its own.

My right hand jerked forward. It dove into her pocket. Pulling. Yanking. Everything jamming in the petite pouch of her coat. Thread broke like ladder rungs.

She swayed. We grunted. I kept tugging. Until one metal can wiggled out, like a newborn. Then another. And another.

She stared at me, her mouth hanging open.

I stared back, rooted to the ground. "Sorry," I blurted.

Then I grabbed my C rations and ran. I darted between houses, past a row of armored cars, the halmoni's curses trailing away.

That's when I turned my head and saw her, black against a wall—a fleeing shadow hunched over an armful of cans, hair flying wildly behind. A wolf-girl. Moving swiftly. Savagely. I hardly recognized myself.

thirty-one ······

When I returned to the churchyard, I found Youngsoo in the exact spot where I'd left him. He hadn't moved an inch, and the same frown was on his face. I ran toward him, hiding the C rations inside my jacket.

"Youngsoo, you won't believe what I got!" I said, the cold cans pressed against my stomach.

His arms were crossed. He turned his head away from me. A cough bubbled in his chest, but he kept his mouth shut and tamped it down.

I grabbed our pot, then dropped the cans on the ground. "Look! Canned rations! I think there'll be meat and vegetables inside! When was the last time you had meat? And I don't mean anchovies—I mean real meat!"

Youngsoo shrugged. He picked at his fingernail. Flames from neighboring campfires lit up his face.

I took a deep breath, then counted to five. "I went out and risked everything to get this food, and you have nothing to say?"

"You left," he said, looking at the ground.

"What did you expect me to do? Swipe these cans with you on my back like a sack of potatoes? I wouldn't have been nearly as fast."

"Am I just in the way?" He burrowed deeper into his crossed arms. "Is that why you call me stupid?"

"I didn't call you stupid!"

"You didn't say it now, but sometimes you do." He started coughing up all the mucous he'd been keeping down.

I thought of Omahni in the kitchen, shaking her head at me when I'd done something wrong. I knew that I sometimes did the same to Youngsoo. Had I always done that to him? Or did it start only after Omahni had pulled me out of school?

A flash of light shot through the night sky. Blasts rumbled in the distance. I snatched the pot and cans and stomped away.

There had to be an abandoned firepit in the churchyard, and several feet away, I found one. I set the pot beside it, then examined the metal can. It was sealed shut, with only a small key glued to its top—where was the keyhole? "How do you open this thing?" I said to myself, pounding it against the pavement.

"Yah! You're going to ruin a perfectly good can of food!" the woman with the stew called. "Come, give it to me. I'll show you how to open it."

I went to hand it over slowly, not wanting to let it go. I watched her crank the key around the can, miraculously peeling away a thin strip of metal. "There you go. That's how you open it," she said, grinning.

"Thank you." I stared at the sausages floating in a light red liquid. Though it nearly killed me, I added, "Would you like some?"

"No, no, that's for you and your brother," she said, shaking her head.

I didn't argue. Shame burned through my skin for not wanting to share.

I turned my attention back to the firepit. The coals were still hot, so I poked the embers with a stick and blew on them until an orange glow blazed brightly. When the fire seemed hot enough, I set the pot on top and dumped the contents of the can in. My mouth watered, and I had to swallow.

A cold wind blustered through the city as our dinner cooked, and a blanket of snow began to cover all the rubble in a clean, white sheet. Though I knew what lay underneath, I thought it looked almost beautiful.

Finally, I took the pot off the heat and carried it back to Youngsoo. He wouldn't look at me.

"Here, try some," I said, bringing a spoonful to his lips.

Reluctantly, he opened his frowning mouth, but then burst into tears. Coughs tore from his chest.

I patted him on the back, the bones of his spine protruding. It hurt to look at him.

"Sorry, Youngsoo," I whispered. "Sorry about leaving you and being so mean."

I wanted to tell him that he was a good kid, that he wasn't stupid, that it wasn't his fault that Omahni had pulled me out of school, that nothing had ever been his fault, but I only stuck my tongue out and crossed my eyes at him instead.

Through shuddering breaths, he forced a smile, though the corners of his mouth kept pulling down. A huge bubble of snot blew in and out of his nose, and we finally started laughing.

I stirred the soup, then slurped a spoonful, keeping my mouth ajar to blow out steam. It wasn't as delicious as Omahni's kimchi stews, but it was still good. The pink meat had a salty, pork-like flavor. "Youngsoo, really, try it. It's good."

Youngsoo breathed in deeply before swallowing a piping hot mouthful. Instantly, he sputtered and coughed, then lay down and held his hand up, refusing another bite.

I didn't understand how he could turn down this food, and I nudged him on the shoulder, but he only turned his back to me. A funny squeaking sound came from his lungs.

❄ ❄ ❄

It was late. Campfires in the churchyard turned the cardboard houses into glowing lanterns. Youngsoo fell asleep. I covered him with a blanket, then fed the fire with sticks and trash to keep him warm.

I stared at the shimmering air above the flames. It blurred everything in sight: mounds of rubble, a woman pounding her chest in prayer, a girl curled up like she was back in the womb, an old man crying out for his wife of sixty years. I never once let my eyes wander from the wavy lines of the fire's looking glass. Outside of it, the broken buildings and suffering people were too sharp, too clear.

We were almost there. Just a train ride away from Busan.

thirty-two · · · · · ·
December, 1950

The next morning, Youngsoo vomited. It set my heart racing.

"Are you okay?" I asked, wiping his mouth with the edge of his blanket. But he could only cough. I patted his back, my hand shaking. "You probably just gagged because of all that coughing."

I stood up and looked around. There was no one here to help us. Most of the fires had sputtered out in the night, and smoke rose like ghosts across the churchyard. Almost everyone was gone. My breath was white, and I shivered.

More explosions boomed. The loudspeaker crackled the same instructions to head to the train station. I wondered if the woman's voice barking orders on the other end was a recording; I hoped she was real, because then we wouldn't be completely alone.

"We've got to get on that train," I said, gathering our things and hoisting Youngsoo onto my back.

Rays of morning light cut across the barren roads, and wind-whipped embers swirled in the air. There were street signs, and eventually, other refugees emerging from broken buildings and making their way to the station. I followed them, past debris and shattered storefronts and crumbling concrete, to a big building that had collapsed in on itself.

This couldn't be it.

A woman ran past, and I grabbed her sleeve. "Where can I find the train station?" I asked.

"Are you blind? You're standing right in front of it," she said, her eyes darting wildly.

My heart dropped. The station was nothing but a mound of rubble. Were we ever going to get out of this city?

"Now let go of me!" she said, yanking her sleeve away. "The Reds are getting closer!"

Her urgency sent fear pulsing through me. But it wasn't until I ran to the side of the building that I heard them: *Move it! Watch where you're going! It's the last train!*

The words stopped me cold.

Last train of the day? Last train forever?

What does it matter? The Reds could get here today!

I looked at my bloodied shoes and socks. Two hundred miles to Busan.

If we didn't get on *now*, we'd never outrun the bombs and guns, never survive that much walking. Ai! Why hadn't I gotten up earlier? Was this why the streets and churchyard were so empty? Because today was the last chance to escape the city? I tightened Youngsoo's legs around my waist and ran toward the tracks behind the station.

Throngs of people surrounded the only train left—the last train leaving Seoul. They swarmed in and out of every carriage like ants through the eye sockets of carrion. I hurried closer, the roar of the crowd intensifying—then took a deep breath and barreled into the crush.

Bodies closed in on me like floodwater. I tunneled through the mob, stumbling over tracks, over soft flesh underfoot. My eyes flashed downward—I saw an arm, a leg, a back—all part of the unfortunate few who had tripped and fallen. I reached down to help someone, a girl, but the stampede swept me away.

Suddenly we were flush against the train. "Is there room for two?" I yelled, moving up and down the line of cars, squirming through the press. Could anyone even hear me?

But my cries didn't matter—a swarm of people teetered up to the edge of every open door. The train was full.

I looked up. Roof riders were clambering to the top of the train, and my mind started racing. There was no space inside, so what choice did we have? We would be roof riders too. I climbed the rusty ladder on the side of a boxcar, Youngsoo clinging to my back.

Mounds of people covered the rooftop. From up here, the scene below writhed and pulsed like something out of hell. Underneath us, a mother frantically screamed for her son whose hand had slipped from hers, the crowd pulling him down until he vanished completely.

I hurried forward, tripping over legs and feet. A teenage girl searched the flat top for something, anything, to fasten her blanket to—one end was knotted around her ankle, the other end to nothing. My stomach twisted as I realized that the rooftop was as dangerous as that mangled bridge by the Taedong. Once the train gathered speed, we would fly right off—Youngsoo first, with his willowy arms and spindly legs.

I turned around.

"Noona, where are you going?"

"We need to get down! We need to get down!" I said, rushing back toward the ladder.

I stumbled over a woman, my foot catching and my hand scraping against her wooden crate. Youngsoo flew off my back onto a pile of luggage as I fell. The woman pushed my head, and I shoved her back, struggling onto my knees. "I need to get my brother!" I shrieked.

Youngsoo scrambled toward me, like a crab winding sideways, his arms and legs like pincers. For a second, I flinched, wanting to run from him as much as I wanted him to reach me. But I waited, and when he clamped onto my back, I got up and lurched toward the top of the ladder.

Last train. The words kept looping inside my head.

Arms shaking, I climbed down and started sprinting alongside the tracks, ducking and pushing through the crowd. "Is there room in here?" I shouted into a boxcar.

"No! We're full!" a woman yelled back.

A charge of panic shot through me. I ran faster.

"Any room in here?"

"No!"

"How about here?"

"No!"

Always no. I howled in frustration.

The train started rolling. I blinked. Was it my imagination?

No. Slowly, slowly, it went. Slipping past my reaching fingers. Outpacing my stumbling feet. Youngsoo tightened his grip around my neck.

Then, from somewhere, a man's cry: "That's the end! That's the end! We are full!"

All at once, doors closed up and down the row of boxcars. A loud roar rolled off the crowd in a wave.

In the half second that followed, the throng on the platform swept forward like a storm. Hard pushing and shoving. My shoulder mashing against the side of the train. I was getting carried off my feet. One slip and fall, and I'd be crushed under the rolling wheels.

"*Help!*" I screamed into the boxcar in front of me.

This was it.

The end.

All that my life would ever be.

"Squeeze in! We need to make room for these children!" someone shouted overhead.

A hand reached down. It was a young man in the doorway of the car above, a newsboy cap slanted over his eyes. He grabbed my arm. I clamped on. And with one guttural cry, he hoisted us up, lifting high until we slithered on board.

I slumped onto the floor; Youngsoo spilled off my back. We were saved.

Inside, there were no seats, only the sliding door and one tiny window. The bodies of strangers pressed up against me. An old man reeking of urine started leaning on my shoulder.

The man with the cap held his hand out to a mother and her son.

"Shut the door already!" screamed a woman clutching a baby to her chest. Her eyes darted back and forth over the mob rushing for the train, pouring out of the concourse, covering the station yard. I saw them, too. From here, the crowd looked like black ink spilling toward the freight car. I couldn't stop shaking. We had no more room.

But the man with the cap gritted his teeth and kept the door open, extending his arm to desperate strangers.

"Shut the door, cap boy! We'll suffocate with too many people! Who made you gatekeeper of the train!" a man hollered from the back.

The crowds started climbing the car like fast-growing ivy. Some pushed inside, frantic to claim their space. A scream started bubbling in my chest. I wanted the cap man to shut the door, give us room to breathe, leave the rest behind—even though I'd been on the other side just a second ago, on the ground, reaching. The cap man looked at me, but I didn't know what to do. Should we shut the door? Let more people in? I yanked on my hair and let out a sharp cry. Why was it so hard to do the right thing?

"We're going to do the right thing," Abahji had said, tying a sack of rice and swinging it over his shoulder. "Come follow me." Myung-gi and I looked up from our books, bleary-eyed, waking from our story world into the blinding light of this one. We were ten and twelve, reading under a tree, uncomplicated friends.

"Even Myung-gi oppah?" I asked.

"Yes, especially Myung-gi. I need him to help me carry another sack of rice," Abahji said.

We followed Abahji across the field to Mr. Choi's house. Abahji knocked on the wooden gate.

Mr. Choi answered, his eyes more sunken than the last time I'd seen him. "Eh, Pak Sangmin, what are you doing here?" he asked.

"To give you two sacks of rice." Abahji set the bags by Mr. Choi's feet.

"You don't have to give me rent. I'm not your landlord anymore. You know that," Mr. Choi said. His voice shook with an old man's tremor. "That piece of land belongs to you and the state now. Under the new law. A glorious law," he added tightly.

"I can't let you and your wife go hungry after all that you've done for us over the years."

"What did we do?" Mr. Choi asked, his face softening.

"Please, accept the rice," Abahji said.

When Mr. Choi wiped his eyes and smiled, my heart pinched. "Thank you, Sangmin-ah. You've always been like a son to me," he said, dragging the rice bags inside the house.

We walked back home, Abahji's arms around our shoulders.

"Abahji, do all the farmers still give rice to their landlords?" I asked.

"No, but I don't want land that was stolen from another man and handed to me. Besides, Mr. Choi wasn't just a landlord, he was more like a father. And as sons, what wouldn't we do for our fathers, right, Myung-gi-ya?" Abahji patted him hard on the back.

Someone yanked my shirt.

"Please!" a young woman cried, reaching up. She was so close, I could see the pores on her face.

The cap man grabbed her hand, but his arm shook, and sweat dripped down his cheeks. The chorus of complaints grew louder: *Shut the door! There are too many of them! We're going to topple! He's not listening—push him off!*

Electricity thrummed under my skin. I jumped up and latched on to the cap man's arm, then pulled until my face turned red, until my feet skidded to the open edge, until we got that woman on board, and the door ground shut.

Everything turned dark.

No one spoke. Muffled cries from outside echoed eerily against the tinny walls. The train gathered speed, and those outside ran along the tracks, banging against the metal door as if hurling rocks at it. The boxcar bumped and swayed, and chilling screams rang from above as people fell off the roof. I covered my ears and squeezed my eyes shut.

The train hit its stride. All banging and shrieking ceased.

I opened my eyes. Soon Seoul would be behind us.

A sliver of light trickled in through the one tiny open window. Someone's hot, sour breath blew across my face. The scent of urine poisoned the air.

I counted the long wooden planks that ran across the length of the car ceiling, over and over, until a thud and scream from overhead made me lose my place. I wondered about the roof riders, the people running alongside the train, everyone left behind. What would become of them all?

I burrowed deep inside my coat and felt the map in my pocket. My hand stung from the scrape on top of the train; when I looked, it was pink and raw. But no matter. We were safe.

Youngsoo's warm body leaned in close against mine. The light from the tiny window began to dim, and the steely rattle and clack of the train faded to a murmur. My head started drooping like ripe millet in Abahji's field.

For the next day and night, I slept as if pinned to the floor, my leaden arms unable to keep Youngsoo from slumping to the ground.

thirty-three · · · · · ·
December, 1950

It was a rotten stench that woke me.

I opened my eyes and saw a thin stream of morning light through the small window. My back and neck ached from sleeping upright against the boxcar wall.

"What is that awful smell?" a woman wearing a headscarf shouted from the opposite end of the freight car.

I looked around and spotted a dark brown stain on the old man's baggy pants.

"Aigoo," a husky-voiced woman cried. "Harabuji, did you soil yourself? Now everyone has to endure this nauseating smell!"

Groans filled the train.

"Shut up, all of you," the old man said, his cheeks a slight pink.

The foul stench reeked of sickness. It smothered me in someone's dying. I gagged and covered my nose with my coat. The old man rubbed the back of his wrinkled neck, his eyes shifting side to side as if he didn't know where to set his gaze. I couldn't help feeling sorry for him; a harabuji shouldn't have to sit in his own filth.

"I say we kick him off at the next stop," the headscarf woman said.

As much as the old man stank, the idea of casting him out scared me. It was cruel. And did I smell so much better? Did any of us?

A grandmother clapped her hands once, fiercely. "Yah! Everyone, show some respect!"

"How about if he shows us some consideration and gets off the train," a man yelled.

A small child wailed into the stifling boxcar.

"Just great. Now the baby's giving me a headache," someone said.

The husky-voiced woman got up and stood in the middle of the group, her eyes hard and black like watermelon seeds. "Calm down, everyone! We will not behave like animals."

The tight space. The stench. The screaming.

Panic surged to the top of my head. I needed to get off. When would we reach Busan? Pungent smells filled my nose and mouth, suffocating me. I grabbed Youngsoo's hand and rose toward the door, but he tugged me down. Where was the window? At the very least, I needed to see the window. My eyes darted toward the light, and I concentrated on that single ray.

The baby's crying weakened to a whimper. He and his mother sat to my left. I tore my gaze from the window and dared to look at him. The infant was tiny, his body no bigger than napa cabbage. He coughed—wet and crackly.

"The baby's hungry," said the husky-voiced woman, taking a seat behind the mother.

"But he won't eat." The mother's face twisted in worry. She

offered him a slice of sweet snow pear, but he sucked on the end for only a few seconds before gasping for air. The mother thumped his back, a deep crease down the middle of her forehead.

The canned food. I had nearly forgotten. I pulled one of the C rations out of my coat pocket. "Here, you can give the baby some of this." I held it out to the mother.

She examined the label. "I have some of that already. He won't eat it either," she said, her eyes damp.

"Oh." I was so sure I could help. I looked at the baby. He was probably only three months old. How unlucky to have been born in the middle of a war.

Youngsoo sat crumpled against the wall, his face pale. It was no way anyone would normally sit, and I felt an urgency to do something, anything.

"Are you hungry?" I asked.

He shook his head.

"Well, you have to eat." I twisted the key around the can, peeling away the thin metal edge. The lid popped off. More sausages in a light red liquid. I dipped my pinky and tasted the juice—sweet and tart. I fed a sausage to him, and he nodded that it was good.

"These sausages remind of Ahjuma's husband and his fat fingers," I said, holding one up to the light.

Youngsoo choked and coughed, hardly able to catch his breath, and I wondered whether laughing was worth all that trouble. It took him five minutes to settle down.

"Noona," he said finally, looking up at me, his eyes dark and steady. "I don't think what Ahjuma's husband said was true. Sons aren't better than daughters. No one's better than anybody."

I smiled faintly. But what Youngsoo believed didn't matter. Everyone else thought it was true—Ahjuma's husband, Joonie's mother, even Omahni. Everyone, except that ponytailed girl. But she was only one person—and just a tan-skinned peasant girl, like me.

The train rumbled along the tracks for hours before stopping at a small village station.

"A bathroom stop," someone murmured.

"Anyone need to use the toilet? If so, looks like this is where you get off," the cap man by the door shouted.

I had hardly eaten or drunk for the past few days, yet still I felt the urge to go. How could I, though? What if the train left without me? What if someone took my spot? I looked around. Not a single person in the car moved to leave, not even the harabuji. There were a few grumblings, but no one forced the old man off.

The cap man slid the door shut. Only the sound of someone peeing into a metal bucket echoed against the walls.

❋ ❋ ❋

By morning, my bladder was full and my head pounded. The baby had cried through most of the night but finally quieted.

"What's wrong with him?" Youngsoo asked, leaning his head against me.

"You heard what they said. He's hungry."

Youngsoo grew silent and stared at the baby's tiny body.

"How's he doing?" the husky-voiced woman asked, nodding toward the child.

The mother stared off into the light coming from the tiny window, the baby's face pressed into her padded coat. A puddle of urine flowing from the direction of the old man soaked her long skirt, but she didn't flinch. "The baby's fine. I'm sure of it," she said, a distant look in her eyes.

"Someone pass me the bucket," the headscarf woman said. I watched as the urine pail sloshed its way across the boxcar to her. She snatched it, then hitched up her skirt and squatted in front of everyone. I looked away.

"I'm next!" a boy around Youngsoo's age shouted.

My face felt hot. I had to relieve myself too, but not in front of a crowd.

"Empty it out the window, then pass it to me after you've finished," an older man said.

Sweat poured from my head. I couldn't hold it for another second. The scrape on my hand throbbed. But there were men, boys, and girls my age, all close enough to watch. Tears squeezed out from the corners of my eyes.

"I'll take it after you, sir," I said, squatting on my haunches.

PART III

❄❄❄❄❄❄❄❄❄

BUSAN

thirty-four · · · · · ·
January, 1951

The train's clanking slowed, and my body lurched forward.

I opened my eyes. The cap man sat straight up. Everyone froze. There was a hissing sound followed by a whistle.

And then the train stopped.

The door slid open and a searing light flooded the boxcar. I shielded my eyes and squinted. Where were we now?

The bustling sounds of a city rushed in.

Throngs of people walked up and down the platform; a man carrying two large oil drums shuffled and sloshed his way to his next delivery. Terraced hillsides stood out in the distance.

"We made it! We're in Busan!" the cap man shouted, his shiny face glowing.

Everyone gathered their belongings, talking in animated voices. But the young mother gave a piercing scream, her baby limp in her arms. She groaned from the gut, from somewhere deep and dark. The husky-voiced woman lowered her head and prayed, and a few others stopped to help the mother, but nothing could console her. She rocked back and forth, faster and faster, her horrible moan unending. We passed her and her baby on our way out, and I swallowed hard. Youngsoo clung to my back, trembling, as I climbed down from the train.

People poured out of the freight cars. A few lowered themselves from the top. I sighed in relief that some of the roof riders had made it, but the sickening thud of bodies hitting the ground and slamming into tunnel entrances kept sounding in my ears. I knew I would never forget it. My knuckles turned bony and white as I clenched my fists; I had to shake my hands loose.

Men and women dropped to their knees and kissed the ground. One woman strode past, holding papers with the address of her destination; another looked dazed, stopping and turning, unsure where to go next. I was grateful that Omahni had a brother in Busan. What had Abahji said to Mr. Kim about finding Uncle Hong-Chul's house?

Just a few miles from the Busan station. South of the Gukje Market. He's got a fish stand there, house number 8818.

A gentle breeze rustled my hair, and I took a deep breath. The air smelled different here, like rotting seaweed and fish. It didn't help my sudden anxious queasiness. "What's that awful stench?"

"What stench?" the cap man said, laughing. "That's the smell of the ocean, the scent of freedom!" He jumped down from the boxcar, swung a bag over his shoulder, and went whistling on his way. I watched him go, a small tug in my chest. He was gone before I could thank him for saving us.

I shifted Youngsoo higher on my back, following the crowd out of the station into the city. People bustled in the streets. There were wide roads, sidewalks, and clusters of houses with clay-tile roofs. A line of three-story brick buildings stood in the distance—not a single portrait of Kim Il-sung or Stalin hanging from any one of them. I passed a trolley, women carrying baskets on their heads, and shoeshine boys polishing the boots of American GIs. It had been a long time since I'd seen Americans.

"Excuse me, mister," I said to a passing stranger wearing a fedora. "How can I get to the Gukje Market?" I set Youngsoo down; he had to lean against a skinny electrical pole.

The man shook his head and looked at us as if we were two worms turned inside out on sticks. I tucked the hand with the fleshy pink scrape behind my back; even Youngsoo tried to hide the bloody bottom of his pants with his blanket. "I'm assuming you two just came into the Busan train station," the man said, finally.

I nodded.

He reached into one of the pockets of his wool coat. "Here, catch," he said, tossing me a bunch of coins. "If you go back to the station, you can get on a bus to the Gukje Market. It's only about a thirty-minute ride."

"Thank you so much!" I said, bowing. I couldn't believe we'd be at Uncle's house in less than an hour. Every hope that had been simmering below the surface came bubbling up. Abahji, Omahni, Jisoo. Clean clothes and warm beds. Delicious foods. And more than that, no more running; we were as far south as we could go.

We went back to the station and found a bus to the Gukje Market. An old woman in the front seat clucked her tongue at the state of us, muttering "Aigoo."

I sat by the open window, Youngsoo leaning against me. This was far more comfortable than the freight train. The bus started rolling, and a cool breeze blew in—not nearly as icy as the winter winds back home. We stared out the window, our eyes weaving back and forth over the sights: shorn hillsides, jeeps and trucks, steep roads crowded with shops.

"Noona, look!" Youngsoo pointed past a row of houses.

Something blue shimmered between them—like sky, only deeper. I leaned my head out of the window, staring. The buildings blurred past, fewer and fewer, until finally, I had a clear view.

The ocean.

It was alive, churning and roaring against the rocks. A massive blue sprawling out as far as I could see. Nothing could contain it. We were only a hundred feet away, close enough to taste it in the back of our throats.

Youngsoo and I looked at each other and shook our heads in disbelief; it was the open sea from our dreams. My heart ticked faster.

We passed a port. Gray warships, several stories high, floated like steel mountains. How did they stay afloat? I stuck my neck out farther, the wind whipping my hair. One large ship moored at the pier had the flag of the United States at its stern—red, white, and blue flickering in the wind. American soldiers walked along the wharf, a familiar swagger in their stride. I waved out the window, shouting "Tootsie Roll!"—the only English words I knew. Some of them waved back.

The bus turned inland again, and I pulled myself inside. We drove by wooden-fronted houses, restaurants with sun-bleached signs, a concrete police station, a middle school with an iron clock and blue-glass windows. Students wearing uniforms crowded the sidewalk, loads of books in their arms. One girl had tan skin and long, wavy hair, like me. "Youngsoo, are you seeing all of this?"

He coughed and nodded, his eyes red and his nose drippy. I tightened the collar of his jacket, then closed the window. "Don't worry—now that we're in Busan, you'll get better soon," I promised.

The bus slowed to a stop.

"Gukje Market!" the driver shouted.

"We're here!" I said, grabbing Youngsoo's hand. "We finally made it!"

thirty-five · · · · · ·

Gukje Market. It was the kind of place where you couldn't think.

Colorful signs wrestled for attention. Merchants called out their prices; customers bargained them down. Here, no one was afraid of being called *capitalist bourgeois pigs*. The chatter was as loud as a thousand squawking birds.

Youngsoo and I slowed as we walked past small wooden storefronts on a narrow dirt road, staring in wonder at the clothes, dishes, and foods set up on crates and blankets: mounds of white yam, heaps of thick carrots, racks of rice bowls, bolts of white linen, folded Western pants.

"Hey!" a teenage boy shouted. He wore a tattered coat. Aside from being cleaner than us, he didn't look much better off. "You need shoes?" He pointed to the only pair of women's sandals on his blanket. "How about some kitchen things?" His stack of pots and ceramic bowls were mismatched and chipped. When I didn't answer, he held up a framed black-and-white newspaper clipping of a white woman with rolls of shiny hair. "You like Grace Kelly? She's a famous American movie star. Pretty, like you. I'll give you a good price!"

I shook my head; I couldn't believe he had a framed picture

of an *American*, as if that movie star were as important as Kim Il-sung himself. "No, thank you. But could you tell me where Kang Hong-Chul's fish stand is?"

"Kang Hong-Chul?" he asked. "This isn't some tiny village where everybody knows each other's names. Do you know how many people are in this city—including all the new Northerners?" He laughed. "Sorry. There are probably a hundred people with that name!"

"Thank you," I said politely. Youngsoo and I walked on.

How strange it felt to be in a busy marketplace! The air was different here, not the same as by the bus station, and I had the peculiar feeling that something was off.

I watched a man hang a wooden sign—Fruits and Vegetables—above his small storefront, hammering it in with nails. His wife hugged him from behind, while a little girl squealed, "Apah! Apah!" at his heels.

And then I knew. Here, people were no longer running; they were setting up shop. Instead of screaming, there was haggling and selling. No explosions roared in the distance. No shots rang out from behind. Yankee soldiers strolled the stands, ogling the pretty girls and punching each other in the arm as if they were silly schoolboys. I breathed in the bustle, and sighed in relief.

Boys played chase up and down the road, and Youngsoo tugged my arm, as if he wanted me to stop them long enough for him to join. (Which he couldn't; we both knew that.) But when I looked closer, I saw that as they wove through the crowd they cut slits in women's bags, stealing money. A gang of bigger boys, dirt-smudged and barefoot, knocked over a woman's apple stand, grabbed handfuls of fruit, and ran off, the edges of their shirts drawn up and cinched into lumpy bags. Another crew grabbed handfuls of dried squid before scattering in all directions, hopping around like hot oil in a pan. Youngsoo sat on an empty crate, laughing at their antics.

One of the squid boys turned to Youngsoo. "What are you looking at?"

"Nothing," Youngsoo said, turning still and quiet.

"This is *our* market," the boy said, stepping closer, fists drawn. "You and your sister need to get out of here!"

Who did he think he was—this kid no bigger than me, wearing a shirt and pants two sizes too small? *His* market? My laugh exploded like a bag of flour—*pah!*

The boy glared. "Do you think *this* is funny?" he asked, and—while keeping his gaze fixed on me—punched Youngsoo in the stomach.

"Hey!" I screamed. That sound of fist hitting flesh—like the back of Omahni's cleaver pounding fresh suckling pig—made my stomach turn.

Tears sprang from Youngsoo's eyes. He doubled over, gasping.

In a flash, I lunged forward, my body nothing but shoulders and fists. Pummeling. Grabbing. Tearing. The hard bone of his jaw against the rock of my hand. Voices crowded around: *It's a girl! A what? Get her off him!* Arms pulled me back, stopped my knuckles mid-swing.

I looked around.

So many boys, red-faced and huffing, stood in a circle, staring at me. "She's crazy," one of them said. "Yeah, a possessed witch," another answered. The boy I'd hit said nothing; he only blinked and cupped a hand under his bloody nose. And before I knew it, he and his friends were gone.

"Are you okay, Youngsoo?" I asked, kneeling beside him.

He nodded. I helped him up on his feet. My hands throbbed, covered in small cuts. I took a deep breath and leaned against someone's display, the adrenaline draining from my body. I was tired of fighting.

"C rations!" an old, sunbaked woman cried, sitting squat on the ground, a toothpick wedged between her teeth. Dark metal cans covered the top of her wooden crate. "American C rations! Delicious!"

"Excuse me," I asked her wearily. "Can you tell me where I can find Kang Hong-Chul's house?"

"Eh? Kang Hong-Chul?" The toothpick bobbed up and down as she spoke. "Are you another one from the North he's helping? Thousands of you are coming into our city, and now there's a water shortage! What do you say to that?"

"So you know him?" I asked, flushed with excitement.

"Tell him that he owes me another game of *baduk*. He's probably afraid of losing again." She laughed, baring gums with missing teeth. "His fish stand is at the end of this row, but his house is down that side street. Now unless you're going to buy some C rations, get out of my way, kids. I'm trying to earn a buck here."

❄ ❄ ❄

I thought I would run, but I found myself walking down that road, slow and steady, thinking of a sunset and how it never rushes. It was late afternoon, and the light was already changing. The air dimmed and thickened, like in a dream. All market noises fell behind, and in the hush I could hear only Youngsoo's wheezing.

"Get on my back," I said, stepping in front of him.

To my surprise, he shuffled past me. "No, I don't want them to think I'm a baby."

"Don't be ridiculous. It'll be easier if I carry you," I said, grabbing his hand.

He pulled away. "No, I want to walk by myself!" His voice was strained, like thin glass on the verge of breaking. Blue veins showed through his white skin. Normally, I would've yelled at him for snapping at me, but something about the way he whined—like an infant born too soon, its pink lungs still forming—kept me quiet.

I let him go and trailed a step behind. We passed clay-tile roofs and low stone walls, the house numbers inching higher: 8810 . . . 8812 . . . 8814. We needed only to find house number 8818, and this long journey would be over. Everything I'd hoped for would finally come true.

Every so often, Youngsoo bent to catch his breath. When he coughed, he winced and put a hand to his chest—something I'd never seen him do before.

He wiped his eyes with the back of his hand in a single swipe, then threw his arm down in frustration. Another coughing fit overtook him, leaving him quiet and limp. "Noona, will you carry me?" he asked in a small voice.

"Of course." I knelt and let him climb on my back. Light as air.

thirty-six ······

House 8818. I stood on my toes and peeked over the stone wall. Inside the courtyard, a man sat by a small firepit roasting squid inside a wire fish basket. I couldn't see his eyes, only the back of his neck, which was caramelized from the sun.

Youngsoo and I peered at him, unblinking, our necks stretched long. We looked like ghosts, bony and dirty, our hair tangled like nests—only we didn't know it until Jisoo spotted us from inside the courtyard and screamed like a pig being slaughtered.

"What did you do to him?" Omahni had said, bobbing Jisoo up and down as he cried.

I wasn't sure why I'd done it. Sometimes grown-ups pinched babies because they were too cute. Sometimes kids pinched each other when they were annoyed. For me, I think it was a little of both.

Abahji gave me a funny look, then tousled my hair. He turned to Jisoo and kissed him on the forehead. "Happy first birthday, my son. What will you pick for your doljabi?*"*

Omahni had set the birthday objects on the floor: a spool of thread, a pencil, a book, money, and rice. When I had turned one, I had chosen the book, which meant that I would have a studious mind. At Youngsoo's dol, he grabbed the rice, a sure sign that he would never go hungry. And today, we would learn Jisoo's fate.

"Happy birthday, Jisoo! I can't believe it's already your dol," Mrs. Kim said as she helped Omahni decorate the table with rice cakes, fruit, and dates.

Jisoo tugged on the sleeve of his pink-striped jacket and at his blue vest with the gold pattern. Abahji set him on the floor in front of the different things.

We watched and waited.

Jisoo sat, then held his arms up toward Abahji. Everyone laughed.

"No, son," Omahni said. "You have to pick something." She stood behind the row of objects and waved her hands to entice him.

Jisoo started crawling. He looked at all the choices, then at Omahni as if to ask whether he was really allowed to touch such things. Omahni nodded. Jisoo smiled, then grabbed the money.

Everyone roared.

Jisoo burst into tears, his eyes wide in alarm. Tiny droplets darkened the front of his bright blue vest.

"Wah! One son will be rich, and the other son will never go hungry. Two blessings! Now you'll never have to worry about begging in the streets!" Mrs. Kim said to Omahni.

At which Omahni covered her teeth and laughed, her eyes tearing.

The room burst into celebration. Jisoo reached up for someone to hold him, and when no one did, I picked him up, sorry for what I'd done, his soft, fuzzy head warm against my cheek.

❄ ❄ ❄

Jisoo. The same fuzzy hair, the same stick-out ears, the same bloodcurdling shriek. He was longer and thinner, but it was still him. Why wouldn't he stop crying? The man whipped around and looked up at us. His face changed color.

I lost my balance and toppled against rock and pavement. Youngsoo slid off my back. My side would bruise to deep purple days later, but for now, I could feel no pain. We lay there, stunned by the fall and what we had just seen: *Jisoo, our baby brother, back from the dead.*

The gate flew open, and the man rushed to our tangled bodies. Keeping his gaze on us, he turned his head slightly over his shoulder and shouted, "I think they're here!"

He pulled us up with one arm each, and when our faces came close, I could see eyes like Omahni's staring back at me. "Uncle?" I whispered.

He laughed and didn't look like Omahni anymore. "That's right, it's me, Uncle! We thought . . ."

But then his face crumpled like brown paper, and rivulets of tears ran down the folds.

Youngsoo and I leaned on him, watching. It didn't matter that I'd never met him before—in that instant, he was part of the same family-shaped lump that had permanently lodged in my throat. Uncle wiped his eyes and guided us, hobbling, through the gate.

There was a garden on one side and a storage shed and outhouse on the other. Large earthenware jars lined the base of the courtyard wall. And hiding behind one of those urns was Jisoo, still wailing.

Uncle picked him up and patted his back until he quieted. Jisoo stared at us, and we stared back, his eyes as vacant as a chicken's.

He'd forgotten us. I put a hand to my cheek as if I'd been slapped.

Jisoo wrapped his arms around Uncle's neck, then nestled his head against his shoulder as if he'd been doing it his whole life. Youngsoo reached for my hand, and I held it tightly.

Footsteps thundered from inside the house. The front door slid open. A woman stood in the doorway, as sturdy as anyone with crop-picking in her blood. And from behind, a smaller figure pushed her way past:

Omahni.

For a second, our eyes locked, a jumble of emotions rushing through that tunnel of space between us. It was like seeing home—hot soup and rice, the warm ondol floor, even scoldings in the kitchen.

How is it that my daughter got the tan skin? Can't depend on you for anything. You're overreacting—you'll learn how to keep house.

No. What did it matter? We were together again. A spring of joy burst inside me.

"Children! My children! You're alive!" Omahni screamed. She rushed toward us, her long white sleeves billowing like wings and her hands fluttering over our faces. Youngsoo threw both arms around her, and Omahni pressed her cheek against the top of his head. "My son, my precious son," she moaned as Youngsoo held her tightly and wouldn't let go.

I watched and smiled extra hard, ashamed of the sudden ache in my chest.

"Sora-ya," she said, her eyes glistening, "you came; you brought your brother here safely." When she hugged me, all I could think was that I had done a good job delivering what she wanted most.

Without warning, the big-boned woman yanked me close, and I found my face squashed against her bosom. "Thank God, you children are alive!" I heard her muffled voice say. There were long, stifled gasps and hiccups, and when she finally let me go, I could see that she was crying. "Sora-ya, I remember when you were just a tiny baby."

And then I knew. She was Auntie, and I hugged her back.

"Your father is out looking for work, but he should be home any minute now. Oh, you children are going to give him the best surprise of his life!" Uncle said as Jisoo hid behind his leg with one eye peering out.

My heart lifted. Abahji had no idea about us, and we were going to surprise him. Youngsoo and I glanced at each other, smiling, and between coughs he bobbed up and down in excitement.

It was already getting dark. Abahji would be here soon. Lights from inside the house glowed into the courtyard. I was moving through a dream. Floating.

thirty-seven · · · · · ·

"Come inside," Uncle said, ushering us through the front door.

His house stretched in a long line, all the rooms in a row with sliding rice-paper doors separating them. It was even prettier than Myung-gi and Yoomee's house back home. We entered the middle section—the sitting room—sandwiched between a kitchen on one side and a bedroom on the other. A colorful wardrobe decorated with slivers of painted ox horn stood against the wall. We sat on a wooden floor around a low table.

"Your parents and Jisoo arrived about three weeks ago," Auntie said, carrying a tray full of rice, steamed corn, dried squid, and bubbling *daenjang jjigae* from the kitchen. She clattered bowls across the table, hastily filling them with food as if we would disappear in a puff of smoke if we weren't fed soon. "Tell them what happened, Sister-in-law," she said to Omahni.

That was when Omahni told me how they came to Busan: *In a convoy of U.S. trucks, we crossed the Taedong River over a pontoon bridge. Where were you? Only two wool blankets between the three of us. Just enough rice from our pack. Killed a pigeon; roasted it. What did you eat? Crossed the border in the same truck, bouncing up and down, our heads jiggling. How did you get across? Tootsie Roll for*

Jisoo. Cigarette for Abahji. English lesson for me. Were you heading south?

I listened carefully. Across the Taedong River in a truck? Roasted pigeon? Wool blanket? And since when did Abahji smoke? My head spun.

Youngsoo smiled at me.

"Hurry, children, eat," Auntie said.

The smell of soy sauce, garlic, sesame oil, and fermented soybean suffused the entire house. My stomach grumbled loudly, practically talking at the table, and everyone laughed.

"Once your father gets here, you'll have to tell us everything that happened," Omahni said, looking straight at me.

I swallowed.

I took a piece of dried squid and tore it between my teeth. It was warm and savory. My first food in Busan. Nothing would ever taste as good. I started shoveling spoonfuls of rice into my mouth while everyone sat around watching as if it were live theater. I thought I even saw Auntie adjust a small cushion behind her back, so she could be more comfortable as she watched.

Youngsoo only picked at his food.

Omahni began to feed him, but the metal gate clanged outside in the courtyard. Everyone's head pointed toward the sound.

"Your father! He must be home!" Uncle said, getting up to open the door.

I dropped my spoon. My open palms hit the table. Everything inside me started jumping. For a second, I mixed up panic with excitement and didn't know whether I should run to the door or hide.

I heard his voice wafting from the courtyard: *Any word on the children?*

And then he was inside, seeing us. The next thing I heard was him shouting our names, his voice cracking and shaking.

It wasn't until I saw my father standing in the doorway that I realized how much I'd held in for so long. Every glob of grief I'd swallowed, every worry I tamped down came gushing out of me. But more than that, the way his belt cinched his waist to almost nothing got its hooks into the meat of my heart. I wasn't ready for it.

His knotted work hands, their fingernails lined with dirt, reached out and held me.

"Abahji!" I screamed, a wellspring of fear and joy inside me. Bursting.

He still smelled faintly of millet, but also fish and smoke. "Sora-ya, I'm so sorry," was all he could say, touching my face. I burrowed into his shirt. His arms around me shook.

Finally, he wiped the dribble from his nose and sat down at the table, cradling Youngsoo and me on his lap. He kept looking at us as if we weren't real. "Youngsoo-ya, I bet you were brave," he said, squeezing my brother. Then he looked at my dinner plate and said, "Wah, look how beautifully our Sora eats," as if my chewed-up cob were a work of art. Which made me want to sob even harder.

Jisoo stomped over to Abahji and tried to push us off his lap. Everyone laughed through their tears.

"I prayed you two would find your way here," Abahji said, letting us slide onto the floor beside him.

"Tell us what happened," Omahni said, leaning toward me. "How did you get here? Where were you after the bombing? How did you find food?"

Youngsoo and I looked at each other, the hesitation heavy between us. How much did I want to tell? That I'd stolen food from peddlers, scraped it from the bottom of burnt pots, accepted it with cupped hands from strangers? That I sometimes went for days without finding any at all? I lowered my face.

The room quieted.

Abahji rubbed the back of his neck, hard. He gripped the table with one hand, then turned to me. "Tell us everything, Sora."

Omahni sat still, only her mouth twitching.

I cleared my throat. Where to begin? There was too much to say.

"After the bombing on the hill," Youngsoo said, surprising us, "we thought you'd been killed. We looked for you anyway . . . but then there were shots. We ran until there was no one around." Everyone was listening. "We walked across rivers on chunks of ice. We walked through woods in the snow. We stayed overnight in abandoned houses. Then we took a ferry to Seoul and got on a train, just ahead of the Reds. Noona saved my life. She saved it a hundred times." He tried to say more, but his body twisted in a coughing fit.

"When did you pick up that cough?" Omahni asked, concerned.

"After the bombing," Youngsoo said, sipping water.

"That long ago?"

"Yes." He curled inward, hugging himself. "But I'll be fine."

She put a hand to his forehead. "Well . . . good food and rest should fix that." She smiled and patted him hard on the back until I thought his head might pop off. Then she straightened her shoulders and looked at each of us.

"Everything that happened, it's all over now," she said, as if making a royal pronouncement. "Now, eat! We all must eat!"

The stalled room cranked into motion. Food was passed around the table. Everyone talked at once. Youngsoo slid close to Omahni, and she put her arm around him.

"Noona," Uncle said to Omahni.

My head snapped up. How strange to hear someone call her *Noona*. I had thought of Omahni only as my mother, not as someone's older sister. I tried to imagine being grown one day and visiting Youngsoo and his wife in their house, but I couldn't see it.

Uncle placed a hand on Youngsoo's head and said, "A mother without her son is like a turtle without its shell. You are a lucky woman, Noona, to have found your son again!"

Your son.

Uncle grinned and clapped me on the back, but his heavy hand suddenly felt like an iron weight bearing down on me.

thirty-eight · · · · · ·

After dinner, Abahji and Uncle went out to the courtyard to finish roasting squid for Uncle's fish stand, and Omahni filled a basin with warm water for us to wash up. Though I craved a full bath, I knew that would have to wait until another day when we could all go to the public bathhouse.

She gave us soap, towels, and the clothes she had packed in Abahji's jigeh before the journey: my white blouse and long tan skirt, Youngsoo's gray undershirt and pants. The clothes draped over our arms like old skins from a previous life. I grazed my hand over the blouse, then pressed it against my face. It smelled like the willow tree after a hard rain.

Youngsoo and I washed our faces first, bending over the basin while trying to keep Jisoo from playing with the water. He'd slowly warmed to us, daring to touch my arm before scurrying back and sucking his thumb. Omahni used a washcloth to scrub Youngsoo's neck. The grime fell away in sheets, turning the water gray.

"Now off with the shirts," Omahni said.

"You can go first," I said to Youngsoo, hoping I'd have some privacy once he'd finished.

Omahni pulled the filthy shirt off over his head.

It was then that I saw it—that we all saw it.

Youngsoo's rib cage stood out like ripple marks on the bottom of a sandy river. Red bumps and open sores wept from his back where he'd scratched at the lice. His chest caved in with every breath. He was white, almost colorless. He looked even worse than he had that day in the wagon.

Omahni stopped moving. Auntie returned with a tray of tea but wouldn't set it down. And Abahji and Uncle were suddenly standing in the open doorway. Quiet.

Something curdled in my stomach. It was so much worse than I'd thought. A nameless fear—a kind of dread—settled over me. What if he didn't get better? Panicked, I turned to Omahni and Abahji. "Youngsoo needs more than food and rest. He needs to see a doctor right away!"

"Yes, we'll call a doctor in the morning," said Abahji gravely. He crossed the room and examined Youngsoo's sores. A few were filled with pus.

Omahni laid Youngsoo's hand in hers. She looked at me. "Did you know your brother was this sick?"

There was an edge in her voice. I stared at the floor, mute.

Had I known he was sick? Of course. I had caught glimpses of protruding bones and reddened scabs, but we wore so many layers of clothing, and we were always walking. There was the constant cough, but I'd grown accustomed to it. Besides,

I had the same itchy scabs, the same sunken belly, and a dry, tickly cough—how could we avoid them? I gnawed on my lower lip.

Youngsoo tucked his chin and looked up at me.

"What does it matter whether the girl knew or not?" Auntie said firmly, stepping in to save me. She set the tray of tea on the low table. "I'll call Dr. Min first thing in the morning. He's the best doctor in town. There are long lines to see him, but we go to the same church; I'm sure he'll give us special attention."

Uncle led Omahni and Abahji by their elbows to the low table. "Try not to worry too much," he said. "The boy's skinny because he didn't have enough food; he can gain the weight back. The sores are clearly from lice, which we can wash away. And his cough is probably just a bad cold; Dr. Min has medicine for that."

Abahji sat cross-legged on the floor, rubbing his thighs. "Maybe you're right," he said, unsmiling.

"I'm sure I'm right," Uncle said.

Youngsoo and I finished washing in silence. Auntie poured tea for everyone. "Youngsoo, drink this. The hot water is good for you."

He took a sip. I thought of the time Ahjuma had given him herbal tea. Maybe this would make his color rosy again. I exhaled and accepted a cup from Auntie too, bowing.

The tea was warm and slid down my throat. I sat on the floor, hugging the soothing cup to my chest. I looked around the room—warm wooden floors, yellow blankets folded against the wall, a pearlescent sheen on the rice paper doors. So safe and cozy. Jisoo lay curled in the corner, asleep on the floor, his head probably filled with dreams of playing and eating.

I knew Youngsoo was sick, but he would get better in this place. He would. I couldn't forget we were in Busan.

"Ah, I see the warm tea is making you drowsy, Sora," Uncle said gently.

I tried to nod, but my eyelids drooped under the weight of the long day. In minutes, I was set adrift. . . .

I was nine and freshly bathed, my tummy full of dumpling soup and rice. My new undershirt and pants had no holes and felt soft against my skin. I snuggled against the heated ondol floor, tucking my arms and legs inside a warm, white blanket. Moist air left over from steaming bowls of rice clung to the inside of our windows.

The cold wind roared outside in the dark.

But we nestled close to one another, all of our mats laid side by side. On this night, I got to pick my favorite spot—between Abahji and Youngsoo. A single kerosene lamp still glowed as Omahni finished rubbing apple peel on her hands to smooth out her rough skin. In the soft light, she looked luminous.

My new schoolbooks sat on the floor beside the low dining table. The large dresser that Abahji had made stood handsomely against

the mud walls. I stared up at the thatched roof and wanted to curl my
arms around it all—the house, our things, my family.

Omahni blew out the lamp.

In an instant, I was asleep.

Lost in visions of warm beds, clean clothes, and new school-books, I couldn't have noticed when Youngsoo fainted and collapsed on the table. Only Auntie's droning voice drifted from far away: *The children! We must get them to bed.*

thirty-nine · · · · · ·
January 2, 1951

That night, I dreamed it again.

I graduate at the top of my class.

Clapping rises everywhere, and I have the distinct feeling of floating. Of course, Yoomee is there too, watching with envy.

But this time, instead of a certificate, the principal hands me a worn, folded piece of paper. I open it.

It's the world map that I tore from Youngsoo's history book.

My eyes opened.

A soft light seeped through the window. Our family had slept in the study. It was clean and bright. A tall, skinny bookshelf stood in the corner next to a low writing desk. Folded mats and blankets sat on top of a wooden chest. A woven bamboo pillow hung on the wall. The aroma of daenjang jjigae, kimchee, and squid lingered in the morning air. A silky yellow blanket covered me—I was cleaner than I'd ever been in the past two months, and the smooth fabric felt slippery against my skin.

Just a day ago, we were sleeping in a cramped train rank with urine and death. Had it all been a bad dream? What about Youngsoo?

My head snapped toward his direction. He'd slept on the

opposite side of the room, beside Omahni—far enough away for his coughing not to have woken me. Had Omahni patted his back when he wheezed in the middle of the night? And what about a cup of water? He would've needed a cup of water.

Muffled voices wafted through the sliding paper door: *They're alive? Yes, showed up last night. Oh, what a miracle!*

I got up and rubbed my eyes. Omahni and Abahji had already gone, their mats and blankets neatly folded and tucked away in the corner. I tiptoed toward Youngsoo. He was still sound asleep. I slid the door open.

"Sora!"

There, in the kitchen, stood a ghost of a woman and her daughter.

"Mrs. Kim? Yoomee?" I asked, blinking.

Mrs. Kim had chopped off all her hair, and deep lines fanned out from the corners of her eyes. She rushed to hug me, no longer smelling of honeysuckle and soap—only musty, unwashed scalp.

"Thank God you and Youngsoo are safe! We've all been so worried!" she said. I hugged her back, thinking how strange it felt to see her here, in Busan. I had thought the Kims were dead.

Yoomee stood off to the side, watching. She'd grown taller, thinner; other than her shiny hair, everything about her had dulled. I wriggled one arm away from Mrs. Kim's embrace and extended it to her, hoping she would know from this small gesture everything that I'd seen—charred lumps with braids, blue fingers frozen stuck on ice, gifts of a wooden cart and dried anchovies—and understand how it had changed me. How it sat heavy in my throat and stayed there. How it made me miss everyone I'd ever known, even her. To my surprise, she tightened her fingers around my hand and held it.

And then I knew—she'd probably seen the same, maybe even worse.

"How long have you been in Busan?" I asked.

"About five months." Yoomee stared at her feet, then at the ceiling, looking nothing like she had at the church picnic when the girls called her a spoiled brat. A tear started rolling, and she wiped it.

Mrs. Kim said, "If it weren't for your uncle and auntie, we wouldn't have found a place to stay. They even helped Myung-gi get a job."

"Myung-gi? A job?"

"Yes, he's fetching water and delivering it to people's homes," Auntie piped up. I'd hardly noticed her in the corner, cutting apples. "He even brings us a bucketful here. With so many refugees in the city, there's high demand for water. He's got steady business."

I couldn't picture it—Myung-gi fetching water. What about his books? Was he going to school? Would he be excited to see me?

Auntie poured a hot cup of tea. "Sora, bring this to Young-soo; he needs to drink it. Your father is at the Gukje Market with Uncle, and your mother is out buying ingredients for Young-soo's rice porridge. I need your help here."

"Yes, you should tend to your brother," Mrs. Kim said, putting on her coat. "We'll stop by again soon. It's a shame you can't see Myung-gi today; he's so busy working. But I know he'll be so thrilled to see you, Sora. Your arrival here gives us all hope."

I smiled, holding that cup of tea to my chest, the hot ceramic warm against my heart.

Before leaving, Yoomee turned to me. "I'm glad you're here."

"You are?" I said, my eyes widening.

"We all are." She stared at her feet. "Maybe we could get together sometime. My mother taught me how to knit; I could teach you too."

"Sure," I said. "I'd like that."

Yoomee buttoned her coat, and for the first time in my life, I was sad to see her go.

I headed back to our room. Youngsoo lay on a mat beside the pile of our coats, his breathing whistling in and out like a noisy flute. I knelt beside him.

"You should drink this tea." I slid my arm under his neck, raising him slightly.

He opened his eyes and reached for the edge of the cup with dry, cracked lips.

"Guess who was here?" I asked. When he didn't answer, I told him about Mrs. Kim's new haircut, Myung-gi's job fetching water, Yoomee's same straight-across bangs. I prattled on about how strange it felt to make plans with her, as if we'd always been friends. And maybe we had been—I just didn't know it at the time.

"Youngsoo, I have to show you something." I grabbed my coat from the pile and reached into the pocket. The paper map's corners had softened and rounded, and creases along the folds nearly cut right through the sheet. I held it up for Youngsoo to see. "There," I said, pointing to Busan. "Can you believe we made it? We're on the coast . . . the very edge of the world."

Through wheezing breaths, Youngsoo beamed at me, a genuine glowing smile.

"Do you know what this means?" I bit my lip, hardly believing what I was about to say—the words that he had always said aloud that I'd only silently wished. "We're not far from Hawaii. Maybe we can sail across the ocean one day." I was breathless. "You can go fishing in the ocean, too. Can you imagine the kinds of fish that live deep in the sea?"

He stared out the window. Treetops swayed in the wind. Only the sound of rustling leaves settled between us.

forty · · · · · ·

"Youngsoo's cough sounds strange," Omahni said, after she'd returned from the market. "Thank God we have a doctor coming to the house."

I watched her mince a mountain of carrots, onions, and zucchini for the rice porridge she was making for Youngsoo. "Yah, Sora-ya, wash the rice."

I poured several cups of rice and water into a bowl, then swirled and rinsed the grains. I wanted to stay with Youngsoo, but he had fallen back asleep, and I couldn't ignore Omahni. I looked around at the stove, hooks, and ladles; the mortar and pestle on the counter; the wooden grain bin in the corner. Auntie's kitchen looked like Omahni's, and I felt as if I had never left home.

Auntie sliced melon on a wooden board.

"Sora-ya," Omahni said. "Do you know they have a temporary school here that is not too far? You could walk there in thirty minutes. Isn't that right, Sister-in-law?"

Auntie nodded, chewing on a piece of the fruit.

I stopped washing the rice.

Had I heard Omahni correctly? Was she going to send me

to school? My ears pounded, and I could hardly hear beyond my own breathing. I kept my eyes fixed on the pearly wet grains. Don't breathe. One wrong move and everything could fall away like petals at the end of their bloom.

Omahni didn't look at me as she scooped the minced vegetables into a large pot. "Youngsoo has missed more than half a year of school because of this wretched war. Once he has recovered, he can resume his studies, but until then I'd like you to go to school for him."

It was a strange request, and I wasn't sure I completely understood. "Go to school for him?"

"Yes. You know, attend his third-grade class, bring home his work, and show him everything that the teacher taught during the day. There may be a small fee for tuition, but Uncle said he'll cover it."

Omahni chopped the garlic—*taaak, taaak, taaak*. The rhythm throbbed in my temples. *Go to school for him.* I repeated the words inside my head. Omahni was not sending me to school for my sake, but rather, for Youngsoo's. Something cold slithered into my stomach.

Yet still, wasn't this my chance to finally attend school, even if only to sit in a third-grade class? When I was in North Korea, hadn't I been content to eavesdrop on Miss Chun's lessons and learn from Youngsoo's books?

My cheeks flushed. It was as if I'd walked in a huge circle, returning to where I had started: By the river doing laundry. In the prison of my mother's kitchen.

"Omahni," I said, taking a deep breath, "I don't want to go to school."

A sharp pain pierced my heart. I couldn't believe my own words. I wanted to go to school, but not like this—what Omahni suggested was too much.

"What? You won't go to school for your brother?" Omahni said as she stirred the sizzling vegetables in the pot. She stopped to look at me.

"It's not that Sora doesn't want to help Youngsoo," Auntie said, arranging melon slices on a plate. "Isn't that right, dear? She'd rather stay by your side and help you in the kitchen. What a dutiful daughter."

I stared into the murky rice water. Once Omahni added the grains and liquid to the pot, she would have to stand there and stir it for hours to prevent everything from scorching. Had she ever made rice porridge for me? A quick radish soup, maybe, when I was nine and had drenched my nightclothes in fever. But never the loving, labored devotion of rice porridge.

"I suppose that's for the best," Omahni said. She took the rice from me and dumped it into the pot, then turned her attention to the gasping fish on the cutting board. "In a few years, we'll start meeting with the matchmaker, and you'll need to learn so much before then."

"You are the best teacher, Sister-in-law," Auntie said. "If she learns from you every day, she'll be well prepared for her future."

My mind spun in confusion. Omahni was picking up where she had left off. Back to the old life. Back to tradition. Back to a lifetime ago. How could I stay by her side all day, every day? Cooking. Cleaning. Fumbling everything. Something heavy pressed down on my chest. My skin felt hot and tight, as if I'd outgrown myself.

A sharp crack.

Blade against wood.

I jolted.

Omahni chopped off the fish's head. Its body flopped and twitched on the board. I stared at the headless fish, covered my mouth, then ran out the door.

forty-one · · · · · ·

Later that afternoon, Dr. Min came to the house. He walked briskly across the courtyard, wearing a black coat and felt hat. In his right hand he carried a leather case.

I stood watching from the main room, my fingers drumming against my legs. Surely, the doctor would make my brother well again.

But it was true that by the time Youngsoo recovered, he would have fallen behind at least a year in his studies. Maybe I was being selfish, not helping with his lessons. After all that we had been through, what wouldn't I do for him? I rubbed my forehead.

Abahji greeted the doctor, bowing and thanking him for coming. Politely, I lowered my head as they walked past. Dr. Min returned the greeting with a nod and a brusque smile, smoothing the thin mustache curling down on his lip.

My parents led him into the room where Youngsoo slept, and everyone followed, including Uncle and Auntie, but when I tried to slip in, Abahji held up his hand. "It's better if you wait here and keep an eye on Jisoo for us." Then he slid the door shut.

Jisoo stood beside me, gazing up with curiosity.

"Shush," I warned. "The doctor is here for Youngsoo." To my surprise, Jisoo sat still.

I listened carefully. Through the thin paper door, I heard everything: *pneumonia*, *lungs*, and *fluid*; instruments clacking; Omahni's rising voice; and Abahji's solemn questions, to which Dr. Min finally answered:

"I'm sorry, it's very advanced. He doesn't have much time left."

I'm sorry, it's very advanced.

He doesn't have much time left.

I slid to the floor, stunned, the doctor's words ringing in my ears. What was he saying? Youngsoo didn't have much time left? How was this possible? He was only nine. He had a lifetime.

Then I heard a long wail, part animal, part human. It came from Omahni.

The door slid open. Dr. Min handed Abahji several bottles of medicine.

"I'll go to school for him! He won't fall behind, I promise!" I blurted.

Abahji acted as if he didn't hear me, then turned away to hide his face. Without thinking, I leapt in front of him, needing to see his smiling crescent-moon eyes, to know everything would be all right. But Abahji's face was contorted like a grotesque mask.

I couldn't breathe.

Uncle walked the doctor out of the house and across the long courtyard to the street, and I watched them with a feeling of being caught in a dream. Once we reached Busan, Youngsoo was supposed to get better, but now he was dying. *Dying*. From inside Youngsoo's room, sounds of grief rose like floodwaters. I clasped my ears, tensing every muscle in my body.

The pounding in my chest grew louder and harder until I could do nothing but run out the front gate.

❆ ❆ ❆

On blistered feet, I ran to the busy Gukje Market. Different sounds rushed me now—hard-edged haggling, the dueling calls of merchants. I passed a stand full of ceramic bowls and had the urge to smash them to the ground. My face felt hot, and I tugged hard on my shirt collar.

It was the war's fault. Because of those Reds. The color of murder. If we hadn't had to trek across the country, if North Korea had been fit to live in, Youngsoo would've never gotten sick. Where could I enlist on the side of the South? I'd do it right now. Just give me a rifle, and I would rage into the middle of a battle.

Then I had a terrible thought—it was all *my* fault.

If I had sided with Omahni, then we would have stayed home, and Youngsoo never would have caught pneumonia. Or, if I had gone straight south instead of heading back north, we would've found Omahni and Abahji sooner. Or, if I had taken better care of him on the journey—fed, clothed, carried him more—he wouldn't have grown so ill.

I stared into some shiny metal pots. My face was ashen, as

pale and gray as a round moon in a midnight sky. "Fine pots! Fine steel pots!" the pot-seller shouted, taking a wooden spoon and clanging them like a bell.

But I could hardly hear. My long shadow stood beside me as the sun slipped lower on the horizon, the doctor's words echoing in my head. *He doesn't have much time left.* I needed to go back to Uncle's house. Back to Youngsoo.

I darted through the marketplace, bumping into strangers, crashing into a crate. An avalanche of oranges tumbled down. Glazed bowls shattered into pieces.

"Yah, crazy girl!" someone shouted from behind. "You've ruined everything!"

forty-two · · · · · ·

When I reached the front gate, the house was quiet. I lifted the metal latch and walked across the courtyard.

Maybe it was all untrue—a misunderstanding.

Maybe Youngsoo was fine.

I took off my shoes and stepped into the sitting room. No one was there. I slid open the door to our bedroom.

Omahni sat on the floor beside him, pounding him on the back, urging him to "cough it out," but he only moaned in protest. I cringed.

"Where is Abahji?" I asked.

"Your father went out with Uncle to get herbal medicine," Omahni said. She wouldn't look at me, just continued slapping Youngsoo on the back.

"Omahni, I don't think that's helping," I said.

Youngsoo glanced up at me gratefully.

"Don't tell me what to do," Omahni said. "He's my son. I haven't done enough for him."

"But you've done everything for him."

"I haven't!" Omahni jumped up and gripped me by the shoulders. "Sora-ya, listen carefully. When you were traveling with Youngsoo, did you make sure he was warm enough? How much food did he eat? At what point did his cough worsen?"

I stood frozen. Had I kept him warm enough? How much food had I given him? I could've done more. I should've done more.

"Enough, please, Sister-in-law!" Auntie said, stepping into the room. "Listen to your daughter. Slapping Youngsoo on the back isn't doing any good. You're just making it more difficult for him."

Omahni dropped her hands to her sides, looking lost. "But what can I do?"

"Come with me, and let me pour you some tea. Sora can sit with Youngsoo for a little while."

"No," Omahni said. "I'm not leaving his side."

"Sister-in-law," Auntie said, her voice softening. "Sora wants to be with Youngsoo. Let the children have some time together."

Omahni's face crumpled. Auntie led her from the room by the arm, as if she were a small child, and shut the sliding door behind them.

Bottles of strange tinctures and dark-colored drinks with gangly roots floating inside lined the floor. My map sat in the corner, neatly folded and tucked under the edge of a tray where I had left it. Just this morning, I had shown it to Youngsoo, pointing to the shores of America and making grand plans. How stupid of me. To assume that after all we had been through,

Youngsoo would be well, and we would be happy. Was it too much to ask?

I reached for the map, unfolded it, then crushed it into a tight ball and threw it on the floor. It lay in a twisted clump. I collapsed beside Youngsoo, hugging my knees.

He lay on his mat and stared at the wrinkled-up paper. "Noona, will you go to school here?" He could hardly get the words out between breaths.

"I don't know. That's not important now."

"You should. You're the smartest person in the whole world."

I forced a small smile.

Did he know? Had he heard the doctor? Why wasn't he afraid? I looked at him and thought that his ears had grown terribly large, but in fact it was his face that had grown terribly thin.

The sun had nearly set, and all at once, I felt an urgency to play games with him, to talk about fishing and favorite foods, to get in the dirt and make mud pies. To show him just how much I loved him. I searched the room for something—anything—and found a flat box on top of the chest: a board game we had played back home.

"Youngsoo, do you want to play yoot?"

He nodded.

I put the game on the floor and opened the box. The pieces looked just like the ones we had when we were younger.

"Noona! Set the game here!" Youngsoo had said, his chubby hand patting the picnic blanket on the grass.

"Okay, but I go first." I opened the box, set up the pieces, then flipped the wooden sticks so high that they landed in every direction, including in the bushes.

He bent over laughing, his five-year-old body rolling on the grass.

Now Youngsoo lay still. Only his eyes shifted across the board.

I grabbed the short wooden sticks and threw them up in the air. They landed with a clatter across the wooden floor. I moved the flat, round piece two spaces. Maybe if we both stayed awake, the day would go on forever.

"Your turn, Youngsoo."

The sticks landed in a tangled heap.

"You got a lucky five!" I said.

"Wah . . ." The tiniest stream of air slipped past Youngsoo's lips. His face lifted briefly, a small glint in his eyes. How could something so small make him smile at a time like this?

"Lucky five! I got a lucky five!" he had said, jumping up and down. "Noona, did you know this is my favorite game in the whole world— no—the whole universe?"

Youngsoo sucked in long breaths. I flipped the sticks in the air. Another loud clatter. Two more spaces.

"You're still ahead of me, Youngsoo."

The waning sun cast a warm glow in the room, turning everything golden. Youngsoo, bathing in that light, looked up at me and smiled. I had to remember the straight lines of his lashes and the way his hair spiraled in that one spot on the crown of his head.

"I don't want to play anymore. I know you're going to beat me," I had said, crossing my arms.

"It's okay, Noona. I still might lose."

He tossed the sticks, and they barely lifted off the floor, landing facedown.

"Lucky five, again!" I said. But my voice sounded hollow and faraway. Desperation edged its way into every syllable. "You're winning, Youngsoo. You're still winning."

forty-three · · · · · ·
January 3, 1951

The next day, on a blue-skied Sunday morning, I found myself lying on my mat.

A thread dangled from my blanket, and I twirled it around my finger until my nail turned purple. The study was bright, the sun already hanging high in the sky. I was alone and couldn't remember how I'd gotten here. I last remembered staying up beside Youngsoo.

I scrambled out of bed and ran to the main sitting room.

Everyone was inside.

Omahni sat on the floor, cradling Youngsoo. She swept his hair to the side of his face, then smoothed his wrinkled shirt. Her shoulders rocked back and forth. She laid his hand on top of hers and stared at his fingers as if she were noticing for the first time how small they really were.

Abahji stood over Omahni, blotting his eyes with a handkerchief, his face red and puffy. Uncle stood off to the side, sniffling and clearing his throat while Auntie sat on the floor, hugging Jisoo on her lap.

A prickly feeling scurried up the back of my neck. "What's going on?" I cried out from the doorway.

Omahni jerked and dropped Youngsoo's hand. Everyone looked up in surprise as if they had forgotten I was in the house.

Then I knew, from the way his hand fell.

He was gone.

My stomach plummeted. The air was sucked out of the room. Uncle and Auntie said something, but their voices were just muffled sounds. They moved toward me. Arms curled around my shoulders. I shook them away. *Don't touch me*, shot into the room. Had it come from me? My mouth hung open. Pleading voices filled the air. *Sora, please calm down.*

A sob welled in my throat. This wasn't supposed to happen. Not yet, not ever. There was still more I needed to say. Had he known that I never minded taking care of him, not really? That it wasn't his fault I couldn't go to school? That there was no one else I would've rather had by my side? I tried hard to remember if I'd ever told him this.

"Let me die, too!" Omahni wailed. She thumped herself over the heart and wouldn't stop.

Auntie jumped up, and Jisoo tumbled off her lap. She wrapped her arms around Omahni, soothing, embracing, and restraining her all at once. Jisoo lay frozen on his back, staring up at me, too afraid to move. *Get up*, I wanted to scream at my littlest brother. *You're a baby. Do something cute, make everyone laugh.* But when he wouldn't, my heart slid down faster.

Abahji walked over and pressed my face into his chest. His shirt smelled medicinal, like desperation and dying. And for once, I turned my face, not wanting to breathe in Abahji's scent. "It'll be okay, Sora-ya," he whispered. But his voice broke when he said it.

I knew nothing would be okay. I had lost my brother, my best friend.

From the edge of my eye, I could see Youngsoo lying on his mat. Maybe Omahni and Abahji were mistaken. They weren't doctors. Had they checked his breath?

But as soon as I went and looked at his face—so slack, so hollow—I knew every trace of him was gone. My head started lifting like a balloon, detaching from myself, looking down on the tiny room as if it belonged to a dollhouse, all of us nothing but toy figures.

We would never talk again, never see each other grow up. There would be no fishing, no grand gestures offering me any catch in the sea.

I took in a shuddering breath.

Although I had known it was coming, nothing could've prepared me for this moment, this feeling of utter loss and loneliness.

forty-four ······
January, 1951

The days passed in a fog.

Everyone rushed around the house preparing for the burial. I did nothing to help. From morning till night, I sat in the corner of the sitting room beside the colorful wardrobe, my eyes round and ring-tailed. My one task, given to me by my father: keep my face angled away from the study where Youngsoo's body lay.

"Why don't you take a break? It's dark outside," I overheard Abahji say to Omahni in the kitchen.

Omahni's hands blurred in a chopping frenzy, bits of minced garlic falling to the floor. "Everyone will come after the funeral, and I still need to prepare the dduk and *yukaejang* soup," she said, not looking at him. Pots and pans covered every cooking surface. A slab of raw meat dripped blood over the edge of a cutting board, and I thought I could feel myself draining the same way.

"Why isn't Sister-in-law helping? Where is she, anyway? I'll go find her," Abahji said, heading toward the door.

"Don't. She has been helping."

"Then let her do the rest."

"No, I have to make his food. No one else. Just me."

Abahji held the sides of her arms and stared into her face, his eyes searching. "Please, stop fretting over the food. Just stop."

That was when Omahni shrugged his hands off her shoulders like a wild, bucking horse, and Abahji stumbled backward.

"I need to do this," she said, her voice low and steady.

Abahji looked at her and nodded, his unshaven face long and drawn. "Fine, I'll leave you alone. I need to get ready for the funeral as well." When he walked out, he glanced at me sitting in the corner, then lowered his eyes and continued out the front door.

Omahni stopped chopping. I heard a snuffling sound from the kitchen.

I curled myself into a tight ball, covering my ears and squeezing my eyes shut. I didn't want to picture her standing still, the back of her hand to her lips, shoulders shaking. I gritted my teeth.

❄ ❄ ❄

The next morning, I woke in the same crook of the room, a blanket covering me. Everyone had already gotten up. It seemed like no one slept anymore.

I opened my mouth wide to stretch it after not talking for days, and my lips cracked and bled. When I got up to get a cup of water, I found Omahni still cooking, her eyes red-rimmed and bloodshot. I pretended not to notice and hurried back to my corner where it was safe, where I could sleep endlessly, where no one saw me, even when they walked right past my legs splayed out like a rag doll's.

Later that day, I ate four bites of rice. Auntie wouldn't leave the kitchen until I'd finished chewing every grain. *So skinny*, she'd said. *Eat more. You're disappearing.* But the rice clumped in my throat like cotton balls; I could hardly swallow. I just wanted to return to the corner. So, I moved my jaws up and down like a piston to earn my pass back to solitude.

With Auntie's approval, I returned to my usual spot. But something in the room had changed. I could sense it, like a dog with its ears pricked. The back of my neck stiffened, a pounding droned in my ears, my palms turned slick.

Youngsoo's door was slid open.

My head snapped away from that opening as if something had jumped up and bitten me on my other side. I didn't want to look when only his body lay in that room, like an imposter. I stared at a knot in the wooden floor, even put my finger in it, but when slippers started shuffling inside the other room, I let my eyes wander toward the sound.

Omahni sat on the floor, swaddling Youngsoo in white hemp like a cocoon. She took her time, wrapping and unwrapping, then wrapping again, until the binding was perfectly taut. I stared long and hard at those bands of cloth stretched over the shape of my brother, wishing that he would emerge like a butterfly from its chrysalis. A sickly sweet perfume came from his direction, permeating my nostrils even in the main hall, and I wanted to stop breathing.

Omahni tied the last knot in the hemp. The cloth covered

him from head to toe, like an extra skin between us, and I could feel him slipping even further away. Omahni must've felt it too, because she grabbed the one thing we had left of him—his coat—and brought it to her face. After a few seconds, she laid it flat on the floor, smoothing one sleeve, then the other, and straightening the front. I knew she would want to fold it into a perfect square to keep forever. Her hand grazed over the pocket, then paused in midair.

I leaned closer toward the door.

Omahni reached inside the pocket and pulled out a cluster of objects: a spinning top, a handful of river rocks, fishing net string, and twigs. I stared at the unexpected treasures—we both did. Were those the things he grabbed when Abahji had told us to pack only the essentials? And on our way here, after walking all day, our knees shaking, had he carried handfuls of rocks in his pocket?

I clamped a hand over my mouth, not knowing whether to laugh or cry. It was like seeing Youngsoo again, his small, grubby hands touching all of it.

I blinked, the fog lifting briefly. Pieces of him had followed us here and were now staring up at me, saying that I'd fed him enough, clothed him enough, carried him enough, and that he had been happy. I laughed and snorted, not even caring about the snot dripping from my nose, because it was the first sound I'd uttered in days while sitting trapped inside myself.

Omahni cupped the objects in her hands and sniffed deeply.

I wanted to step into that room and do the same, but I didn't, a part of me still afraid. Whether I touched those things or not didn't matter. More important, we needed to preserve Youngsoo's belongings in a special box for the safest keeping—on this, I knew Omahni would agree. We just had to find a box. As if she could read my thoughts, Omahni got up and searched the room, and when she couldn't find what she wanted, she put Youngsoo's things back into the pocket, then resumed folding his coat.

"Omahni, we can get a pretty box at the Gukje Market," I said from the other side of the sliding door.

But she continued only folding.

forty-five · · · · · ·
January 6, 1951

The next day was the funeral.

Abahji and Uncle carried the coffin on a wooden bier. They stopped once at the gate and lowered it three times before heading toward Yongdu Mountain—a gesture to mark Youngsoo's final departure from this house. They stared at the ground as they walked, stoic as two monks, though I could see the line of Abahji's clamped lips quivering.

I looked up at the fresh blue sky. It felt like spring in the middle of winter—like that afternoon by the Imjin River, before it had turned bloody.

Nothing seemed real. I felt weightless as I trailed behind Abahji and Uncle, my arms stuck at my sides. That morning, I had searched Abahji's eyes for reassurance, but he looked right through me as if I were dead too.

Finally we reached the hill path outside the city. Morning sun filtered through the pine trees, scattering circles of light onto everyone's bodies. Omahni squinted, a hundred tiny wrinkles on her face as if she'd run a fine-toothed comb over her skin. I didn't dare reach for her hand, though I noticed it hanging limp, waiting for someone to hold it—Youngsoo, maybe Jisoo.

Jisoo rode on Auntie's back, his hands clasped around her neck. He glanced at me blankly, then turned to stare at the evergreens towering overhead. I wondered if he understood all this, then remembered that he'd just turned only three. For the first time, I considered our ten-year difference—without Youngsoo to bridge the gap between us, I felt even more alone.

As we walked higher up the mountainside, the pines thickened and the sunlight could barely reach us. Omahni, stepping in and out of stray beams, disappeared for longer and longer in the shadows. The air turned bitter cold.

"Youngsoo-ya! Our Youngsoo-ya!" Omahni cried up to the sky. Auntie put her arms around her.

I watched them, dazed.

I wanted to hear his voice again, see him fishing in the river. I pictured his face—before sickness, before war—back in the beginning.

"Come, Sora-ya. You're a noona now. Meet your new baby brother," *Abahji had said.*

For days, I had been at Mr. and Mrs. Choi's house, waiting for you to come. I ran inside our thatched-roof cottage as fast as my chubby legs could carry me.

In Abahji's arms, swaddled in a white blanket, was the tiniest face I'd ever seen. I didn't realize I was holding my breath until you opened your eyes, and I gasped when I saw those beautiful, silvery-black pools. You looked at me as if you already knew who I was.

"He's so cute!" I cried, reaching with clumsy hands toward your jewel eyes.

"Ah, careful, Sora-ya," Abahji said, holding you high. "You shouldn't touch the baby. He's still too small."

"I promise, I won't touch. Let me see again," I said.

Abahji lowered you. And I looked once more. You were the most beautiful baby in the whole world. Those cherry lips, that fuzzy hair, the little bean nose. I couldn't resist. The tip of my lips kissed the soft top of your head.

I loved you, immediately.

The memory pressed on my bruised heart.

Along the path, camellia trees were greening. I couldn't stand their buds—so fat and ripe and ready to bloom—as if they were rushing toward spring, toward a season Youngsoo would never see again. He would never enjoy their pretty colors.

The willow tree back home was probably still buried underneath a blanket of snow. I had the sudden urge to see our old house, the sparkling river, the schoolhouse on top of the hill.

After a long walk, we came to a clearing. Trees circled it, sheltering it the way parents watched over their children. I could see Mrs. Kim and Yoomee, dressed in white, the color of mourning. The others were strangers—Uncle and Auntie's friends—and I wondered why they had come; they didn't even know him. *How old was he? How did he die? Was he their only son?* As soon as they saw us coming, they stopped their gossiping and weeping and split apart like curtains, revealing that deep dark hole in the ground, as if it were the final act of their show.

My heart shrank back, but my legs kept walking. It was deeper than the pit in my stomach, blacker than the insides of my eyes when they were closed. Yet Abahji and Uncle lowered Youngsoo's body into it. Inch by inch, the coffin slipped from view, and my breath quickened. I couldn't lose sight of him. Not even for a second.

I rushed closer to the edge. And when I looked down, I could see the casket again.

The pastor stood before the grave with a straight back and a rock-steady voice, the way only a professional funeral-giver could. I thanked God that this dry-eyed man would carry us through the ceremony. He led us in several hymns, and Uncle sang extra loudly to make up for Abahji's and Omahni's thin tones, but even his voice wavered at the refrain: *All things bright and beautiful.* Then came a sermon that I couldn't remember. Omahni tried to say a prayer, but her voice frayed after the first words, and Mrs. Kim rushed to her side. My throat thickened into a lump of clay.

Abahji stepped forward and bowed before tossing the first clump of earth over the coffin. Then the men buried Youngsoo.

My eyes stayed fixed on the pine box, watching until every bit of it disappeared under the dirt. I couldn't believe that my little brother lay in the ground.

Everyone began leaving.

Mrs. Kim dabbed under her eyes with a handkerchief. "Sora-ya, how are you, dear?"

No one had asked me that before, and I didn't know what to say. I was frozen until Myung-gi stepped forward and bowed to Omahni and Abahji. He had grown several inches taller, into someone leaner, more muscular. Behind his wire-rimmed glasses, his face had hardened. I wouldn't have recognized him if it weren't for the long, familiar look he gave me, full of so much kindness that I had to hide my face as it twisted into an ugly sob.

forty-six · · · · · ·

Everyone headed down the mountain in twos, but I walked alone. With no one by my side, the wind buffeted me, and I swayed like a tree ready to snap.

We went to Uncle's house. Auntie hurried into the kitchen, and when Omahni and Mrs. Kim followed to help, she chased them out. Omahni didn't object. Uncle patted Abahji on the back as they settled on the floor around the low table. The rest of us joined them. We sat in painful silence, no one daring to speak first.

Finally, Abahji told Mrs. Kim that her short haircut looked nice, then broke into tears.

I listened to my father howl like a lonely wolf and thought I'd shatter into a million pieces if I stayed in that room. So I got up and walked out the front door.

In the courtyard, Myung-gi and Yoomee sat beside the row of guests' shoes on a raised wooden platform. Yoomee held Jisoo on her lap, cuddling him like a puppy.

"I'm sorry. For everything," she said, looking at me.

I sat beside her, wondering if Jisoo thought she was his older sister. I held my arms out to him, but he wouldn't come. He would probably go to anyone else—even Mr. Kim—rather than to me.

Mr. Kim. Wait.

"Yoomee . . . where's your father?" I asked, realizing in that instant that I hadn't seen him since we arrived. I couldn't remember if he had even been at the funeral.

"They took him," Myung-gi said, talking to the ground, his hands between his knees. "The night before we left. He told us it might happen. He told us to go, no matter what. So we did. That's why I've been working instead of going to school. I'm head of the house now." He swallowed once, then slumped deep into his lanky, big-footed self, nowhere near done becoming a man.

"But we'll see him again," Yoomee said, sitting up straighter. "If they sent him to a labor prison, I'm sure he escaped. He's the cleverest man alive, my father. He'll come here, just like you did." She stopped and bit her fingernail.

I pictured their father—like the Man Who Was Not My Uncle—with a rifle in his back. A wave of nausea hit me. What had happened to Mr. Kim? Where was he now? Was he even alive?

"I'm so sorry," I said. But even still, to me, missing was better than dead, and I envied Yoomee for having something to hold on to. I knew that Youngsoo would never come home again.

Tiny sparrows flitted around the courtyard, and I wondered how something so frail could be alive while my brother lay cold in the earth. They danced all over the grounds, chasing each other, and I followed them with my eyes, concentrating only on their game.

"Youngsoo was a sweet boy," Myung-gi said.

Yoomee wiped her eyes with the back of her hand while Jisoo pulled on her straight, silky hair.

The sparrows teased me with their comings and goings, these birds that were now a part of this fateful day. Then, without warning, they took flight, fluttering so high that I could no longer follow them. They too were gone. Early evening owls began hooting, and I wondered how the afternoon had already passed.

Guests from the funeral began trickling in for the dinner. Myung-gi, Yoomee, and I jumped to our feet and led them inside where Auntie had set a table full of grilled fish, pickled side dishes, spicy beef soup, and rice cakes. Everyone crowded the small room, murmuring condolences and remarks about how handsome Youngsoo looked in the photograph by his shrine. We hadn't brought any photos from home, but luckily, Uncle had found one in his house. It was taken when Youngsoo was a baby. We had a better picture back home—one of him fishing by the river—and I wondered whether we'd ever see it again. Someone poured Abahji a glass of soju, and he drank it, then asked for more. The room continued filling with people, and soon I could hardly find a place to stand.

"Come on, there's space over there," Myung-gi said, pointing toward the back near the shrine. Yoomee and I followed, weaving through the crowd.

I couldn't see it before—not with all the people in my

way—but up close, Youngsoo's shrine sparkled. A shiny silver frame held the baby photo that Uncle had found. Beside it sat a glossy black lacquered box, inlaid with mother-of-pearl cut in the shape of flying herons. And inside the box, on top of the black velvet lining, lay all of Youngsoo's things.

"I remember that spinning top," Yoomee said, looking at the open box. "He loved that toy. Every time we went to your house, he'd take it out and show us."

I smiled faintly. I hadn't realized how much he'd carried in his coat pocket. So many rocks and twigs and string, and underneath them all, a folded piece of paper. "What's that?" I asked.

Myung-gi and Yoomee drew closer.

My hand shook as I pulled it out.

But I already knew, even before the picture of oceans and continents and rivers unfolded before our eyes. "My map," I said, staring at the smooth sheet that I had once crushed into a tight ball and thrown away. "What's it doing here?"

"Sora, you shouldn't touch those things. They're part of the shrine," Auntie said, swooping in and taking it from me.

"But how did this get here? It wasn't in his coat pocket," I said.

"What do you mean? It belonged to Youngsoo. He was holding it the night before he passed, smoothing it against his chest to get out all the wrinkles. Someone must've crumpled it by accident. Poor thing. He was so tired, but he just wouldn't quit until it was perfect."

Blood drained from my face. He'd wasted his energy fixing something I ruined. He should've saved his strength for another game of yoot or a final glimpse of the starry night. Anything but this.

Auntie set it back in the box, then returned to the guests.

"That map was yours, wasn't it? It was the one you always looked at back home, when we still went to school together," Yoomee said, her eyes widening.

"I crushed it and threw it away," I whispered. "In his room."

"And Youngsoo found it and smoothed it out?"

Congratulations, detective, yes, I wanted to say. For a second, I glared at her. I wished she would mind her own business. I should've thrown it in the fire where he couldn't find it. Then he wouldn't have wasted his final night on that worthless, stupid map.

It was then that Yoomee put a hand on my shoulder. I looked at her in surprise.

"He did it for you, Sora," she said. "So you would keep looking at the world. He didn't want you to give up on your dreams."

forty-seven · · · · · ·
February, 1951

Over the next few weeks, Omahni spent her time lying on a mat and staring out the window.

Auntie prepared the family's meals after long days of working at the fish stand. No one asked Omahni to help around the house, and for once, she never offered. I didn't know what to say to her, and, believing that she blamed me for everything, I said nothing.

Abahji went to work at his new job on the dock even though he could hardly get out of bed. I knew he stayed up all night smoking cigarettes, sipping soju, and gazing at the stars. And although he'd come home pounding his aching back, he never complained about hauling heavy military supplies from a conveyor onto trucks. There were plenty of other men willing to take his spot, according to the supervisor.

During the day, I helped take care of Jisoo, and even Omahni, who now always had a headache. Chores helped me get through the hours. I helped Auntie make soup and rice for breakfast, cleaned the dishes, and fetched water from the neighborhood well. I bathed Jisoo and changed the wet towel Omahni kept draped over her forehead. At midday, I would make a simple lunch and clean up, and not much later begin preparing rice for dinner. Although Auntie sometimes scolded me for turning the rice into mush, the housework kept me from falling into the abyss that now consumed my mother.

I never mentioned Youngsoo, knowing that Omahni and Abahji couldn't hear his name without falling apart. But I wished I could tell someone how he'd once made me laugh until water shot out of my nose. How he'd built a tower of rocks that was as tall as me. How one time he'd scored higher than his classmates on a math test—it couldn't have been a mix-up; he had earned it. How he would've caught a two-foot-long trout in his net, if it weren't for the kids splashing into the river. *He was great at fishing*, I wanted to say, *because aren't patience and perseverance most important?* And he was smarter than we all thought too, sometimes surprising us with his observations. *Animals don't hate, they just fear.*

But my days were wordless, and by evening, my lips were glued shut with dried saliva.

❄ ❄ ❄

One day, over dinner, everything I wanted to say and everything they could never hear collided.

"Sora! Will you set the table for me?" Auntie called from the kitchen. Pots and pans clanged. Her slippers swished across the floor.

"Yes, Auntie." I grabbed the chopsticks from the chest and set them around the low table in the sitting room.

"And get your father and Uncle. It's time for dinner."

I walked out to the courtyard. The evening air was cool and comfortable. Uncle roasted squid over the firepit while Abahji ran the dried pieces through a small press. The aroma had become so familiar that I hardly noticed it anymore.

They were talking about the war and the fighting near the thirty-eighth parallel. I had almost forgotten there was still a war; the American soldiers strolling through the marketplace were as unguarded as the rest of us, and with Youngsoo gone it didn't matter anyway. I cleared my throat. "Abahji, Uncle, please come to dinner."

"Okay, Sora-ya. We'll be right there." Abahji dusted his hands and shirt of dried squid flakes.

I returned to the main room. Omahni sat at the low dining table. Her eyes brimmed as she stared at the chopsticks across from her.

Auntie walked in carrying bowls of noodle soup, then looked at Omahni. "Aigoo . . . Sora, how could you be so thoughtless?" she asked.

Omahni sobbed.

What is she talking about? I followed Auntie's gaze, and counted the chopsticks around the table—seven. I had set down seven pairs. Blood pounded in my ears.

"Noodle soup was Youngsoo's favorite," I blurted.

Omahni cried harder.

"It was what he wanted on his last birthday," I continued.

Auntie blinked at me, her mouth pinched into a thin line.

"What's going on in here?" Uncle asked as he and Abahji stepped through the door.

"Sora put down seven settings instead of six, and it has upset Sister-in-law," Auntie said, looking as if she had just bitten into a sour plum.

"That's not Sora's fault. You should know that was an honest mistake," Uncle said.

"Did I say she did it on purpose? I was just saying that she shouldn't be so thoughtless! Especially to her mother, especially these days!"

"She's not being thoughtless!" Abahji shouted, spittle flying from his mouth.

"Brother-in-law, please," said Uncle. He rubbed the back of his neck. "Why is everyone shouting? Aren't we all suffering enough?"

Jisoo burst out crying; Omahni scooped him up and ran out the door, Auntie following close behind. Abahji patted his shirt pocket and stepped into the courtyard, fumbling to pull out a cigarette. And Uncle shook his head, then went to his room.

I was alone.

We had gathered together, the Paks and the Kims, dressed in our finest.

Shiny fruits and colorful cloths filled the house. We ran in and out of every room, playing hide-and-seek. The top of Myung-gi's head poked out from inside a chest. Yoomee's small silhouette showed from behind a folding screen. Ha, I found them both!

"Happy Chuseok, everyone!" Mrs. Kim said. She passed out plates of sweet rice cake.

"Thank you for inviting us. Dinner was delicious," Omahni said, holding three-year-old Youngsoo in the lap of her dark yellow dress.

Abahji sat on the floor by the low table. "Oh, I'm so full." He patted his stomach.

We came out of our hiding places. The evening light cast a soft glow on all our faces. I closed my eyes and wished this house could be mine.

There was laughing and drinking and talking. About the pears that were so ripe this year. About the beautiful sound of our Korean names. About the good health of family and friends. I listened, my heart soaring.

Soon, my own words swept up and rushed out: Did you know there are ten vowels and fourteen consonants? My favorite color is orange. Tag is more fun than hide-and-seek. I'm going to be a writer when I grow up. My harabuji once lived in America; he's dead now. There's a girl in my class who thinks she can fly. I love fried dumpling. But my brother's favorite food is noodle soup.

A scream balled up in my throat. I sat in the seventh spot, digging the tip of Youngsoo's chopsticks into my palm.

forty-eight · · · · · ·
April, 1951

Somehow time marched forward.

I sat on the stone wall at the back of the house. The mountains had turned a velvety green, their sharp edges softened by new grass. Rows of cherry blossom trees exploded in a pink-petal snowstorm. My eyes stung from staring, and I closed them.

"Sora-ya! Where are you? I need your help!" Omahni walked out of the kitchen and into the courtyard. Her hands were red with hot pepper flakes and wet with kimchi juice. She had begun cooking again, not wanting to burden Auntie any further.

I watched her from behind but pretended not to hear.

Omahni checked the outhouse, then the storage shed. She called my name again as she turned to look on the side of the house, the bottom of her long skirt swishing. It was then that she saw me.

She marched up with her hands on her hips. "Yah, why didn't you answer me when I called?"

I shrugged.

Something in her face wound tighter, and for a second, I

worried that she might unleash all her pent-up anger in a slap across my cheek.

"Get down from that wall, right now," she said, gritting her teeth.

I started to climb down the stone wall, thinking of the time when I'd scrambled off the roof of the train. Youngsoo's panicked face flashed in my head. I tugged at my long skirt, which now fell short above my ankles. I was growing taller, already different than I was on that day, while Youngsoo would always remain my nine-year—

"Hurry up!" Omahni grabbed my arm with her red-pepper-flake hands and snatched me off the wall. My elbow scraped against the rough stones. I caught my mother's gaze as I stumbled to the ground and thought I saw a flicker of recognition in her eyes, as if she were seeing herself in my face and punishing us both for it. My eyes stung.

"Go to Uncle's fish stand and bring home several squid right away. I'm going to teach you how to make a squid dish tonight to go with the birthday dinner," she said in a flat tone. Her face sagged as if she were made of wax, and melting. She went inside.

Birthday dinner? Whose birthday? I had to think.

Oh, it was my thirteenth birthday. Why couldn't Omahni have just said so? But as soon as I asked myself, I knew by the way she could hardly look at me or be in the same room for too long.

It should have been me instead of Youngsoo.

He was such a good kid, much better than me. Always trying to make everyone happy. Her precious son. It was no wonder that Omahni loved him more.

But still, I was here. And I didn't know what to do about it.

❅ ❅ ❅

The Gukje Market bustled with the Saturday afternoon crowds. Glossy pottery, bright fabrics, and ripened fruits and vegetables—cabbage, chives, tangerines—covered the tables. The earthy scent of spring hung in the air. Uncle's fish stand was at the end of an aisle. I headed toward it.

"We've got fresh carp and squid caught today," Uncle called out to passersby. He didn't shout or haggle. On his table, silvery fish with mouths agape poked out from small buckets, and bulbous squid lay in rows, their tentacles draped over the edge like wet, braided hair.

"Uncle," I said, walking toward him. "Omahni asked me to bring home squid for tonight's dinner." For some reason, I couldn't say it: *birthday*. My birthday.

"Of course. You turn thirteen today. Here, I'll give you the biggest, freshest ones." Uncle winked at me and dumped the slimy, curling masses into the burlap bag I had brought.

How could he be so different from Omahni? I bowed. "Thank you, Uncle."

He smiled. "You know, when your mother and I were kids, we would go with our father on his fishing boat. We'd always come home drenched! Sometimes, as a special treat, our father would give us each a persimmon—your mother's favorite. We ate them in our fists. The juices dribbled down our arms and chins, but it tasted so good. Your harabuji would laugh at our messy faces. Those were some of my happiest memories." He patted my back.

I couldn't imagine Omahni playing or having a messy face. I shifted my weight, wanting to leave.

"Did you know that before a persimmon turns sweet and orange, it starts out green, and so sour that it makes your mouth dry? Kind of like your mother sometimes," Uncle said, chuckling. "But if you're patient and give it a chance, it turns into a totally different fruit, well worth waiting for. Hold on, let me see if my friend is selling any at his fruit stand today. I'll be right back."

If I had left a second earlier, then I wouldn't have heard it— the words that turned my stomach inside out and set me on the warpath as I headed back home.

"It's bad luck, of course, to have a child die," Auntie said to a woman at a nearby cabbage stand. "It's best just to move on, and not think or talk about it."

"You're right, you're right. Better just to forget. Thank God, at least she still has one son left," the woman said, clucking in sympathy. "Can you imagine if she'd lost her only son and was left with nothing?"

I listened intently, my entire body buzzing like a struck metal gong. *At least one son left? Better to forget? Left with nothing?* Auntie with her big mouth and stupid friend!

A strange metallic taste washed over my tongue. I left before Uncle returned, before he could tell me more about my mother and fistfuls of persimmon and playing on a boat. All of which I could hardly believe. Omahni would never let me be as free.

A different street. Unfamiliar houses. Wider roads. I didn't know where I was going, only that I was tired of running away. I'd risked everything—including my brother's life—to get here, thinking one kind of freedom would automatically lead to another, that I could go to school, that I could write, that we would be happy. But I was wrong. Nothing was guaranteed.

A part of me would stay trapped, no matter where I went. It started raining, and I squinted through the water pelting straight down, the answer coming to me out of the mist.

Arriving in Busan was only half the battle; the other half was in Uncle's house, working in the kitchen, red kimchi juice dripping down her arms.

forty-nine . . . . . .

"Did you get the squid?" Omahni said. She stared blankly at the bulging bag in my hand.

I stuck my arm out and handed it to her.

Omahni took the bag, then headed inside the house. "Come, I need to teach you how to cook," she said over her shoulder.

When I stepped into the kitchen, Mrs. Kim and Yoomee were already preparing food, their heads down and elbows moving. Omahni rolled up her sleeves. "Sora-ya, watch carefully. I'll teach you how to clean the squid."

Omahni grabbed the tail with one hand and twisted the head off with the other—entrails and the black ink sac slipped out. Then she tore off the outer speckled skin, peeling it away to reveal a smooth, milky surface.

The next squid came slapping down on the counter in front of me.

"Now, your turn," Omahni said.

I clamped down on the squid's body and grabbed the head, but the tail slipped out of my grasp. I tried again—digging my nails in this time, slimy juices covering my fingers—and yanking harder. It came apart, the insides oozing out and black liquid leaking everywhere.

"Aigoo! You popped the ink sac." Omahni reached for a bowl of water, her face crinkled in annoyance.

I stepped back to let her finish the preparations. She rinsed the squid in the bowl, and the water turned black. I snuck a glance at Yoomee's squid. It was as pristine as Omahni's, of course. Yoomee looked at me with sympathy.

Omahni had rushed around the kitchen, her long hair fraying from her bun. "Help me, Sora-ya. I have so many dishes to prepare today. I'll never finish in time."

I chopped the cucumber into slices, my small, clumsy hands holding the knife in a fist.

"Not like that. Slice it paper thin. Hold the knife like this," she said, putting her index finger over the top of the blade. The knife in her hand echoed—rat tat tat tat—against the cutting board.

"Omahni, it's only Halmoni coming to visit. Do we need to make so much food?" I wanted to go outside and play.

"Ha!" Omahni snorted. "Do you know your father's mother? Nothing is good enough for her. The last time she was here, she told me my rice was hard and your father looked too thin and maybe my cooking didn't suit him. That maybe I didn't suit him." She fried scallion pancakes in the cast-iron pan.

"Couldn't you just ignore what she says?" I looked out the window. Blue sky and green grass beckoned me. How much longer did I have to stay indoors?

"Easier said than done. You'll understand one day, Sora. Except I will make sure you are perfection in the kitchen. No mother-in-law will be able to find fault with you. I'll guarantee you have a good life."

Omahni froze. I followed her gaze to the cutting board. My cucumber slices were thick and all different widths, scattered like chunks of chopped wood. Her face reddened. "Aigoo! What is this? Mrs. Kim tells me Yoomee can make a pickled cucumber salad all by herself!"

I stood there like an overgrown tree sprouting in the middle of the kitchen, getting in everyone's way.

Omahni clipped my shoulder as she reached for the seasonings. She mixed garlic, soy sauce, red pepper flakes, and sugar in a small bowl, stirring with her fingers. With just the feel of her hands, she added more salt and pepper. Before rushing off to prepare the noodle soup, she handed me an empty bowl.

"Now you try," she said.

I hadn't paid close enough attention. The ingredients were scattered across the counter. I poured and sprinkled everything into the bowl.

Omahni stopped to dip her pinky into my sauce. "Aigoo. Too sweet. It's like candy." She poured more soy sauce into the mixture to counter the sweetness. After another taste, she shook her head. "Still no good. How will I ever get you married off one day? Start over."

I stared at my bowl full of too-sweet sauce.

Everything slowed as if underwater. This bowl had come all the way from home; I'd held it a hundred times before. But today, as I watched myself pick it up, I was amazed at how easy it was simply to open my hand and let it go. I watched it drop like heavy fruit cut from its branch.

The terrible crash caught everyone's breath. Shards of white pottery exploded across the floor. Dark, oily liquid splattered onto the walls. But I did not flinch.

"Yah, Sora!" Omahni said. Her face twisted in anger. "You're such a clumsy girl! Aigoo . . . God have mercy on the fate of such a hopeless daughter!" She bent to pick up the broken pieces.

Hopeless daughter—it shot like an arrow and lodged in my heart. The hurt bloomed across my chest.

"Omahni," I said, hardly able to speak past the knot in my throat. "You have no right to call me that."

"What did you say?" Omahni said. She stood and flung the ceramic shards back to the floor.

A small piece hit the side of my face, but I refused to rub it. The room fell silent. Something stirred inside me, murky and fierce. I felt it gather and rise, turning my face crimson.

I looked at her. "You weren't there. I took care of Youngsoo. I kept him alive. I protected him. He believed in me."

"Uh-muh! So you're saying it was all my fault because I wasn't there?"

"I never said that."

"Have you lost your mind talking to your mother this way?"

Auntie ushered Mrs. Kim and Yoomee out. Omahni grabbed a wooden spoon and smacked the back of my knees.

I drew in a sharp breath. My legs throbbed. A slow tear carved a path down my cheek.

"You're always going against me. You never do as I say!" Omahni said, whimpering and striking out, almost as if she were terrified.

"What do you mean? I always do what you say. I stayed home from school to watch my little brothers, didn't I?"

Another whack.

I clenched my teeth and stared at her white skirt. A small soy sauce stain had splattered there.

"You selfish girl! Talking back to me!" She raised the wooden spoon once more.

"Uncle told me that you used to play on your father's boat. You had a messy face," I blurted.

She lowered the spoon. Her eyes were searching me. "What are you talking about?"

"Nothing has changed since we came to Busan," I said, my voice shaking. "You're still forcing me to be someone that I'm not."

Omahni's face snapped back into a snarl. "Oh, really? Who

are you then? Do you think becoming a storyteller who doesn't even know how to cook bean pancakes will give you a secure life? How about your future mother-in-law—would she take kindly to an incompetent girl like you? Wake up, Sora, I'm trying to prepare you for the rules and expectations of this world!"

"I'm not incompetent," I said, tears now running over my chin. "I just want to do something different. Don't you ever want to do something different?"

She chuckled, as if she couldn't believe I'd said something so stupid. "What would I do? Don't be ridiculous."

"I don't know. You could learn how to paint or go somewhere unexpected," I said, wiping my eyes and frantically searching the room as if the answer were hidden behind the walls. "Like Egypt."

"Egypt?" She snickered again. "Why would I go to Europe? Hitler destroyed almost all of it."

"No, Omahni. Egypt is in Africa."

Omahni's cheeks turned bright red. "Is that what you learned from your fancy books? You've had your head in them too long. You don't know how to do anything else! If I don't teach you the practical things in life, you'll never survive!"

"I want to go back to school," I said.

"Well, you can't." The words lashed out of her mouth as fast as a whip.

My eyes met hers. "But there are some things you can't teach me."

She laughed, the sound of splintering wood, and I covered my ears. "So, I'm not good enough for you? You're too smart to follow in my footsteps and learn from me?"

"Stop putting words in my mouth. That's not what I meant," I said, my voice rising.

Omahni threw the wooden spoon on the floor, her eyes flashing. "Why do you hate me?"

My face blanched. I couldn't believe I'd heard her right. It was the same question I'd been asking *her* inside my head all along.

"You'll do anything to go as far from me as possible—anything to be opposite of me! Always talking about going to school, going to university, going to America," she said, spittle flying everywhere. "You're ashamed of me, aren't you? Ashamed of your uneducated mother who couldn't even save her own son!" She stopped and let out a deep-throated moan. "This is why you were always my least favorite!"

The room started spinning. Hurt, as heavy as a concrete block, slammed into my stomach. I couldn't breathe.

"Oh, God. Oh, God. I'm sorry, Sora! I didn't mean it," Omahni cried.

My voice was a rasp, like black smoke. "I know you think it should've been me instead of Youngsoo. Then you wouldn't be nearly as sad." My face was slick with tears. "And you'd still have two sons."

"That's not true. How could you say such a thing?" Omahni

reached for me, her arms trying to tangle around me like an octopus.

I stayed clear of her grasp. My chest heaved up and down. A buzzing sounded in my ears. I knew this would be hard— maybe even as hard as my journey to Busan—and I braced myself.

"You can't stand to look at me. You blame me for everything. *But I'm worth something.*"

Omahni's eyes pleaded with me. One hand closed around my wrist. I pulled back, but she held on. "Sora, you are not to blame for Youngsoo's death. If anyone is to blame, it is me. I was his mother."

"You're wrong, Omahni. It wasn't your fault either. It wasn't anyone's fault."

That was when my mother shriveled, as if I'd thrown salt over the thin, tear-drenched membrane of her body. She wept.

The angry knot in my chest unraveled, but her words had left a deep mark that was tender and sore. Through my watery eyes, Omahni blurred into an imperfect shape. I knew I would forgive her, and over time, maybe even forget—but a small part of me would always wonder whether there was some truth to what my mother had said.

"Sora, I push you because there are things a girl must know how to do. How will you survive if I don't teach you?"

"Don't worry, Omahni. I'll survive."

"But how will you do that?"

"The way you've always taught me. By being strong and working hard."

"My only daughter," she whispered. "I can't lose you, too."

I reached for her, touching her arm. "You won't lose me, Omahni. Not ever. Not even when I go back to school."

fifty · · · · · ·
May through August, 1951

The following week, Omahni gave me a journal and a pencil for class. The school year had begun in March, but it didn't matter. She told me to head south, halfway toward the beach, where there would be big tents that I couldn't miss.

I ran. My muscles had softened, but their memory was strong, and pounding against dirt roads was familiar. I felt as if I were back in the frozen valleys, the empty villages. Only now, I wasn't running away. I was running to school.

The Busan provisional school was inside an army tent with a green canvas roof and mesh windows. It didn't look like a classroom, but I didn't care; the smell of chalk hung in the breeze. I waded through the crowd of unfamiliar faces, wondering whether I'd make any friends.

"Sora, over here!" Yoomee called, waving her arms by the entrance. Myung-gi stood beside her.

A wave of relief washed over me. I waved back and headed toward them. "Myung-gi oppah, are you back in school?" I asked.

"Nah, I'm just here to see about another job—translating." He took off his glasses and wiped them against his shirt. "If I save money over the next few months from this job and the water job, there should be enough for Yoomee and Mom to live on for a while."

Without his glasses, I thought he could be any one of the boys running stalls at the Gukje Market. "Where will you be in a few months? Are you planning on going somewhere?"

He put his glasses back on; his eyes were magnified and dark. "Once I turn sixteen, I'm going to enroll in the South Korean army. Then I'll go find our father and bring him back."

"I think it's a bad idea," Yoomee said grimly. "Oppah, you shouldn't go."

"I have to go. I'm the only son. What wouldn't I do for my father?"

Abahji's words.

Something constricted in my chest. "But you're a scholar, not a fighter. What about your studies? I thought you would go back to school as soon as you and your family got settled!"

"My studies can wait. I need to find my father." He glanced at the students heading inside the tent, their book bags slung over their shoulders, and his gaze didn't even linger.

In that instant, I knew that it was never his smooth, tan complexion or good looks that I liked. It was his habit of always carrying his bag of books that had made me look for him wherever I went.

I wanted to tell him that he was too young, that the whole idea was far-fetched and dangerous, that he needed to study, that he was more than just my friend's older brother—he was my friend too.

But I knew he had no choice. I would've done the same. So I said nothing.

Inside the tent, a hundred-plus children of all ages sat on the floor, sharing textbooks in groups of four or more. Yoomee and I sat with three other girls, their smiles wide and welcoming. Between the five of us, we had enough pencils, paper, and textbooks to get by.

Over the next few weeks, I caught up in my studies, making up for the year I'd missed. It was as if I had a gnawing hunger for knowledge that I couldn't stop feeding. Curiosity led me from one topic to another, to another, to another—until I found myself reading late into the night with a kerosene lamp in the courtyard, everyone asleep inside.

Our American teacher, Miss Foster, talked with outstretched arms and moving hands. She kept a pencil stuck in her hair and pulled it out like a pistol from a holster whenever she needed it. She had a small following everywhere she went, the younger children always clustering around like a cloud of dust. When she laughed, she tilted her head back and opened her mouth as wide as a sea bass. When she walked, her curly hair bounced up and down. I watched her, mesmerized.

One day, in a meeting, Miss Foster looked at my grades, then wiped the chalk off her hands onto her tan trousers. She grinned at me tight-lipped, as if holding back a mouthful of pride. "You smart girl," she said in broken Korean. "I, for your sake, will find some books." I giggled at her funny sentences.

But she stayed true to her word. Every week, I went home with a bag full of books and magazines—none of which were about communism, the revolutionary struggle, or the Great Leader, although I'm sure if I'd asked for one, Miss Foster would've given that to me too. Instead, I read about Amelia Earhart, the television set, and tectonic plates. I visited other worlds in *The Lion, the Witch and the Wardrobe*; *The Little Prince*; and *The Call of the Wild*. I met Ingrid Bergman and Katharine Hepburn in *Harper's Bazaar* and saw shiny red Pontiacs that gleamed in the sun. I learned that people lived in rows of pretty white houses and cooked something called Minute Rice in just ten minutes. In this way, I spent my summer, always reading—under a tree, on the concrete wall, in the Gukje Market.

On a Friday, Miss Foster pinned a map of the world onto the canvas wall for a geography lesson. She talked about boundaries and continents, currents and oceans, and how debris from a fishing boat in Japan ended up on a California coast.

"From a Japanese fishing boat to the California coast?" I said, shaking my head. How was that possible?

Miss Foster looked at me and nodded. "That's right. We're all connected. Oceans join and flow together, linking all the continents."

I wondered what Youngsoo would say to that—catching fish from around the world in one great sea.

fifty-one · · · · · ·
September, 1951

Autumn in Busan. I had never given autumn much thought—like so many things taken for granted—but now that it was here, I couldn't stop staring. I lay on the stone wall at Uncle's house, looking up at the canopy of red and yellow leaves hanging over me. When sunlight filtered through, the leaves turned to gemstones, and I imagined I was inside a palace.

I closed my eyes. The air smelled as crisp as the day after a hard rain. I could hear Omahni washing pots in the kitchen and Jisoo wrangling with a pair of too-small pants inside the house. But it wasn't the clanging of pots or the frustrated cries of a toddler that set my heart racing. It was a single word.

"Noona."

My eyes flew open, and I sat straight up.

When had I last heard someone call me *Noona*? I knew. It was on that day. The final day. He had called me Noona for the last time. Bewildered, my eyes darted in the direction of the voice. That was when I saw him.

Jisoo.

Sitting beside me.

Holding up his too-small pants for me to see.

"Noona," he said, again. "My pants too small."

How had he gotten up here? Then I saw the clay jars beside the wall. Omahni had positioned them from largest to smallest like steps.

His belly button poked out underneath his shirt. When had he grown so much? When had he learned to say those new words? Every time I walked past him, he always sat alone, just a silly baby engrossed in trying to get his foot into a sock or pull a shirt over his head. It struck me that in those moments, he was trying, always trying, to grow up, and I had never even noticed. Had anyone?

"How could you lose him?" Omahni asked, frowning. She stepped into the house carrying a basket of persimmons. They were still slightly green, picked too soon. "I asked you to watch him because Abahji and I were busy!"

"He was here a second ago. In that corner, playing with socks! Like always," I said, putting my hands to my lips. I couldn't have lost him. He couldn't be very far.

But what about the well in the courtyard? Could two-year-olds climb into wells? Something hit me in my gut. I ran outside.

He was there beside Youngsoo, crouched in the grass, their heads leaning toward each other. An intricate village of twigs and rocks sprawled out before them. I let out a long breath.

"Jisoo, put this one on top of the tower," Youngsoo said, handing him a short stick.

"He's too little. He won't understand. He'll break it," I warned.

But Jisoo held the stick between two small fingers and placed it gingerly on top.

"Good job," Youngsoo said.

Jisoo beamed.

I went back inside to finish sewing the hole in Abahji's shirt, my mind on maps and books, not thinking of my littlest brother at all.

Jisoo tugged on my arm. He looked up at me with wide eyes, his small hands still clutching his pants.

All at once, a horrible thought popped into my head. *What if he didn't remember Youngsoo when he grew up?* He might have grown out of his baby clothes, but he was still little. So little. I couldn't let him forget.

"Yes, of course, I'm your noona, too," I said.

I climbed down, then lifted him off the wall. Jisoo stared at me with that look of admiration or love or a little of both that happens when looking up at your noona. Then I did something I'd never done before. I held him steady when he stumbled, pulled him up to try again, and helped my little brother get his pants on, one leg at a time.

fifty-two · · · · · ·
February 1, 1952

One week blurred into the next. Holidays came and went. Birthday celebrations made a few of us a year older.

Jisoo was now four, and in two months, I would turn fourteen. Youngsoo would've been ten. I could hardly think beyond homework and friends and exams. And before I knew it, the air had turned from autumn cool to bone cold. Winter was here again.

I touched everything in the lacquered box. It felt good to have something to hold in my hand instead of just memories inside my head—which were already beginning to fade, despite my best efforts. What had he always said about going to America—that he would be my captain or my shipmate? Which fish had he almost caught before he tipped over and fell into the river? What was he wearing the night we left home? I pressed the river rocks against my cheek, so cool and smooth and real, like a drink of cold water. How could more than a year have already passed? It felt like yesterday and a lifetime ago. I put everything back and closed the mother-of-pearl lid, then returned the box to the small shelf Abahji had built into the wall of our new house. Auntie had sadly helped us pack our bags when we first announced our plans to move out, and she got quiet on the day we said goodbye. Uncle had to remind her that our new house was only thirty minutes away.

Last month, we had visited Youngsoo's grave for his one-year anniversary. Last week, we'd started sharing stories about him without crying. And today, we would all gather for a celebration, for today was graduation day.

The house was quiet. Abahji had gone to work, and Omahni was already tending to chores while Jisoo was at Uncle's house, keeping Auntie company because she missed him too much. I slid open the door to the room I shared with Jisoo.

A blue dress hung on the dresser knob.

I held it against me. It was too small for Auntie and too youthful for Omahni. Without anyone around, I slipped into it, poking my head through the square-shaped neck. It fell right on my knees, the shortest hemline I'd ever worn. I buttoned the front and smoothed the bodice; it fit snugly around my waist. When I twirled, the skirt billowed out in the shape of a bell.

The door slid open.

My head snapped up.

Omahni set a bucket of water on the floor. "Ah, I see you found the dress I made. The fabric is a heavy cotton. I bought it at the Gukje Market. It's pretty, isn't it? It fits you."

I nodded slowly, my lips slightly parted, turning over in my mind the incredible notion that Omahni had sewn this dress for me.

"But how can we afford this?" I said.

"We can't. But if you don't have any teeth, then you live by using your gums," Omahni said, repeating an old proverb. "It's for your graduation. Don't worry; we'll make do."

A new streak of gray swept along the side of her hair.

"Come, let me get out your tangles." Omahni grabbed a pearly comb that Auntie had given her and ran it through my hair. I couldn't remember the last time she had combed it.

When she finished, she set the small mirrored vanity in front of me. "Here, see yourself."

I looked, mute with bewilderment, and saw a strange girl staring back at me with a hint of knowing in her somber eyes. A slight rosiness tinged my cheeks and lips. I touched my face lightly.

Omahni stooped to pick up her bucket, and when I turned to look, it was as if I'd caught her essence in a snapshot—hardworking, tireless, devoted to her children, always ready to make another run to the well. It was this image that would stay with me, even years later, sitting inside a church with family and friends and pressing her pearly comb to my heart.

Before the last of my mother's long skirt flapped out the door, I called out, "Omahni, thank you."

But she continued walking, her singsong voice bouncing like a kite finally catching its wind: "Hurry, get ready for your graduation! Sora-ya, daughter of mine!"

fifty-three · · · · · ·

By the time we arrived for the graduation ceremony, the tent bustled with activity. Omahni, Abahji, and Jisoo made their way toward the back benches while I sat in the section for students near the front.

Yoomee plunked down beside me, wearing her red pleated dress from back home. Even though the edges had frayed, and she tugged on sleeves that now fell short, I'd always envied her for having that fancy dress. When I told her, she said that she had always envied my good grades. Which led to confessions of how much we'd once hated each other. We couldn't stop laughing.

Commencement began with the student choir singing "Arirang" and "Land of Hope and Glory." I listened to speeches about parents and children, sacrifices and dreams. And in between the words, I remembered the names of those lost to war, too painful to say aloud, but rising like ghosts nonetheless.

A hush fell over the room once Miss Foster began calling us, one by one, up front to receive our certificates, and I sat up straighter in my seat. We were boys and girls of different ages, some from the city, some from the country. Some of us were proper with long braids. Others had cowlicks and smudged faces.

We shuffled in our fathers' too-big shoes, or stepped lightly in store-bought heels. We bounded toward the stage with huge grins. We took tiny steps, our chins quivering. But we were all here, hoping for something better. And I clapped long and hard until I heard my name.

"Pak Sora."

Yoomee jumped up and cheered as I rose and walked to the front, and it struck me that I had dreamed of this moment for years. But it was not at all as I imagined. From where I stood in the front, I could see everyone at once, smiling back at me. They were happy for me. Even proud.

It took me by surprise, and I tried hard to keep myself from coming undone.

Omahni, Abahji, Uncle, and Auntie rose from the bench, their eyes glistening clear and bright. Jisoo, perched on Omahni's hip, waved furiously. Mrs. Kim sat in the back, clutching her husband's handkerchief, while Myung-gi, dressed in a handsome blue suit, stood beside her. I let my gaze linger on him—so broad and tall now—and thought of the time when we were ten and twelve, reading under a tree, uncomplicated friends. I couldn't believe that he would be deployed in just a few days. I bit my lip hard, blinking fast.

They held me up with their applause, keeping me afloat with the strength and support of a village.

When I walked off, Omahni and Abahji wove through the crowd, rushing to hug me. And we stood there, the three of us, arms wrapped around each other like the petals of a camellia bud, tightly bound but ready to bloom.

Families came together inside the tent, laughing and talking. Fathers embraced girls in blue dresses. Mothers clutched their blushing sons. High-pitched squeals shot out as younger boys and girls played chase, circling their parents. Folk songs played on a radio, singing of youth, love, and growing old. Young women on line at the refreshment table swayed to the music. And I took it all in—this tangle of color and dance and light.

By early evening, a soothing hum fell over the crowd as families prepared to leave, prolonging their goodbyes with another sentence, another laugh, and a final bow. I got a plate of sweet rice cake and headed toward my family standing in a circle.

"When will you come to visit?" Auntie asked Omahni and Abahji.

"Oh, so now you miss them. Before you couldn't wait for them to move out!" Uncle teased, knowing it wasn't true.

Auntie slapped him hard on the arm, and everyone laughed.

Jisoo sucked his thumb and clung to Omahni's leg. I picked him up and twirled around and around until he cackled with delight: "Noona! Noona!" When I set him down, he smiled at me with sleepy eyes ready for a nap.

"Omahni, I'm going to stop by the beach before heading home," I said.

"Okay. Just be home before six. The Kims are coming for dinner," she said.

"Don't worry, I'll be back before then to help."

She looked at me and smiled.

The school wasn't far from the shore. On certain days, it was close enough for the fog to roll in from the sea, dampening the trees and turning their bare branches into black brushstrokes. I walked down tranquil streets lined with small houses, past the sounds of playing children and the occasional barking dog. The air was cold and reminded me of arriving in Busan with Youngsoo.

It wasn't long before a cool, salty breeze rustled my hair, and I breathed it in, that scent of freedom. Shimmering waves lapped against rocks. Pink and orange swirled across the horizon. I could see it: pure, white clouds reaching across the sky like an outstretched arm offering me any fish in the sea. He was here—beside me, above me—my brother, the finest fisherman I'd ever known.

I took off my shoes and walked onto the empty beach. Waves roared and tumbled toward me, clawing at broken shells before being sucked back out to sea. I stepped past the foamy white edge, and imagined that the water against my feet had journeyed all around the world, touching the shores of America and back.

The freezing temperature caught my breath, but I took one step, then another, wading deeper, past my ankles, past my knees, the currents towing hard. I thought of all the rivers we'd crossed—the piercing cold shooting through my bones; his hand in mine, pulling each other through. And even of the river back home, sparkling under the afternoon sun and gently flowing out, somewhere, into the ocean before me.

I could feel it. The tides pulling. The ground moving. The ebb and flow of memories. Next year, I'd be in ninth grade. Four years after that, university. And after that, I could only imagine.

I closed my eyes, ready for the waves to come, ready for the tug on my feet, ready for the moving waters, washing in and out and away.

Author's Note

At its core, *Brother's Keeper* is a family tale, perhaps not unlike your own. Sora dealt with sibling rivalry, an exacting mother, and everyday misunderstandings—all within the setting of an increasingly oppressive North Korea and a devastating war. Like many Korean War refugees, Sora strove for freedom with courage and compassion, both for herself and her family, never giving up hope for a better future.

Although this book is fiction, many of the details and events from Sora's journey did occur in history: city bombings; refugees scaling broken bridges; canoes sinking; frozen rivers used as bridges; violence at the Imjin crossing; cardboard houses; abandoned homes overflowing with strangers; and that infamous train ride to Busan on the Gyeongbu Line, from which many rooftop riders fell to their deaths.

Much of the research for this book came from interviews, memoirs, texts, and rare color photos in John Rich's *Korean War in Color: A Correspondent's Retrospective on a Forgotten War*. It is also partly based on the story of my mother, who was a fifteen-year-old living in North Korea when the war began.

Like Sora, she had a relative executed for committing a crime against the state; wanted to go to college but faced some opposition for being a girl; fled North Korea on a cold November night; experienced that bombing on the hill; took care of one of her younger brothers when they were separated from their parents; passed through Kaesong; passed through Seoul; took a train to Busan with hundreds of other refugees; and then settled as a displaced person there for many years before immigrating to the United States.

Unlike Sora, she was the third of six children (two older brothers, two younger brothers, and one younger sister); her younger brother did not die; she crossed the Yellow Sea rather than the inland rivers; and she was the daughter of a high school principal in Pyongyang, not of a farmer in a small village.

My mother suffered great hardship during her journey to Busan and afterward as a refugee. Through Sora and her family and friends, I have created a story that is, in part, a synthesis of various survivors' experiences—but most especially hers.

As much as I tried to stay true to historical facts, I did take some literary license in altering the minimum-age requirement for the Sonyondan Club from ten to eight, so that Youngsoo could attend. While I open the book with Youngsoo running late to his Sunday communist youth club meeting, these Sunday classes generally targeted junior and senior high students to discourage any Christians among them from attending church. And though it was a rainy Sunday on June 25, 1950, I do not mention this in the story. Lastly, the train Sora rode was not actually the final train leaving Seoul.

The Korean War resulted in the loss of between three to four million lives. Today, North and South Korea are technically still at war, as neither side has signed a peace treaty. While the fighting ended on

July 27, 1953, with an armistice agreement declaring a cease-fire—but no victory for either side—the situation has remained tense for more than sixty years. It was not uncommon for families like the Kims to have been torn apart by the war, never to see or hear from each other again, as any form of communication in and out of North Korea was and is tightly controlled.

The Korean War now takes its place in American history as the "Forgotten War." Sandwiched between World War II and the Vietnam War, this little-known conflict on a tiny peninsula an ocean away failed to capture our attention. And soon, we began to forget what it was even about.

Nearly fifty years after the war, memorials began appearing across the United States honoring Korean War veterans. My gratitude runs deep for the many soldiers who fought and sacrificed so much in the name of freedom. Without their courage, my mother would've lived her life under a communist dictatorship.

While the movement toward remembering the Korean War continues, the stories of refugee survivors remain largely untold—narratives full of courage, love, and hope. As we are all connected in our humanity, and as the same waters still journey around the world, touching every shore, let us listen to their stories and never forget.

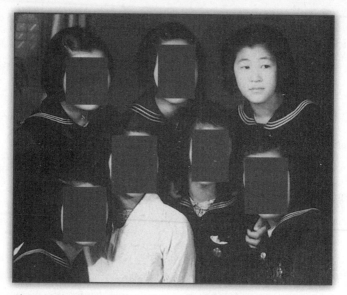

Circa 1947. My mother wearing her middle-school uniform in Pyongyang, North Korea, and posing with friends. She still laments that these friends never left.

Circa 1953. My mother (in the foreground), a high school student in Busan.

Circa 1954. One of my mother's younger brothers wearing his middle-school uniform in Busan. My mother took care of him when they were briefly separated from the rest of the family during their journey from Pyongyang to Busan. Currently, he lives in the United States and remains close with my mother.

Circa 1959. My mother's parents.

My mother graduates from Yonsei University as a music major in February 1960. She went on to teach piano for several years, then immigrated to the United States on September 6, 1970.

My mother, a college freshman.

Glossary of Korean Words

Abahji – Father (in North Korean dialect)

-ah – indicates closeness and familiarity when attached as a suffix to a person's name ending in a consonant, usually by an older person to a younger person

Ahjuma – term to address a middle-aged woman

Ahpa – Dad

ai – sound to express frustration

aigoo – oh no

"Arirang" – a famous traditional Korean folk song, more than six hundred years old, which serves as the unofficial anthem of Korea. Adopted in both the North and South, it was Korea's song of resistance during the Japanese occupation.

baduk – traditional Korean board game involving black and white stones

Chuseok – Korean Thanksgiving Day, which falls on the fifteenth day of the eighth month of the lunar calendar. It is one of the most important holidays of the year, involving a feast and the honoring of ancestors.

daenjang jjigae – stew made with fermented soybean paste

dduk – sweet rice cake

doljabi (dol) – traditional celebration for a baby's first birthday

galbi – barbecued beef short ribs marinated in soy sauce, garlic, and sugar

Gukje Market – international marketplace, in Busan

Halmoni – Grandmother

Hangul – Korean alphabet

Harabuji – Grandfather

janggu drum – hour-glass-shaped traditional Korean drum, covered on both ends with animal skins

jeogori – the upper article of clothing in traditional Korean dress, worn by men and women. For women, it consists of a short jacket characterized by a V-shaped collar.

jigeh – A-frame wooden backpack-like carrier

kimchi – a traditional side dish made of fermented cabbage or radish

kimjang – the communal preparation of large batches of kimchi in late autumn, enough to sustain households through the winter.

Mee-gook – United States of America

noona – older sister of a male person

Omahni – Mother (in North Korean dialect)

ondol – traditional method of underfloor heating using smoke from a heat source such as a wood-burning stove. The heat and smoke pass through horizontal flues under the floor.

Oppah – older brother of a female person. It is also a respectful term used by a female when addressing an older boy with whom she is close.

pansori – traditional form of musical storytelling, usually performed by one vocalist accompanied by a single drum

soju – Korean alcoholic beverage typically made from rice and grains

songpyeon – type of sweet rice cake that is half-moon shaped and served during Chuseok

uh-muh – oh my goodness

wah – more of a sound than a word that is an exclamation similar to "wow!"

-ya – indicates closeness and familiarity when attached as a suffix to a person's name ending in a vowel, usually by an older person to a younger person

yah! – hey!

Yeobo – term of endearment, akin to "honey" or "sweetheart," when addressing one's husband or wife

yoot – popular, traditional Korean board game involving four sticks, rounded on one side and flat on the other; eight markers; and a game board

yukaejang – spicy soup made with shredded beef, scallions, and various vegetables

Timeline of the Korean War

Korea under Japanese rule

1910–1945

Japan annexes Korea and tries to eradicate Korean culture by banning the use of the Korean language in schools and public places. New laws require Koreans to adopt Japanese names in place of their own.

Korea divided at Potsdam Conference

July–August 1945

In Potsdam, Germany, the Soviet Union and the United States, making plans for Japanese-held territories after an imminent Allied victory, agree to temporarily divide the Korean Peninsula at the 38th parallel—the Soviets taking the north and the United States occupying the south.

V-J Day

August 15, 1945

Japan surrenders to Allied forces (which mainly include the United States, the Soviet Union, Great Britain, France, and China), ending WWII and Japan's thirty-five-year colonial rule over Korea.

Soviet post-war occupation of northern Korea

August 26, 1945

Shortly after the Japanese are ousted from the peninsula, the Soviets formally begin their own occupation of northern Korea, ushering in a communist government.

U.S. post-war occupation of southern Korea

September 8, 1945

The United States enters southern Korea and helps establish a democratic government, marking the beginning of a three-year post-war occupation of the region below the 38th parallel.

Syngman Rhee elected as first president of South Korea

1948

South Korea is formally established as the Republic of Korea (ROK) with Syngman Rhee as its first president.

Kim Il Sung established as leader of North Korea

1948

North Korea is formerly established as the Democratic People's Republic of Korea (DPRK) with Kim Il Sung as leader of the North Korean communist regime.

Start of the Korean War

June 25, 1950

North Korean troops cross the 38th parallel and invade the South in an effort to unify all of the Korea Peninsula under communist rule.

United States enters the war

June 27, 1950

The United States and several UN countries join forces to defend South Korea and stop the spread of communism and Soviet influence.

North Korea takes Seoul

June 28, 1950

Three days after the start of the war, North Korean forces capture Seoul, the capital of South Korea.

Battle of Busan Perimeter

August 4, 1950 – September 18, 1950

North Korean forces take over approximately 90 percent of the peninsula, driving back U.S. and UN forces to a 140-mile perimeter around the southern port city of Busan.

General MacArthur in Inchon

September 15, 1950

U.S. general Douglas MacArthur launches a bold amphibious landing at the west coast port of Inchon, South Korea, cutting off North Korean supply lines. This surprise counterattack forces North Korean troops to retreat from the Busan Perimeter.

UN forces take back Seoul

September 16–29, 1950

Riding on the success at Inchon, divisions of the U.S. Army, Marines, and X Corps advance strategically from various locations, pushing north away from the Busan Perimeter, northeast across the Han River, and east from Inchon, eventually linking up with ROK forces to take back Seoul.

U.S. takes Pyongyang

October 19, 1950

Taking advantage of the North Korean retreat, General MacArthur continues to push northward to capture Pyongyang.

"Home for Christmas"

November 24, 1950

General MacArthur orders troops to advance up to the Yalu River, which borders North Korea and China. Confident of a victorious end to the Korean War, he tells his troops they will be "home for Christmas."

China enters the War

November 1950

Fearful of U.S. troops so close to its border, China engages in a strong counterattack on the American advance, fighting as an ally of North Korea.

Communists recapture Seoul

January 4, 1951

As UN and ROK forces retreat, battles concentrate below the 38th parallel. With the aid of Chinese troops, communists recapture Seoul. After this date, North Korean refugees can no longer enter the South and are forced back.

UN forces take back Seoul

March 14, 1951

U.S. general Matthew Ridgway and South Korean general Lee Hong Sun lead UN forces in this Fourth Battle of Seoul, also known as Operation Ripper. UN troops move into Seoul from the east and force communist troops northward, resulting in the fourth and final time that Seoul changes hands during the war.

Stalemate

June 1951 – July 1953

China's large army rivals UN forces, resulting in a stalemate. During this final phase of the Korean War, intense battles concentrate near the 38th parallel as neither side is able to make the massive territorial incursions seen in the first year of the war. Although this period also marks the beginning of truce talks, it results in tremendous casualties and some of the bloodiest trench warfare of the conflict.

Armistice agreement signed

July 27, 1953

After a year of bloody warfare then two years of a grinding stalemate, the principal backers of the war—China, the Soviet Union, the United States, and the United Nations—decide that pursuing total victory would risk a wider global conflict and lead to another world war. As a result, the Korean Armistice Agreement is signed, declaring a cease-fire but no victory for either side. The DMZ (demilitarized zone) is established, roughly following the 38th parallel and permanently separating the two countries. Kaesong, formerly part of South Korea, is the only major city to be taken from the South and given to the North as a result of the agreement. No peace treaty is ever signed.

Acknowledgments

I thank God for the people in my life who made this book possible. To my kind and brilliant agent, Michael Bourret at Dystel, Goderich & Bourret, thank you for believing in this story and taking a chance on this new writer. I'm honored to have you as my agent. Without your guidance, I would be lost. My deepest gratitude is to my talented editor, Mora Couch, who brought this book to a level that I never could have. Your keen editorial insights challenged and encouraged me every step of the way. Many thanks to the entire team at Holiday House for your support and hard work. And to the Atlanta Writing Workshop and SCBWI for providing me with invaluable opportunities and a sense of community in an otherwise solitary pursuit.

Special thanks to my mother for sharing her life story, for bearing with my random questions, for showing me unwavering faith. Your strength paved the way for all your daughters and grandchildren. This book is an homage to you, your family, and your generation. To my father, thank you for sharing your love of writing. There isn't a day when you don't go to your desk and write. By your example, I learned not only of dedication but also of a deep love and respect for the written word. My heartfelt gratitude to my older sisters, Helen, Gloria, and Joyce, who are also my critique group and my mentors. Your encouragement and feedback were critical in shaping this story.

Finally, this book would not have been possible without my three daughters: To Laura, my secret weapon, who read this book more than any person on the planet. You amaze me with your astute insights that show maturity well beyond your age. To Abby, my avid fantasy reader who read through this historical fiction in one sitting, thank you; it meant so much to me. Your bubbling enthusiasm encouraged me more than you know. To Emily, my dear youngest, who showed great patience when Mama was too busy writing. You suffered the most through my obsessive writing days yet always cheered me on; I couldn't have done this without you.

And to my loving husband, Chris, thank you for believing in me as a writer even when I showed you my ugly first draft. You built me up when I felt most tenuous. You didn't let me quit when I said maybe this wasn't meant to be. Without your love and support, I would have never completed this book. You are the bedrock on which I write.